Water

Water

Lloyd Jones

*Dedicated to everyone who has ever
lived at Bryn Clochydd, Gwytherin,
and the good people of Bro Hiraethog*

*Many thanks to Lefi and Alun at Y Lolfa for inspiring me to
write this book, and for their help and advice. I am happy to
acknowledge the influence on this novel of* Baotown *by Anyi Wang*

First impression: 2014

© Lloyd Jones & Y Lolfa Cyf., 2014

Cover design: Y Lolfa
Cover picture: Ray Wilkinson

ISBN: 978 1 84771 818 1

The publishers wish to acknowledge the support of
Cyngor Llyfrau Cymru

Published and printed in Wales
on paper from well-maintained forests by
Y Lolfa Cyf., Talybont, Ceredigion SY24 5HE
e-mail ylolfa@ylolfa.com
website www.ylolfa.com
tel 01970 832 304
fax 832 782

I

TEN HENS. SEVEN cows. Three dogs. Two cats. One farm. Four graves.

Here, at the centre of the old homestead, the farmyard opens in front of us like the palm of a hand; a workworn hand, with blisters and hardpads and scars. This is where the life of the farm is staged every day; the very first act began here many centuries ago. We Welsh people – how many of us started our lives in a place like this, still in our baby clothes?

The old actors went to their graves a long time ago, but their props can still be seen all around us. No, forget those leaning gravestones in the churchyard: think of the walls they raised, the ditches they dug, the roads they carved with their horny hands over an immense period of time, and the enthralling patchwork of little fields they created – each with its own name, its own character. The Water Meadow. Red Acre. Green Uplands. Davy's Field.

The feats performed by those vanished people weren't measured in degrees and diplomas but in sweat and rheumatics, in rasping coughs and fingers twisted out of shape.

And after they went there was silence. The small flowers of the field are their remembrance now.

A time came for the landmarks of the old world to be destroyed. After they build castles in the sand, children usually jump on them, destroy them. That's the nature of children, and that's the nature of mankind too when we enter the dark times.

The old fields and walls and ditches became old and weak. With no-one willing to tend them they wilted and weakened; their only function today is to hold within their damaged folds all the spirits of the old kingdom.

The pig was killed and devoured without thought for the future – and then came the winter.

But there is life there still.

In the back bedroom at Dolfrwynog two little heads are looking through the window, towards a grove of ancient birch trees by the rim of the lake.

'I'm sure I saw something down there last night,' says Huw to his sister Mari. He's a boy of twelve, thin as a whippet and constantly miserable. His shoulder blades stand out like knives and he hurts everyone with his love, passing from one to the other as a pet lamb might do, jabbing everyone with his neediness and his sharp little bones.

He gestures towards the trees.

'A man, Mari, I'm sure of it.'

She guffaws. 'Don't talk rubbish,' she replies scornfully before leaving in a bad mood, spreading a spectral wedding train of dust behind her; it chokes the wintry light eking its way through the window, and leaves a sour smell in the room, as if someone had beaten the battered old carpet under her feet. The room's in a mess, with peeling wallpaper scored by a naughty child's crayon marks. Huw stares at the trees; his eyes dwell on a little cloud of wool – the remains of a lamb which died last year. Nothing stirs there today. Perhaps hunger is playing tricks with his mind.

This is Dolfrwynog. An old farmhouse napping in a pool of wintry sunshine. Some of the stones in its walls are as big as a year-old calf. Today it sleeps in utter silence on its little stage, watching the fields fall away from it towards the lake. Once upon a time the people who lived here saw a rich, broad cwm in front of them – the Valley of the Flowers as it was known in Welsh literature – but that lovely vista disappeared some time ago.

There are four graves in the far corner of the paddock adjoining the farmyard, underneath the plum trees, with a threadbare covering of new grass on them. The decaying remains of a posy of flowers, jammed into an old jar, lie aslant in the soil. A child's prayer rots away in a rusty tobacco tin bearing the words *Golden Virginia* on its lid.

On the windowsill in Huw's bedroom there's a stack of big, heavy books. They smell of the past. In their midst there's a thick book on history, and ancient copies of the *National Geographic*, showing all sorts of strange and distant lands. An Inuit stands by his igloo; there's a row of bare-breasted girls with lots of bangles and exotic tattoos – he likes to look at their pert little breasts while listening all the time for the squeak of a foot on the stairs.

But times have changed, the world has shrunk again. The farmyard outside represents the whole world now for Huw.

When he reads about the Spanish Armada being driven around the coast of Britain in the great storm of 1588, the first image that comes to his mind is that of the geese honking and wandering around the farmyard like ships, slashing his boyish hands with the sharp swords of their beaks.

The cowhouse is across the Atlantic, in the New World, and his family sets sail for it every day with a bucket to fetch a precious cargo of white gold. Huw is mostly spared this arduous journey for the simple reason that he lost an entire shipment during last month's storms: he squeezed a teat on the young heifer too tightly and she gave him such a mighty kick he was bowled over into the manure-laden gutter.

Everyone shouted at him and ridiculed him. Mari took him to the river for a clean-up, but turned her back when it was time to wash his little thingy.

'Nothing much to see anyway,' said his sister sarcastically as she dried him off with a dirty towel, adding: 'You're damn lucky you didn't break the bucket, it's the last we've got.'

Later, during the afternoon, Mari and her mother Elin go upstairs and the daughter points through the window, towards the cluster of trees by the lake.

'Over there.'

Mari looks at her mother's face, waiting for a response. Too much bright red lipstick as usual; she's too old for it. Where does she find the stuff, anyway?

One is a copy of the other, except the older of the two is approaching forty and the other is sweet sixteen; the shape of her body is a daily reminder of the years which have disappeared in a blur for Elin.

'What did he see, exactly?' asks the mother.

'A man, he says.'

The two of them stand there for ages with their arms crossed, waiting for a movement by the lake.

'Well, you'd better tell Wil,' says Elin in a tired voice. 'Just in case.'

Mari observes the two deep lines which have arrived to crease her mother's brow during the last few years.

'We don't want the same thing to happen again, do we?' she adds before turning towards the door.

The whole world has withered to the size of this sombre little farmyard.

At the bottom of the yard there's a dung-heap – Everest. Yes, there's a midden at Dolfrwynog. Huw stands by the house scratching his head, staring at the dung, looking at Everest. He imagines the cockerel planting a flag on its smelly summit. And a memory comes to him from his schooldays, a solitary detail: the original Mr Everest had been a Welshman of sorts.

Then he turns his gaze towards the loft above the stable, where the farm servants used to live in a different age, up a flight of stone stairs, above the warmth of the horses chomping their oats.

Everything's on a different scale now. The stable loft is a continent away, and the farmyard's a vast muddy sea. He imagines a little ship labouring across it, her hold crammed with slaves moaning and crying out in pain; dying slowly, then being thrown overboard. What terrible suffering… not unlike the awful kick he received from the young heifer while he was trying to milk her.

There are no farm boys living in the stable loft nowadays. But neither is it empty. There are frequent signs of life up there. A snatch of song, a few opening bars coming through the doorway when it's open: *Who'll be here in a hundred years* sounds on the airwaves in a wavering tenor voice, touchingly sweet because of its naivety. And sometimes an exclamation.

'Dammit!'

In the night a patch of yellow appears in the little window – an hour of candlelight is allowed before bedtime.

Yes indeed, Uncle Wil has moved to the stable loft to live by himself. The direction of his life has changed. One day he came across an old brass compass and he spent hours faffing around in the farmyard; then he'd marked the four points of his new world: to the North was the hen-hut at the top of the yard; to the East was the stable loft; to the South, at the lower end of the yard, was the dung-heap; and to the West was the gable end of the farmhouse itself.

I'll go to live in the Far East, said Uncle Wil to himself. Then a broad grin spread across his face. He imagined himself standing in the doorway of the stable loft as dawn broke, chanting like a muezzin, calling the people to prayer. He sketched out an imaginary minaret, rising above the roof of the stable.

He chuckled loudly. After all, the only thing that sustained him nowadays was his sense of humour.

'That's settled then,' said Uncle Wil to Huw after a brief pow-wow in the middle of the farmyard, surrounded on all sides by the ogling geese, with the gander shifting his head slowly from side to side like a miniature seesaw.

'I'm off to live in The East,' and he clomped away to his new home.

Following his departure life at Dolfrwynog changed slowly.

Another man, much younger, came to take his place in one of the back bedrooms. No-one could have foreseen that development. How the world surprises us at times! But there will be several journeys across the yard, as Huw visits his uncle in the land of minarets, before that happens.

2

Uncle Wil stood in the Far North, in the snow by the hen hut. It was January – the black month. Terrible storms had blighted the beginning of the year. Day after day they'd been unable to do anything except feed the livestock in the huts and milk the black cow and the heifer before retreating to the house to keep warm. Wil was forced to keep his hens in their hut for three whole days, feeding them with a handful of stale corn every morning. A few seeds each, that's all. One of the hens died and he plucked her in silence inside one of the huts, without a hint of a song or a conversation with one of the dogs, as was his habit. Normally he could be heard every day singing one of the old songs of Wales, in his reedy voice, or he'd have a chat with the collies Jess and Pero, as if they were his children. Every other sentence he'd say something like, *What do you think, Jess?* or, *Why not, Pero?*

He was a friend and a brother to the dogs… but he had a special relationship with the hens, as if they were all members of the same congregation. If Wil was the minister then the hens were his chapel elders. He thought the world of them. He had a name for each of them: Becsan, and Megan, and Bwgan the black one…

He felt sad as he plucked the feathers from Non the old hen, with snow swirling around his face and melting on his nose. There was only half a roof left on the hut and every now and then a small avalanche of snow slid down a gutter and hit his hat, splattering the back of his neck with icy snowflakes.

Dammit! he said, under his breath, every time it happened. He'd worn that hat ever since he was a young man. It had been green originally with a black band and a bit of a feather: but the feather had disappeared some time ago, leaving its shadow – a different shade where it had rested against the felt.

'Dammit!' said Wil. The feathers were sticking to his fingers, which were blue with cold. By the time he'd finished there was a small mound of feathers adorning the white floor of the hut, surrounded by a zigzag pattern from his big black boots. Non had been the bravest, the most daring hen on the yard. She'd gone further than any of the other hens – to the far end of the paddock, where she'd laid her eggs for a while. Among those hens, Non had been their Marco Polo. And because of their wandering habits, Wil seldom thought of them as mere hens. They were the diaspora. At nightfall, when they returned to their hut, they were the far-flung people of Wales returning to their homeland for the great annual festival of song. After all, they sang in harmony together on their perches. The cockerel was the guest soloist. And as a measure of his pride in them, Wil was in the habit of charting their journeys and forays on a huge map he'd nailed to the wall of the stable loft; this chart was made from useless old wallpaper which had been thrown aside – Anaglypta, grooved and patterned, which made Wil's pencil slip and slide away, creating meaningless squiggles.

'Dammit!'

He'd made a map of his little kingdom, the very centre of the farm, with little black crosses to show where the hens had laid their eggs. There was one black cross right at the edge of the map, denoting where Non had made her nest. Today, as he fumbled with her body, Wil knew that she'd never wander again to the farthest reaches of the paddock. He could hear an otherworldly sound in his head – it was Non, clucking long ago on a clear morning in summer with the sun rising above her. Non, young and beautiful. Tears welled up in his eyes as he thought of her. Daring Non, adventurous Non, who had bid farewell to her tribe and sallied forth into the world, travelling further than any of her feathery sisterhood. Inside that hut Wil felt all alone, like Scott of the Antarctic, preparing to bid a sad farewell to the world. Wil also kept a diary. He would commemorate that day with one simple sentence:

Non passed away today.

No-one could ever guess how emotional he felt as he noted her passing in his book, with some of Non's blood and tiny bits of her insides still clinging to his fingers. He wrote the date 10/1/10 by a new red cross on his map, to signify that Non – who had reached the end of the world, further than anyone else – had laid her last egg.

He returned to the house with Non in one hand and a couple of eggs in the other, since one of the young pullets was still laying. He put his offerings on the draining board and returned immediately to his new home in the stable loft. There, in the glimmering light which filtered through the tiny window, he lay on his bed in silence, under two heavy black greatcoats. He shivered occasionally. Afterwards he napped for half an hour, and dreamt about Non, standing majestically on the prow of a golden ship, looking terribly noble with a pagoda and a beautiful palace in the background. There were rows of lovely girls dressed in exotic silks, all of them shading their faces with fans. There was a little bridge too, arched over the water – exactly like the one on the willow pattern plates on his grandmother's dresser. Their sole colour was blue, just like Non in his dream, clucking proudly as if she'd just laid a golden egg. Then the girls went in all directions to look for the egg. One of them returned, holding it in her hand.

'In the paddock,' she said in perfect Welsh.

Everyone laughed. Then, very carefully, the girl put the egg into Uncle Wil's pocket and kissed him. Everyone laughed again. In his dream he could hear the silvery peal of the girls' delicate laughter.

He woke with a pain in his scrawny leg, where a rusty old bedspring had jabbed him; it was this, not a golden egg being placed in his pocket, which had prompted his marvellous dream.

The day descended into a white, swirling hell. Wil could barely see the farmhouse through the blizzard, so he gave up and spent the day in his lair.

That night, while he slept, a cruel wind, cold and sharp, stirred Non's beautiful feathers into the white of the snow, making a wonderful pattern on the floor of the hut. Fine red and yellow feathers, once warm and lustrous, were cooled by the unforgiving snow. A lonely little wind whistled in the cracked slate roof.

At intervals the dogs bayed a song of utter hopelessness. And two orange eyes appeared above four orange paws near the hen hut – a fox. Naturally, the dogs went wild. In the morning Wil noticed a quadrilinear pattern on the perfectly white yard, as if a child had dotted a sheet of paper with a printing set.

3

Huw stood in the open door of the stable loft, a small black silhouette against a white background. His hair and clothes were flecked with snow and he had a hole in his shoe. A thread of snot dangled from his nose and there was a weal of dry blood where he'd scraped his elbow on a rusty nail. Huw had a cold; but there again, he'd had something wrong with him throughout the winter, or so it seemed. Right now his teeth were chattering because of the cold. He held his arms folded across his chest, hugging himself in an attempt to keep warm. He looked like a puppy who'd been stepped on.

'Hurry up and come in,' said Uncle Wil who, though trying to put some warmth in his voice, couldn't hide a note of impatience. The boy was so difficult to like. His own mother couldn't love him, so how could anyone else? Elin rarely spoke to the little lad, other than to chide him for some trifling offence or another. They'd hear her voice barking at him regularly, something like, *Clear off now*, and he'd flee the house. Poor little bugger.

Uncle Wil signalled with his hand, and as quick as a squirrel darting across a branch, Huw dashed across the room and wriggled underneath the greatcoats. The whole contraption squealed and swayed as he joined his uncle in the bed.

After a moment's silence, Wil was heard to say in a patient but laboured voice: 'I don't suppose you'd mind closing the door, would you Huw?'

Huw dashed to and fro again.

After reaching the bed he lay as still as he could underneath the heavy coats, until he warmed up a bit. They lay there for a while, without a movement, neither saying a word.

'I want to to live with you here, in the stable loft,' said Huw after a while in a weak little voice.

Wil allowed a heavy silence to settle on the room.

'I'd really like to live here with you,' said Huw again, his voice a little stronger.

Again, Wil said nothing. He rather hoped that silence would make the problem go away. But Huw refused to read the signal.

'I'm sure Mum wouldn't mind,' he added.

Uncle Wil continued to lie there by his side, as still as a stone statue.

He shut his eyes. Dammit, he'd have to say something. He couldn't ignore the boy: he was so vulnerable, so very miserable.

'Listen,' said Wil finally. He detected his mind searching desperately for excuses. But there wasn't a single excuse to be found…

'Listen, Huw,' he continued. 'You can come here for a few days, to see if we both…'

But before he'd finished his sentence, Huw had raced from the bed. He went through the door as fast as a squirrel darting down a tree. As he raced across the yard he heard his uncle's voice from the stable loft:

'Shut the door, will you Huw?'

And then, *Dammit!,* as Wil got up to shut the door himself.

Huw moved in that very same day, travelling across the ocean of the yard to stay with his Uncle Wil in the stable loft. If anyone had been looking through a telescope (and yes indeed, there really was someone out there observing them) they'd have seen a frail little boat crossing the muddy billows, under a small dark sail – which was little Huw holding his bedclothes aloft, above his head, as he moved from one port to another. When he landed in the loft his blankets were wet and muddy where he'd dragged them along in the mire. Uncle Wil was forced to spread them over the stalls in the stable below, in an attempt to dry them.

The boy could do nothing right; he seemed to make a mess of everything.

'Never mind, boy,' said Wil in his nicest voice. After an hour or two they could hear someone approaching, accompanied by the crunching sound of shoes on the stone stairs leading up to their eyrie. Their visitor was Jack, who'd brought Huw's mattress and a bag stuffed with some of his things. After making a general racket and spreading dust all over the place he retreated again, across the yard, back to the farmhouse.

It was a very subdued supper the two of them ate in the loft that evening, after making a bed for Huw in silence, a yard away from Uncle Wil's bed in the far corner. Wil had scored the candle with a knife, and now he told Huw they'd have to go to bed when the flame had reached the collar he'd marked.

Huw was quiet throughout their pitiful meal. He knew that silence was his best tactic. That was the hardest lesson he'd ever learnt, that silence was the best way to avoid a blow to his feelings.

He ate his bread and cheese without saying a single word. Now and then he nudged the flame of the candle with his forefinger, or gathered a smudge of hot wax on his nail. He loved the dance of the flame, its colours too, and the smell of the wax as it trickled down the pillar of white in hot little boulders. Uncle Wil stayed silent. He too played with the wax for a while, with a matchstick. The silhouettes of their hands danced around on the whitewashed wall by the table, like two little puppets performing a jerky waltz in a children's theatre.

Eventually the flame reached the point where it was due to be snuffed.

'Ah well,' said Uncle Wil, and he made a half-hearted attempt to tidy the table by dusting some crumbs into the palm of his hand. Rather than put them outside for the little birds, as he usually did, he threw them down his throat and coughed dryly afterwards. Huw did the same, copying his uncle's cough. Then he removed his shoes and went straight to his new bed on the floor, without shedding any of his clothes. Parts of his bedclothes were still damp, with animal smells and mud clinging to them.

He shivered for a while, but eventually the clackety-clack of his teeth ceased and he began to nod off. Through a fog he heard Uncle Wil go out for a wee. New sounds came to his ears: the splash of his uncle's urine hitting the stinging nettles under their room; the squeal of a twig belonging to one of the plum trees scratching on the window above his head, and the distant scrabblings of mice somewhere in the wall by his ear. Yes, he could hear them moving about. After all, they had their own little lives in there. Perhaps they had their own tiny bedrooms and a kitchen and a parlour, and even a little gym with miniature bikes and that sort of thing. His mother was forever going on about the gym she used to frequent in the city where they used to live. Every other sentence she'd say something like, *When I was in the gym* or, *When I was shopping one day…*

His mother lived in the past.

Uncle Wil came in and shut the door, then lay an old sack along the bottom to prevent draughts. After taking off his shoes he walked over to the candle and blew on the flame. He failed at the first attempt and muttered, *Dammit!* So he tried again, and this time he succeeded. Finally, he wove towards his bed like a drunk in the dark, very slowly, with his hands fumbling in front of him. Since his eyes were that much better, Huw could see every movement. Uncle Wil looked like a picture of Lady Macbeth in one of the big books. In the caption she was saying, *Out, damned spot! Out, I say…*

When Huw saw those words for the first time he thought she was talking to her dog, throwing him out of the house. Spot was a dog's name, wasn't it? He couldn't understand why there wasn't a dog in the picture, and an open door perhaps, with a tail disappearing through it.

Never mind, said Uncle Wil to himself. After a symphony of squeaks and rattles and coughs the loft went quiet. The two of them lay there like two mummies in an ancient, dusty pyramid which had never been opened. Huw could hear the mice playing inside their own pyramid. He imagined a ceremony taking place in there with mice dressed magnificently like the Egyptian kings, walking in a stately procession through their tunnels… some might have the faces of lions or rams, or hawks, or jackals. Retinues of slave mice in attendance. A loud squeal pierced the plaster and Huw imagined one of the mice being sacrificed to the God of the Mice.

Uncle Wil began to snore gently and at one point said, *Dammit!*, quietly in his sleep. Then he woke with a start.

The two of them lay there for a while in the darkness, listening to the mice as they marched through the walls.

'Uncle Wil?'

The old man pretended to be asleep.

'Uncle Wil?'

His uncle couldn't feign sleep any longer.

'Yes, Huw?'

'Uncle Wil, I saw a man in the trees by the lake.'

'Don't be silly, Huw.'

'But really I did, I saw him moving around down there.'

Wil knew only too well about the man, he'd seen him a week ago. But the stranger had moved on, to a hut above the farm, where they kept turnips. Wil had been trying to decide what to do about him.

'I know, Huw. I've seen him myself.'

Huw lay completely still in his bed and analysed his uncle's statement. Suddenly he felt warm for the first time in ages. Someone believed him. At last, he'd been right about something.

A few minutes passed, then:

'What are you going to do about him, Uncle Wil?'

Silence again. Then:

'We'll go to find him tomorrow,' said Wil.

'We?' said Huw, and a thrill of fear went through him.

'Yes, both of us,' said Uncle Wil. 'You can come too if you keep quiet. I mean very, very quiet.'

Huw allowed the currents of shock and excitement to pass through his feet into the darkness.

'OK, Uncle Wil.'

Hours went by, or so it seemed, before Huw got off to sleep. Uncle Wil had dropped off long ago, and the mice had fallen silent too. He heard a dog baying at the moon occasionally from the doghouse. When he awoke, Uncle Wil had gone and he was alone in their icy loft.

4

B Y THE TIME Huw had yawned and got up, Uncle Wil was ready. Having woken well before dawn, Wil had prepared a detailed plan, ready for their journey to the Far North. He had gone through it step by step. First of all he'd had to make a final decision on whether Huw should go with him.

The lad was good for nothing, really. Perhaps he'd make a racket and disturb the peace of the land. Or maybe he'd start crying, or whingeing, or sulking.

But there again, he'd provide company, and perhaps the time had come to harden him up and make a man of him. He could run for home to warn the family if something untoward happened. *Yes*, thought Wil, *I'll take him.*

Wil had lain in his bed for a whole hour, like a dead body, while he formulated his plan. Then he rose and went out to the nettle patch. Listening to the splish-splash of his urine hitting the vegetation, he stood in the dark for quite a while because he was slowing down; like one of the old tractors rusting away in the paddock, his body was a vintage model, and there were no spare parts available now. His body was on a runaway course towards a cliff and his brakes weren't working.

Wil returned to the loft and started his preparations. He fetched his shotgun from under the bed and struggled into one of the big old coats which also acted as one of his blankets; he belted himself ready for action and slipped half a dozen cartridges into the right-hand pocket.

Finally, he wrapped some old sacking around his trouser

bottoms; he'd done this so often the hessian curled around his shins in a natural corkscrew shape. He slung another sack around his shoulders like a soldier's chain mail in the Middle Ages. A black balaclava completed the picture – by then he looked like one of Scott's men in the snow and ice. He sat at the table, head down, thinking about Scott at the Pole. Hadn't Evans, who died on that fateful expedition, been a Rhossili man? Wil had taken an interest in history once, when that sort of thing seemed important.

A sentence bubbled to the surface of his memory. *To seek, to strive, to find and not to yield.* Weren't those the words on Evans's memorial? He'd been a giant of a man who liked his pint. But Wil certainly didn't feel like a giant that morning, and he hadn't tasted beer for ages. Right now his stomach ached for food, since he'd left the last biscuit for Huw. And he didn't feel particularly brave either. Any journey beyond the farmyard worried him greatly nowadays. Dangers lurked in the fields around them. There were already four graves in the paddock, and he didn't want to see any more there. He looked up at his chart, and he felt a tear coming to his eye when he saw the red cross denoting the death of poor old Non.

By now a small black shape had drifted over to the doorway; Huw was looking out on the sparkling white apron of the farmyard.

'Shut that door, will you lad?' said Wil, whose nerves had tensed in tune with his empty stomach.

'Well done,' he added when the boy did as he was asked.

'Got a coat?'

Huw nodded.

'Where is it?'

'In the house, Uncle Wil.'

'Where's your balaclava?'

Huw dropped his eyes and shuffled about.

'Don't know, Uncle Wil.'

But he knew very well where it was – buried in the paddock. He'd hated it right from the start, tickling his ears and heating up his brain.

'Try this,' said Wil, after he'd fumbled about in a drawer.

The cap was far too big for the boy, but he kept it on. At least it didn't itch, and he could pull it down over his ears.

'Go and get your coat,' said Wil. 'Have you got any gloves?'

'Yes, Uncle Wil.'

'Wear them too.'

'Where are we going, Uncle Wil?'

In response, his uncle chuckled. 'To find the stranger, of course.'

Huw crossed the yard at a gallop to fetch his things. Wil sighed heavily and closed the door behind him, though he said nothing because, after all, it was just as cold inside the loft as it was outside.

He walked down the uneven stone steps and, after putting two cartridges in the shotgun, he stood in the centre of the farmyard. There was no light on in the house so the family were still asleep, presumably. He looked around him. A thin layer of snow had settled on the frozen ridges of muck and manure. The dunghill looked like a miniature Snowdon, or Everest. Hailstones crunched underfoot. He noticed that the ditch which took water away from the house had frozen over so he broke the film of ice with his boots, while watching bubbles of air moving around below the surface. Then he went to the granary to fetch a handful of corn for the hens, in a rusty old bowl. Going to the top of the yard, he opened the hen house door and propped it open with a stave.

'Hiya, girls,' said Wil lovingly.

The hens slanted their heads, as though they were children watching a teacher arriving in class.

'And how are you today?'

Megan moved closer to her master and circled his feet, clucking. She hardly had a tail at all by now, and it was she who received the first splash of grain every morning.

'Don't you go wandering too far today,' said Wil with a fatherly voice. 'Keep to the yard and come home if the snow starts drifting.'

The hens sang a little school-choir song.

Then Wil went to the top of the yard and waited for Huw, who eventually emerged from the house looking like a scarecrow. For a few seconds the two of them stood facing each other in a *High Noon* scene, two scarecrows ready for a shoot-out. But in no time at all they were striding towards the North Pole, leaving the dogs barking a frenetic farewell. Struggling to keep up, Huw thought of a picture in one of his books up in the bedroom, a black and white photo showing Scott and his men with their dogs at the Pole. Hadn't they been forced to kill some of them and eat them? A shiver went through him, because he had no wish to eat dogmeat. Yach!

He followed his uncle up the hill, stepping into the indentations left in the snow by his uncle's boots. And so he struggled on, rolling from side to side as he hopped from one imprint to the next. By the time they reached the top he was puffed and sweating. Following in a giant's footsteps had exhausted him and he had to stand still for a while, holding his sides. He noticed then that the world had gone completely quiet. All the sheep and the cattle had disappeared, and there wasn't a single bird in the sky – as if the snow had made everyone and everything disappear. *Abracadabra,* said Huw to himself in the snow, a little black wizard practising his spells. *Abracadabra...*

By now Uncle Wil, walking in a dream, had moved far ahead of him.

Wil was preoccupied with the farm and his family. The farmyard had become the focus of his life, the equator of his existence. That yard was the centre of civilisation. He rarely left it these days. It was Jack, his sister Elin's partner, who went to work in the fields. Jack was the farmer now, though he asked for advice every other second.

'*What should I do today…*' was his first question every morning. Wil was tired of having to keep an eye on everything. What would happen if he died? What about the rest of them – would they starve to death? Would they have to move away?

Wil walked slowly now, his big hobnailed boots crunching through the white powder. He didn't like going towards the mountain nowadays. It was a white wasteland, cold and dangerous. He imagined a polar bear leaping on him and ripping him to shreds. Blood in the snow, red on white, with a little bit of yellow perhaps, because he'd be sure to wet himself. And there would be some brown too, probably.

Waking from his reverie, he heard a little voice calling to him. Someone trying to warn him, perhaps. An Eskimo shouting *bear* in his own language, and waving his arms about. But no, the cry came in Welsh. A Welsh Eskimo? Impossible, surely.

Wil stopped in his tracks and let the silence settle on him like a mantle. Yes, he could hear that voice again, crying out to him from afar.

'Uncle Wil…'

And then again:

'Uncle Wil…'

He stared in the direction of the voice. *My God*, said Wil, *of course!* Little Huw. Poor lad. Wil had forgotten about him completely. So he started walking back towards the boy while waving, urging him to catch up.

'Come on, m'lad,' said Wil in his warmest voice.

And in a while Huw had caught up. Wil mumbled a few words of encouragement. *Never mind... brave lad... well done...*

Then he grasped his hand and started to lead him through the snow, as patiently as he could. Upwards they went, through the upper fields, with Huw's little hand engulfed in his uncle's massive left paw, while the shotgun see-sawed in the crook of Wil's right arm. In half an hour they arrived at the little quarry which, over many years, had provided stones for the mountain road.

'Right,' said Uncle Wil. 'I want you to stay here. Understand?'

Huw nodded. He was glad of the rest, because walking through snow was hard work and he was tired. Uncle Wil found him a hidey-hole so that he could shelter from the wind, a little bit of a cave. He motioned to the boy with a finger.

'There,' said Wil. 'If I'm not back in an hour, or if you hear a shot, run for home, will you?'

'Yes, Uncle Wil. Can I walk about if it's cold?'

'Of course you can,' said Wil in a nice kind voice, 'but don't leave the quarry.'

'OK, Uncle Wil,' said Huw in a whisper, and he went to huddle in the recess, though he couldn't help wondering how he'd be able to time an hour, since he had no watch. Fine snowflakes twirled in the air outside his lair. One of his books at home showed a bare-breasted young maiden bathing at the mouth of a cave, under a glittering waterfall, somewhere in the tropics. Somewhere warm. He started to shiver...

'By the gods, it's cold,' said Huw, trying to sound grown up.

'Yes, well…' said Uncle Wil, 'I won't be long. We can go and look at the traps on our way home if you like.'

'Okey-dokey,' said Huw, who was trying to act cool. He looked on in astonishment as his uncle pulled an old pair of green striped curtains from under his coat and wrapped them around his boots, tying them in place with some old twine. After checking his gun to see that he'd loaded it, he left the quarry as if he were a poacher following tracks in the snow. A heavy silence fell on the quarry after he'd disappeared from sight, but he returned relatively quickly, his black shape appearing like a huge crow alighting. He stood stock still for a few seconds, and Huw thought of a sheriff in one of those ancient films, lips clamped on a cheroot, following some filthy outlaw all day until he trapped him in a corral. But Wil hadn't raised his gun, and he hadn't spat out of the corner of his mouth.

'You OK, Uncle Wil?'

'Fine.'

'Did you find something?'

'Yes.'

'What, Uncle Wil?'

'Never you mind. How about going to look at the traps? Hell of a job finding them in this snow. Thank God it's not drifting, or we'd have to go looking for sheep.'

Huw emerged from his hideout and they started off for home, the boy going from gap to gap in the hedges, searching for traps. There was nothing in the first four, but in the fifth the wire had tightened around the neck of a young rabbit, which was stiff and frozen hard to the earth. Huw freed her and held her up by her hind legs; he could feel her coldness through his glove.

When they arrived on the knoll above the farm they sat for a while on a tree which had fallen in a storm. Uncle Wil studied the farmyard and the paddock, trying to locate his hens. Then, with a few deft movements, he skinned and disembowelled the rabbit. Huw was fascinated, and revolted, by the small pile of guts left near Uncle Wil's boots.

'Look, Huw,' said his uncle suddenly, while also raising a finger.

'Over there, by the plum trees in the paddock.'

Huw followed the finger and spotted a small black dot moving slowly among the graves.

'Megan,' said Huw.

'Yes, by God,' said Uncle Wil. They fell silent, and Wil realised he'd have to put another cross on his map in the loft, a big X on the yellowing paper, with an M beside it. But he wouldn't draw a miniature egg by it because Megan wasn't laying right now, and in any case she wouldn't lay an egg in the snow.

Huw prepared to ask a question, and he wanted it to sound as manly as possible. A question that a cowboy would ask in a film, through the corner of his mouth.

'What did you see in the high meadows, Uncle Wil, when you left me in the quarry?'

But his voice sounded childish and naive.

'Did you see anyone?'

In the ensuing silence, Wil spat from the corner of his mouth, exactly as a cowboy would.

'Yes,' he replied. 'I saw someone. But there's no need to be afraid.'

'A man, Uncle Wil?'

'Yes.'

Silence fell again, as Huw mulled over the news.

'A man like you, Uncle Wil?'

Wil wasn't quite sure how to take this question.

'What do you mean?'

'Well, was he an old man or was he a…?'

Wil roared with laughter. '… a young man!'

'Where was he?'

'Sitting on the turnips in the shed, up in Morgan's Field.'

'He was in the turnip shed?'

'Yes.'

'Has he eaten our turnips, Uncle Wil?'

'Yes, one or two.'

'Did you tell him off?'

'Yes, Huw, I told him off good and proper.'

Both of them sat looking at the Megan-dot on her pilgrimage among the graves below. She'd be going cluck-cluck-cluck and picking at any specks of food she could find.

'Come on, Huw, let's go home.'

But Huw wasn't quite ready to go. He remained seated, with his head in his hands and his elbows on his knees.

'Tell me about the man, Uncle Wil.'

Wil sat down again on the tree trunk, and after a moment's consideration he told the whole story. After all, wasn't he trying to make a man of the lad? Wil studied the trails of snot coming from his little nose, and his dirty, cold-reddened face. What hope was there of making a man from a child like this? A boy with fine down like a light fall of frost on his upper lip, and the voice of a girl. Poor, poor little mite…

'He was a young man, like you,' said Wil. A picture came to his mind. He'd opened the door to the shed with one quick movement and pointed his gun into the darkness. He'd stood there in the doorway while his eyes grew accustomed to the poor light. After a while he'd seen a figure in one of the corners, seated on a bundle of old straw. He was young, not much more than twenty, with curly black hair and a dark complexion. He seemed very thin, and very afraid. It was clear at once that he wasn't going to cause any bother. But he wasn't Welsh, and he wasn't English either. In no time at all, Wil had established that he was Polish, and that he was close to starvation. More that that, he'd do anything to join the family down on the farm at Dolfrwynog.

5

A COLD, VIOLENT wind blew through the valley that night. Following his evening chat with the hens, when he put them to bed for the night, Wil stood in the doorway of the hen hut in his big black coat and moth-eaten balaclava. The pain in his belly had changed key, like a piece of music, since the morning. Hunger had caused the early pain, but now something else was gnawing at him. When he set foot in that upland hut his stomach had fluttered with apprehension, but now an evening pain, more sinister, gripped his guts with an iron hand. Another spectre had arrived at his table. He ought to see a doctor, but there was no doctor to be seen. He'd have to put up with a pain which arrived and departed like a thief who never knocked or shouted, *Is there anyone at home?* before making off with his health.

The wind was a wild beast, it growled and bared its teeth in the cwm. Wil listened to its express train roar as it screamed past, much too close to their platform at Dolfrwynog. It ripped through the trees above the farmyard and foamed through the leaves; Wil was reminded of a time when he was small, on a beach somewhere, listening to the sea for the very first time. It had been exciting, the waves had been magnificent and wonderful and noisy, sucking and chewing at the pebbles underneath his naked feet. He hadn't seen the sea for ages; in fact, he hadn't left the farm for over twenty years. He was pretty sure he'd never go beyond the cwm ever again. His world had shrunk incredibly: the farmyard was his whole life now. Mud and snow, and the roar of the wind; a strange pain in his stomach, and fear stalking the land. No news had reached them for a long time. He'd shut himself off as the last dribs and drabs of information reached the valley – stories about men with knives and guns killing each other in the cities. Murder and mayhem. It was best not to know. Wil thought about his own little map of the world, on the wall of the loft, with a big new X in the corner of the paddock with an M to denote that Megan had ventured almost as far as Non and Cluck the cockerel. But Cluck was still the champion, master of all he surveyed. Number One.

Pillows of snow were blown to bits around Wil as he stood in the doorway. The wind was white, it was an explosion in an ice cream factory. It knifed him, it blinded him.

Then he started to walk down the farmyard towards the stable loft. It would be terribly cold there tonight. Hopefully there would be some food ready for him in the house. He didn't know what to expect from one day to the next; it could be feast on a Monday, famine on Tuesday. But before turning in he'd have to skin a rabbit caught that evening by the dogs.

And yet – wasn't this a perfect opportunity to teach Huw how to do it? The boy needed to harden up, so he'd give him a lesson in butchery.

Huw was waiting for him when he climbed to the loft. He'd lit the candle and gone to bed in his clothes, though he'd removed his shoes which stood in two muddy puddles by the door. The truth was that he was almost crying with cold. But he'd rather stay with his uncle than go to the house, at least he'd receive a little warmth from Uncle Wil. There wasn't much of that to be had in the farmhouse. Yes, maybe he'd miss his books, his only links with the outside world since the electricity had gone off. His laptop had been gathering dust in a cupboard for some time now, and there was no likelihood that he'd use it again in the near future, if ever. During a short golden age he'd been allowed to enjoy the fruits of technology, and it had been wonderful: so much knowledge, so much entertainment at his fingertips. Such a little machine, such huge pleasure. The universe condensed into a small magic box. His friends always nearby. Friends? Well, one friend anyway. He had no idea where Gareth was by now. He'd disappeared into the void, like everyone else. There was nothing or no-one left in the whole wide world, only his family at Dolfrwynog. The farmyard and the fields and the river and the mountain. And the new lake. Once, during a still summer's day, they'd heard gunshots far away. A hunting party, perhaps. They'd seen nobody, and the usual silence had returned soon enough.

'Hey Huw, give us a hand, will you?'

Huw was almost asleep.

'What is it, Uncle Wil?'

'Give us a hand, lad.'

Huw lifted his head to look at Wil, who was standing by the door with the rabbit in his right hand.

'Can you shut the door please, Uncle Wil, it's fierce cold in here,' said Huw innocently.

Wil laughed out loud. The cheeky little brat. But he shut the door before walking over to a cupboard in the corner of the room, where he kept a big sharp knife for flensing animals.

'Come on, Huw.'

He placed the rabbit on an old plastic sack on the floor and left the knife by the body.

'Do you want to know how it's done?'

By now Huw was standing beside him, throwing his shadow onto the rabbit.

'Nope.'

'Well, it's time you learnt.'

Wil grasped the boy's shoulders and moved him aside, so that the rabbit could be seen clearly. Then he lifted the knife and put it in Huw's right hand.

'Start with the legs, cut them off halfway up, at the joint.'

Wil sat down heavily in his chair but he kept an eye on the boy as he started to dismember the dead animal. He was pretty cack-handed at first, but eventually he managed to saw one of the front legs in half.

'Well done, lad,' said Wil. 'Be careful, don't cut off one of your fingers. Cut away from you always with the knife.'

Huw cut off each lower leg in turn, becoming a little more adept each time. Wil showed him how to make an incision and then peel the skin from the body, and he lavished praise on him when he'd completed the job.

'Go and wash your hands now,' said Wil when he saw the boy standing around ghoulishly in the candlelight, smelling his own fingers like a cannibal.

'Hey, Uncle Wil, I've just remembered something.'

'Yes, what is it?'

'They want a pow-wow in the house tonight.'

'Damn them!' said Wil. He hated their meetings and all their empty talk. That Jack was full of daft ideas. For instance, he'd found an odd little stick one day and brought it home.

'This is our talking stick,' he'd declared at one of their meetings. He'd adorned it with pheasant feathers and a coil of beads.

'You can only talk when you're holding the stick. Got it?'

Stupid berk. Him and his stupid talking stick.

One day I'll light the fire with your bloody talking stick, was Wil's unspoken response.

He didn't want any bullshit tonight, not in the slightest.

'Pow-wow... why tonight?' Wil could hardly believe it. He

wanted some food in his belly and a good night's sleep, no more and no less.

He let out a low moan. 'Oh bloody hell…'

What on earth had happened to necessitate another meeting? And why did they have to 'talk' when the answer was probably staring them in the face?

'Come on then – we'll wash our hands and go over there for a bite to eat. Bring that rabbit with you.'

'There's no point in me washing my hands if I'm going to carry the rabbit,' said Huw quite sensibly.

Wil groaned yet again, and grabbed the rabbit. They descended the steps, and Huw washed his hands in an old bath which collected rainwater from the farmhouse guttering, what little was left. The water was icy.

When Wil walked through the door, his sister Elin was standing in the kitchen, dressed in an old duffel coat with a scarf wound around her head, as if she had toothache. Her lips were bright red, as usual. Where did she find that stuff? She hadn't been near a shop for ages, yet she always seemed to have a supply of cosmetics. She couldn't face the day unless she had war paint on her face. That's what Wil had called the stuff since they were both children and she'd come down the stairs with a bucketful of slap on her face. Women. It was impossible to understand them. Elin had escaped to the city as soon as she could, she couldn't wait to see the big wide world: the process of finding work, a husband, and a Facebook ring of friends had come to her as naturally as breathing.

She'd returned home occasionally, all hair and high heels, to laugh through the weddings and to cry through the funerals. His own sister. Always laughing or crying; without moderation, without Welshness. Then, one day, she returned with a new husband and a new hairstyle, both of them shorter and plainer than the last. And here she was again, in the kitchen of her childhood, scowling at her brother and his rabbit, labouring over one of her eternal stews, more turnip than anything else worth eating.

'Don't bring that thing anywhere near me,' said Elin fiercely. She moved as far as she could from the rabbit.

'Yach!'

Elin longed for Marks & Spencer food, nicely packaged and ready for the microwave. Raw meat made her feel sick. Jack could prepare the rabbit, or whatever that disgusting thing was in her brother's hand, tomorrow.

'Come on, Wil, here's a bit of stew for your supper,' said Elin, and she spooned half the contents of a saucepan onto one of the family's ancient willow pattern plates, which had stood once upon a time on the dresser. Over the last three years those lovely, traditional rows had developed gaps like black holes in a set of teeth.

Wil studied the food dispassionately. He knew that it would calm the pain in his insides, and then reignite it. He went to sit at the far end of the long table and started to chew on his meal. Everyone else sat around the open fire, poking it or fiddling with the burning logs. He'd tried to teach them how to handle a fire efficiently, but no-one had listened.

This was their entertainment now – looking for patterns in the flames, or listening to the hiss of the burning wood as dampness rose through the grain and then sizzled like a gob of spit on the surface. A single candle in the centre of the table lit the scene. Wil chomped away without much appetite, and considered the silhouettes dancing on the walls around him. The outlines he saw weren't those of his sister, her partner or the children; rather, in his mind's eye, he was looking at the shadows of his parents and himself as a child, sitting in front of the fire at Dolfrwynog half a century previously, when Wales was going through one of its periodic convulsions, one of so very many over the years…

He stared at the table with its gathering dust and dirty plates. But what he actually saw was a scene from many years ago: his mother scrubbing the wood to whiteness in readiness for shearing day; an abundance of food stacked high – fresh bread, yellow butter, cheese, cooked meats, frothy cakes… and yet there was a similarity in the shadows. These people had the same shapes; yes indeed, Elin his sister seemed to have the same shadow exactly as his mother. He laughed lightly and then a soft sad moan escaped from his tired mouth, since the small amount of meat in the meal had been tough and hard on his jaw.

'Dear God,' spluttered Wil, and a tiny shower of food fell onto the table.

No-one took much notice.

'What's up, Uncle Wil?' said Huw, turning towards his uncle.

'The shadows,' said Wil. 'They're exactly the same as…'

But a fit of melancholia came over him and he fell silent.

'Any bread left?' he asked nobody in particular.

'No,' said Elin in a little voice from the corner of the fireplace. She was playing with a stick, wafting it around and trying to create a smoke-alphabet. In fact she was trying to write NO FOOD in smoke-letters. But she wasn't being very successful, because by the time she reached the second letter the first had already lost its shape.

Jack straightened and rose to his feet slowly. He walked over to the table and sat at the end, opposite Wil. That made them both heads of the table, in a way, though Wil was the unofficial leader because he was the only one who knew how to run a farm and grow food. It was they who had known everything at one time. But Wil was Number One now.

'You can take your balaclava off if you want to,' said Jack in a reasonable voice. He didn't speak Welsh, and although he understood a great deal of it he spoke English as a general rule and everyone answered him in Welsh – everyone except Elin, who always spoke to him in English. In fact the family way of life was a bit of a stew all round – their clothes were a mix of old and new, with everyone wearing any old thing that fitted; there was one big communal drawer for the socks, and nobody bothered much if any item matched the rest, in terms of size or colour. Shirts and socks were shared without restraint by now.

Wil kept his balaclava on his head, and stuffed his hands into his coat pockets when he'd finished his meal, to keep them warm. He'd almost dozed off when Jack went over to the dresser to fetch the talking stick.

'We need to talk…' he said after he'd sat down again.

'Need to talk…' said Wil like an echo. He saw no reason to discuss anything. What was the point of it? They had very little choice in what they did, so why bother talking nonsense? He looked contemptuously at the stupid talking stick in Jack's hand. *Ha! A prick with a stick…* but he bit his tongue rather than say anything nasty. It was important to keep relationships on an even keel.

'Let's have a chat about today,' said Jack. He struck the table with his magic wand. 'We need to get a few things sorted.'

Slowly, everyone rose and sat around the table, without any enthusiasm. Huw lowered his head onto his arms and went into his own world for the rest of the meeting.

Jack went over the day's activities. He'd moved the sheep to the lower meadows on Wil's advice because the weather had taken a turn for the worse, and he'd given them some hay. Jess the dog was about to whelp, and they'd have to decide if they wanted to keep one of the pups because Pero was getting old. He jumped from one topic to the next, then finished and offered the talking stick to the others, but no-one wanted it so he placed it in the centre of the table, next to the candle.

'You got anything to say, Wil?' he asked pathetically.

Wil shook his head.

But almost immediately Huw mumbled something through his sleeves.

'Pardon, Huw?' said Jack. 'Can you sit up and speak properly?'

Huw spoke again, sleepily. 'The Pole,' he mumbled.

'The pole?' said Jack. What d'ya mean *the pole*. What are you on about?'

'The Pole,' said Huw again, feebly. 'Ask Uncle Wil...'

His uncle cursed him under his breath. Hadn't he told the boy to keep shtum about the man in the hut? Or had he forgotten to warn him?

'The pole?' said Jack to Wil, as if to prompt him.

Wil removed his balaclava slowly while trying to think what to say. He'd intended to keep mum. What was the point of saying anything? The story would merely frighten everyone, especially the women.

They all turned towards him, everyone except for Huw.

'We found someone in the upper meadows,' he said eventually.

'Us?' asked Elin.

'Me and Huw.'

'What, did you take the boy up there with you?'

'Yes.'

'You bloody fool...'

'Well, he'd rather be with...' started Wil, but then he bit his tongue.

'You found someone there?' asked Jack.

A little red devil stirred inside Wil.

'You're not supposed to talk without holding the talking stick,' he responded.

Jack laughed out loud. 'One nil to you, Wil,' he said, which made Wil smile. Fair play to the chap, he could take a joke.

'Well, spill the beans then,' said Jack. 'Don't keep us up all night, some of us have beds to go to.'

Without taking hold of the talking stick, Wil revealed his news without withholding anything.

'And then what happened?' asked Jack.

Wil relaxed, and started fiddling with the balaclava.

'He wanted to come and live with us.'

'Thank God you didn't bring him here,' said Elin. 'There isn't enough food as it is.'

'No there isn't,' said Wil. 'But perhaps we'll see him again. There's a possibility. An outside chance, as it were. Hundred to one.'

'Why?' asked a shy little voice which hadn't been heard so far. Mari was staring at her uncle with disbelief. A young man? Had Uncle Wil driven a young man away from this awful place, her prison?

Wil realised what was going through her mind.

'Don't worry,' he said. 'If he's man enough he'll be with us soon enough.'

'Why?' asked Elin.

'I gave him a choice,' said Wil as he stood up and walked towards the door.

'I told him he could come and live with us if...'

He turned and looked at the little group sitting at the table.

They were all staring at him, all except Huw, who'd fallen asleep.

'I told him he could live with us if he brings us horses,' said Wil. 'Big horses, good horses.'

And then he went out, shutting the door quietly behind him.

6

THE SNOW STOPPED falling and the stormy weather abated at the end of January. Dolfrwynog basked in a dry and sunny spell; suddenly they were all walking around in their shirts. Huw could be found sitting on the top step by the stable loft door, with his eyes closed and his face tilted towards the sun. That was the month's most powerful image; Huw sitting in the sun, worshipping its yellow warmth, with Megan the red hen nearby quite often, scratching around for crumbs. That's how Wil would remember February: a little boy giving himself to the sun, worshipping it. Wil imagined them all living in the Stone Age, transported back in time. He saw a cromlech rather than a farm, with Huw dressed in animal hides, sitting on the capstone, adoring the sun. It was easy to imagine such a scene when they themselves lived in such primitive poverty.

'I don't understand this weather at all,' said Wil to Cluck when they met by the door to the hen house one morning. Wil was resting with his back to the wall, scratching his head. His disintegrating balaclava had gone, revealing a mess of gingery-silver hair badly cut by his sister Elin. Wil had been as wild as his wild red hair when he was young. He'd been the strongest and most unruly member of the local young farmers' club. The most stubborn and wilful of them all. The biggest drinker and the loudest singer in the pub. If a television company had ever made a programme about the notorious Red Bandits of Mawddwy they'd have gone straight to Wil for a prototype and then taken on a hundred like him. He'd appeared like a rocket on Bonfire Night – bright and colourful and magnificent. But that was way back in the past. By now he was a finished machine. Half a century of hard work had almost killed him.

Yet though his life seemed short he'd seen many changes. Some big developments had occurred, and many smaller ones. Some had come quickly, others as slowly as a snail climbing a wall. A long time ago, when he was a little boy, he'd seen a very different vista at the lower end of the farm: verdant green fields, rolling in graceful dips and curves towards the floor of the cwm. Dolfrwynog had been fecund and prosperous, thriving on grants and nitrates. But that had been replaced by failure and poverty and sadness. Bad news had dribbled into the valley, like the cold, unforgiving water which had gathered into a lake below the farm. Hour upon hour, week after week it had flowed through a gap at the mouth of the cwm until it had swallowed the lower fields. Then it had grown as silently and malignantly as a tumour. By now it was big enough to supply a large city. Millions and millions of gallons, it was huge. And Wil had watched it happen, gradually, over many years. He'd looked at it that morning, as he always did, and noticed that the body of water had massed and become yet more sinister. It was growing again, creeping towards the farmyard, swallowing yet more land. By now it was lapping around the small grove of birch trees where he'd seen the young Polish man for the first time, shortly after Christmas.

The Polish man. He wondered what had happened to him.

'What do you think, Cluck?' he asked the cockerel. 'What's your professional opinion on what happened to our little friend from Poland?'

Wil opened his right hand and offered Cluck a single corn seed. The cockerel slanted his head from side to side while examining this offering in Wil's grimy palm. The old man hadn't washed for weeks and all the lines were etched with dirt. They looked like hedges around small fields of flesh; indeed, Wil thought he recognised some of the field shapes at Dolfrwynog: Red Acre, and Morgan's Field, and Lime Kiln Field. He saw the seed as a single sheep, and Cluck was maybe moving his head around because he'd heard a tiny bleat coming from the miniature animal.

Suddenly, Cluck plunged his beak into his hand and the seed disappeared.

'Was that nice?' asked Wil.

Cluck replied with a sweet little song. The big black cockerel wanted more. But there was none left.

'That was the last seed in the whole wide world, Cluck,' said Wil apologetically. But he wasn't being entirely truthful. Very seldom did Wil lie openly to his hens, but he'd just fibbed. The truth was that he'd secreted a bag of seed corn in the stable loft, held by a rope from one of the beams, to keep it dry and safe from rodents. A twin sack hung from a beam in the house. It was their insurance against calamity. Fire, water and theft. And acts of God. But God hadn't shown his face for some time. That was Wil's take on events. Elin was the only one who said her prayers these days. The rest had turned into pagans. That was the impression he'd got, anyway.

The door to the house opened and Mari emerged with a basketful of washing.

It was she who did the housework nowadays; her mother had given up on life generally except for an occasional spot of cooking. Elin seemed to be spending more and more time in bed. She'd become very depressed, according to Jack. It was hardly surprising. But Wil had been unable to raise the issue with her. As soon as he opened his mouth to say something, when they were alone together, the words froze between his lips; a device like a baleen veil in his throat prevented the words from emerging, as if important matters were too large to emerge through the filter of his emotions.

He watched Mari as she pegged out the clothes; she'd washed them in the bath after an overnight soak. There was no soap left and she used cold water only. Though it didn't clean the clothes properly it got rid of the sweaty smells. She'd tried to make a sort of soap out of wood ash, which she'd read about in one of her grandmother's old books, but the process had proved too complex.

Mari was pegging out the last item – a small pair of red knickers – when Wil sensed that something was wrong. Nothing obvious, but she looked downcast and her body had drooped.

He rose and went down the yard towards her. Mari noticed him and changed her stance; her chin went up and a false smile spread across her face. But instead of fooling her uncle she betrayed the fact that she'd been crying. And soon enough there were more tears rolling down her cheeks.

'What's wrong, little Mari?' asked Wil in his softest voice.

She turned her back on him and flounced back to the house. As he stood there watching her, the red knickers fell to the ground. He stooped to lift them up and as he did so someone walked out of the house. It was Jack, who stood with a sarcastic look on his face before putting his hands on his hips effeminately.

'Don't think red's your colour, dearie,' he said mockingly.

'Bugger off,' said Wil. 'And instead of standing there like a lemon how about finding out what's wrong with Mari?'

Jack's demeanour changed and his face clouded over.

'Howdya mean?'

'Never mind,' said Wil as he turned away. Although Mari had tried to keep her tears a secret, Wil would find a way to question her later on.

That afternoon Cluck went further away from the farmyard than ever before. In his own leisurely way the black cockerel wandered from one molehill to another until he reached the middle of the field below the farmhouse. Wil heard him crowing proudly far away, on a vantage point, as if he were an explorer who'd just claimed the territory for the Kingdom of the Hens.

Cock-a-doodle-do... his clear trumpet call was heard all over the valley.

Wil went down the field towards him.

'Hey Cluck, what are you doing here, boy?'

Jack lolloped down the field to join them.

'Wil, we've got to talk, man.'

We've got to talk... but that time had ended. It was time to *work* and *make*.

'What's wrong, Jack?'

'Bloody hell man, can't you see? We're starving. There's hardly anything left. Apples finished yesterday. Only a bag of spuds left. The grain's nearly all gone. What the hell are we supposed to live on?'

Wil stood looking at Cluck as he pecked for food in the soil.

'We've got to do the same as him,' he said in a tired voice, pointing downwards. 'We've got to scrounge around for anything we can find. I'll show you how tomorrow. What are you doing today?'

'Same as you told me. I've been mending that fence and checking the snares. Two more rabbits so far.'

'Make some more snares like I showed you and peg them down along the hedge at the top of Red Acre,' said Wil patiently.

'We've still got plenty of *rwdins* left.' He couldn't remember the English word for turnips.

'I'm sick and tired of bloody rwdins,' said Jack.

The Welsh word had entered his vocabulary. He'd never forget it. The letters R-W-D-I-N-S were engraved on his heart and the lining of his stomach. Just saying the word made him feel sick.

'Don't stay here for too long,' said Wil to Cluck. 'Make sure you come home before it's dark.'

'You think more of those bloody hens than us,' said Jack.

'Maybe that's because I like them more,' answered Wil bitterly. 'They're not so needy… they can look after themselves, and they don't come running to me every minute of the day, asking me what to do next.'

Jack stomped back up the field in a bad mood. How should he know what to do? He'd been a computers man, a specialist, best in his field. An incredible wage. He'd stayed at the best hotels, flown all over the world. Hah! Flown all over the world indeed. He'd never see all that again. No, never again…

Darkness came again to enshroud the valley. Someone lit a candle in the house and blew the fire back to life. Jack laboured over another rwdins stew. Elin had stayed in bed all day reading her old magazines. They were a comfort to her, full as they were of nice clothes and cosmetics, though they were falling apart now.

'Where's Mari?' asked Wil between spoonfuls of stew. Jack was right – the turnips made him feel nauseous too.

'No idea,' said Huw. 'In her room, I think.'

'Pop up and see if she's OK, will you lad?'

Huw glowered at his uncle. He was reading one of his old books, which had pictures of the ice at the North Pole, and

Inuits and polar bears. Dampness had caused the pages to stick together and spots of mould made the polar bears look like mutants, half-bear half-leopard.

'Do I have to, Uncle Wil?'

His uncle rose slowly to his feet and climbed the stairs, trying to avoid the squeaky planks. When he got to the top he knocked on Mari's door. God knows what's wrong with her, he thought. Was she ill maybe? Starving away? Feeling low, like her mother?

He knocked again, but there was no reply so he opened the door slowly.

'Mari? Are you there, little one?'

No answer. He pushed the door wide open and looked inside.

No-one at all, no sign of her.

'Jack!' shouted Wil from the top of the stairs. 'Come here, Jack,' he said again.

Soon Jack and Huw were at the foot of the stairs, looking at Wil's ghostly form dancing above them.

'What's up, Wil?'

Then Elin rose swiftly and joined Wil on the landing. Now there were two wraiths wavering in the semi-darkness.

'It's Mari,' said Wil. 'She's not here.'

They all stood still for a while, looking at each other. And then a horrible stench reached their nostrils. A nasty, burning smell.

'Dammit!' said Jack, and he ran towards the kitchen like a madman.

He'd left the stew on the fire.

As Wil walked slowly downstairs he reflected on the fact that Jack had started saying *Dammit!* just like he did whenever something went wrong.

7

JACK WENT NORTH and Wil went South, both carrying guns, as the dawn edged towards them from the East in pink and grey stripes. After a few words had floated from their mouths in little white cloudlets of cold vapour, they separated in the centre of the yard. They'd looked everywhere, in every nook and cranny, in every hut and bedroom, but Mari had vanished. Some of her clothes had gone too, together with her old backpack, with its two little teddy bears on silver chains which had swung from side to side as she walked down the hill towards the school bus. One of them – Daddymonkey – had been a lucky charm given to her when she went up to the big school, and indeed it had brought her luck in the exam room. The other – Mummymonkey – was a memento of a family holiday in Sweden, where they'd gone before the world vanished. A third teddy, Babymonkey, had been lost when she wrestled with Paul Symonds and rolled down the big green bank by the bus stop one morning. Paul, a new boy in the village, had been too friendly…

Wil walked down the field below the house with his gun rocking in the crook of his arm.

'You silly old fool…'

He was talking to himself, about himself. Because during all that commotion the previous night he'd forgotten to shut the hen house door.

He'd remembered round about midnight and had gone up there with a candle in an old jampot to count his hens. One, two, three, four… he reached nine and then started again. And then again, but no matter how often he counted he still fell short. It wasn't a hen that was missing, but the cock himself, Cluck. The last time he'd seen him, Cluck had been standing on a big molehill in the field below the house, singing *cock-a-doodle-do…*

That morning, as Wil walked away from Jack, he'd expected to see an explosion of feathers in the field. But then he heard Cluck shattering the morning silence with a blast from the direction of the lake. Joyfully, Wil went down to the birch grove and discovered Cluck standing proudly on one of the branches, safe and very much alive.

A wave of warm relief swept through Wil and his face cracked into a broad grin.

'Well, who'd believe it, Cluck, you're alive, thank God. Well done, lad. But what are you doing here, when you're needed at home?'

Cluck stared at him, slanting his head as usual. When Wil made a gesture with his right hand the bird flew down to join him, then followed him across the field; he fell back now and then, doubting Wil's ability to feed him, but then danced back towards him again.

That was a nasty little trick I played to fool Cluck, thought Wil when they reached home so he reached for the grain sack hanging in the loft and opened it, then scattered a handful by the door. As the cockerel pecked away in the weak morning sun, Wil returned the bag to safety and said a thank-you prayer to no-one in particular.

'Don't do that ever again, will you lad?' said Wil in a nice kind voice. But at the same time he realised it was foolish to keep just one cockerel, it was too risky. He'd have to invest for the future, despite their shortage of grain. One of the hens had gone broody, so he'd let her sit on her eggs. True, it was very early in the year, but the weather was all over the place anyway so it didn't matter very much. Something else was worrying him too. When they'd lifted the potatoes last year he'd made a clamp for some of them in the hen house, covering them in straw and earth. This was a secret stash, ready to be planted again in the spring. But their eating potatoes had all gone, and now he was in a quandary: should he keep his secret, or reveal that he had food available? If he did that, however, there wouldn't be any seed potatoes left. The problem gnawed at his insides.

In the meantime, Jack had made his way towards the mountain, also with a shotgun. Since the coming of the lake there was only one escape route from the farm, and that was northwards over the hills. As he climbed upwards he could see the lake in its entirety; by now it was a huge sickle of silver curved threateningly around the lower meadows. Greedily, it had bitten into more of their land since he was last up here. When he arrived at the mountain gate he leant on it for a while, resting. He didn't like it up here; it was barren and shadowy and threatening. Jack had sat in front of a computer for most of his life, and the world within it had seemed much more comforting and attractive. The world of Google had been a shangri-la, a place of abundance. Slowly, without anyone realising, everyone had gone to live in their laptops. It was a plentiful place, beautiful and fascinating. Fewer and fewer had come back from their visits to this bounteous virtual world; and if they did, they'd been like spirits babbling about wonderful colours, unimaginable wealth and an everlasting paradise inside the magical realm of the motherboard.

Yes, Jack missed his old life. The New Reality had been an awful shock to him, and almost everyone else too. One of the worst things was the silence. Ever since he'd arrived here he'd found it difficult to deal with the quietness of the cwm. It actually hurt his ears, that silence. No tractors, no cars, no machinery of any kind to console him. No music wired up to his ears. Sometimes, when he knew he was completely alone, he'd scream as loudly as he could, just to hear a noise. Any noise.

After resting he started to walk along the old mountain road, through the heather, with the two dogs behind him. Wil had ordered Jess and Pero in his most commanding voice to follow Jack, since they naturally wanted to go with their master, and they made several attempts to creep slyly homewards. Here on the mountain they followed Jack hesitantly, without much faith in his leadership. In an hour or so they reached the top of Gorse Hill, and the dogs lay down panting while he recovered. He looked all around him, from the North to the East, from the South to the West, and then all around him again but he failed to see any movement. The sheep were all on the farm and the mountain ponies had vanished. High grey clouds raced overhead, and Jack guessed that the vista hadn't changed much in hundreds of years, ever since all the trees up here had been felled by the early farmers. And the silence, broken only occasionally by the sad call of a curlew sheltering in the reeds somewhere, was overpowering.

He and Elin had come here for a picnic shortly after they'd moved to the farm, on a lovely summer's day. They'd made love in the heather, but that sort of thing didn't happen any more. Elin had turned her back on the world, and on him too. She couldn't tolerate the cold and the harshness of life at Dolfrwynog. She often slept through the day, or she'd read in bed. Then she'd come down for supper because Jack had refused to take her food up to the bedroom.

'You've got to face the world, Elin,' he told her. 'It's the same for all of us. Think of Huw and Mari. Try to be an example…'

But his ploy didn't work. She'd begun to lose her sanity, that's what the grown-ups suspected. Her religious streak had strengthened; she insisted on saying grace before every meal, and she forced Huw to say his prayers on his knees at bedtime every evening – that was one of the reasons he'd decided to live with his uncle in the loft above the old stable.

Quite simply, she'd lost interest in the world.

One day Jack had lost his temper after finding the remains of a meal – a bit of meat and turnip chunks – thrown out for the hens.

'Bloody hell, Elin,' he'd hissed at her as she cowered under the bedspread, 'you never stopped talking about bloody food when we had plenty of it, never stopped looking at those bloody cookery programmes on TV – I think you went on about food more than people who were starving. Now look at you…'

And here he was, in the middle of nowhere, on his own. Hell on Earth. One of the dogs loped over to him and he stroked it. The pink tongue was warm and comforting inside his hand.

'Well done, boy,' he said quietly. 'Good dog.'

He wondered what he should do next. Carry on? But to where? He rose from the heather and started walking along a sheep-run through the wilderness. Onwards he went, trying to remember the slight changes in the topography around him; a shift in the far horizon, or the appearance of another hillock, or a stream, or an ancient sheepfold. This went on for hour after hour and he began to tire. He had no food or drink with him, though occasionally he'd been able to drink from one of the little streams and this had killed off most of his hunger. Later that afternoon he was to be found sitting on a spur of yellow mountain pasture, worrying about Huw's future, when he noticed a group of standing stones in the distance, about a mile away from him. His eyes weren't as good as they used to be so he had to really focus hard to see them properly. Yes, they looked like relics from the Stone Age, pointing to the sky, some of them thick and some of them thin. He couldn't remember seeing anything like that up here before, but there again, he'd never travelled this far into the moorland wastes.

He continued to stare at the stones, because something about them aroused his interest. Or perhaps he was beginning to lose it like Elin, maybe his brain was beginning to warp through lack of food and hope. Surely he'd seen one of those uprights move. He dropped to his knees behind a pillow of heather. He shut his eyes, and after resting them for a while he opened them again, staring with renewed intensity at the menhirs. By now they seemed to have moved, yes they were all moving. He realised that they were alive, and he took fright. He started shaking and a cold sickness gripped his insides. Squatting behind the vegetation he gathered his thoughts, while also noticing that dampness from the ground had spread up through his clothing in a dark, chilly stain. Then he looked again: the group was coming directly towards him, along the path. By now he could hear voices, and laughter. And was someone singing?

Yes, Jack could hear a young female voice singing a pop song happily. Then he heard a horse neighing. A horse… so that explained the bigger objects, and he heard the occasional thud of a hoof on the compacted peat. Another voice chimed in with the song, a young man's voice, and then the two voices interplayed merrily. The girl laughed naturally, boisterously. But hang on! He knew that laugh, he would recognise it anywhere. It was Mari's trademark giggle-roar. He raised his head above the heather and saw that the group was within a stone's throw. By now he felt confident enough to rise to his feet, though he raised his gun too, just in case. The party approaching him stopped, and they all stared at each other.

What Jack saw was Mari, leading a horse, followed by a tall young man leading another two horses. They looked happy and alive, until they saw him standing there. Then the old silence returned to gag them all, and to deaden the wastelands around them.

8

'DAMMIT!'

Wil was standing in the middle of the farmyard, talking to himself as usual. He was cursing because rats had raided the broody hen's new nest and stolen her eggs, right from under her. All that was left was the china egg he'd put there to prompt her at the beginning. To exacerbate matters the rats had gnawed at the seed potatoes too. Damn them! Wil had spent an hour finding their hole, then he'd sealed it off with broken glass and shingle from the river, rammed home with a lump hammer. He and the hen would have to start all over again. Naturally, the hen didn't know what was going on. She had no idea that her children-to-be had been destroyed. Now, standing on the yard, Wil pondered the fact that mankind's greatest curse was to understand death. Coming to terms with one's own mortality could be very difficult, but worst of all was the knowledge from early on in life that the grim reaper visited all and everything; humans had to wait around for him like kids at a bus stop expecting the school bus. Everyone knew they'd die some day, and the fact nestled like a nest in the branches of their brains right from the spring of their lives. Their own children would die also, and then their children too, ad infinitum. For ever and ever, till the End of Time. But the hen didn't understand that sort of thing. It would start another little family without shedding a tear. Cluck would drop by to visit her; in no time at all she'd be singing a little devotional song in the hen hut and a brand new egg would pop out of her bum.

Wil himself had never fathered a child; he had never witnessed a woman going cluck-cluck-cluck before laying a baby at the hospital. He'd never had a chance to walk proudly around the village like the other new fathers, looking like someone who'd just won ten gold medals at the Olympics. Sure, he'd chased the local girls like all the other lads when he was young, but it never went further than that.

Wil was never certain why one of his paramours had never joined him in his smelly bed at Dolfrwynog. He'd been a bit wild, maybe that was the reason. There hadn't been a How to Love a Woman course at the agricultural college, no gentle words of advice like, *Change gear at this point and go slowly for a while,* or, *Warm your hands before you touch her udder or you'll get a hell of a kick...*

There wasn't a hope in hell of receiving counsel from his father, because he knew little more than his son. The old man still blushed if he saw a young cow's virgin teats. Shy? Everyone in the neighbourhood had been vastly surprised that Wil's parents had even managed to hold hands, never mind beget children.

Wil's antic mind returned to the rats. Perhaps they had little pink babies at the end of their tunnel; if so, they would all die now that he'd sealed the entrance. A cloud came over him, not because he'd murdered the little rats but because he was aware that countless little lives were arriving in the world every second, while he himself had failed to create a single offspring...

On the other hand, perhaps that was a blessing if one considered the state of the world. The bull had well and truly gone through the china shop. His mind followed the word *shop.* The village shop had closed years ago, it felt like centuries. By now his thoughts were chugging around in his head like windmill sails in a gentle breeze. He listed his favourite sweets, when he was a nipper visiting the village shop: he could see them now, in a row behind the glass counter near his little face. Mrs Jones the Shop, as she was known to everyone, would ask him how his father was, and his mother, and his sister, and she'd go through a litany of other matters, always in the same order. Every morning she'd get his news somehow, she worked faster than the Gestapo.

This was the way his mind worked nowadays, reflecting on the past and idling over countless meaningless trifles. He was happy to loiter for ages, musing and reminiscing. After scouring the lower meadows he'd forgotten all about Mari. Was that the essence of growing old? Standing in strange places, experiencing cloud-thoughts? Reappraising? Regretting?

But what else could he do? He studied the farmyard's hard surface. This was the surface of his individual planet now, as it had been during his childhood. His life had begun here and it was about to end here too.

To the North he observed the hen house, door ajar. A hen clucked a new egg into the world. He turned to face the East – his home in the stable loft. Huw was sitting on the steps, worshipping the sun.

'Hey, Huw,' shouted Wil, 'you'll get piles if you sit on those cold stones for too long. Do you hear me?' Huw took no notice. Adults were always chewing his ear about something or other. They'd tell him to do this and then that. Why? What was the point?

A new sound came from the North, to shatter the silence and to impinge on Wil's reverie. He raised his head to find out the cause of all the fuss and commotion approaching from the top of the hill. He heard human voices, and another sound which he recognised with a flood of joy…

It was Jack who came into view first, with his gun slung over his shoulder. He walked with his head down, looking at his feet, evidently very tired; in fact, he could barely walk. Then, Wil saw a wan little face, smiling victoriously. It was Mari's biggest smile for ages. Her hair had escaped from her red bandana, her cheeks were aflame and her eyes shone. Her shoulders had also risen, as if the weight of the world had been lifted from her. And what was that behind her, coming into view slowly between the branches of the rowan tree – a horse? By the gods, yes it was. A handy-looking cob by the look of it, with a halter on its head. Then he saw more horses descending the hill towards him, fine chestnut ponies with packs on their backs, as if they belonged to an explorer crossing a hostile, uninhabited continent. The man leading them was tall and dark; Wil recognised him immediately. Of course, he didn't know his name; they'd exchanged only a few words that day in the turnip shed.

Wil's mind went back to the day when he'd aimed his gun at the lad in the shed and asked him: 'Who are you and what are you doing on our land?'

The lad had looked at him in amazement, unable to understand Welsh.

Wil had asked: 'You English?'

'No. Polish.'

'What are you doing here?'

'Food... I am hungry.'

'Why are you here?'

Haltingly, the lad had explained. He'd been on a visit from Poland, with his father. It had been a final trip down memory lane, since his father had worked in Wales many years ago, cockle-picking on the mudflats. Already close to death, the old man had fallen ill and his son had stayed by his side at a British hospital. The father had died but by then there was no money left and the lad had been forced to live from hand to mouth while he tried to make arrangements for the funeral, and in the way that bad luck often arrives in a convoy, he was mugged in the street. The cities had become dangerous places by then so he'd fled to the countryside, trying to scavenge for food; that's how he'd found himself in the Welsh countryside.

But although Wil had been moved by his plight, he'd also felt that he had to be hard-hearted.

'You go away now or I shoot,' he'd commanded.

The lad had fallen to his knees and pleaded.

'Please let me stay with you. I work hard, I am strong.'

Wil's feverish brain had gone through all the permutations. Perhaps, indeed, the lad might bring benefits. But he'd have to earn his keep, and produce more food than he consumed. He looked quite fit.

He'd come to a quick decision that day in the hut. He'd challenged the lad to complete a mission, so that he could prove himself worthy. If he failed, they'd never see him again, hopefully.

'You can stay with us if you bring horses,' Wil had said to him. 'Good horses, and food… anything you can get. If you come back with horses you can stay.'

After that he'd shooed him out of the hut and watched him trudge away through the snow, with Wil's double-barrelled shotgun pointing at him. And here he was again, back at the farm, standing on the yard at Dolfrwynog: at the centre of their world, and already part of the family. He'd forced himself into their lives, and now he was about to take his place at the long white table inside their old Welsh homestead.

9

W IL KNEW AT once that everything was about to change
again. He stood apart, watching this burst of activity and
listening to their young, excited voices. He felt estranged and
old, but he tried to be friendly and welcoming.

'His name is Nico!' said Mari exuberantly. She was standing
as close as she could to the newcomer. 'He's Polish,' added Mari.
'He's coming to live with us.'

Mari looked at Uncle Wil in a way which said, Don't you
dare say anything, I won't let you spoil this moment…

A bedroom window squealed open and Elin's head
appeared.

'What's going on? Who's that man?'

She vanished, but then appeared again just as quickly, joining
them on the farmyard. Wil noticed that she'd managed to apply
some lipstick in the few intervening minutes. Women. They
were incomprehensible. He felt out of place amid the hubbub.
What if this lad was a bad 'un, prepared to kill them all in their
beds as they slept? Had anyone else thought of that possibility?
They ought to be more wary; perhaps he belonged to one of
the marauding gangs and was merely a frontrunner, assessing
the situation. Wil tried to decipher his young, handsome face.
Maybe he was OK; maybe he was honest and open and guileless.
Maybe. Only time would tell. Wil took the horses and released
them in the paddock; they'd be fine there overnight. The three
of them snorted and pranced around their new home for a bit
before settling down to graze. It would be wonderful to hear

them from his loft, neighing and cropping the turf. He loved horses – their odour, their bulk, their old-world dignity. They'd been one of the Celts' chief animals. Strong and dignified, a noble beast. Items of horse tackle still lay around in the stable, vomiting old straw through cracked leather. Massive collars and clinking bridles. There was an old cart too, sitting in a nest of stinky old straw and hen shit. It had belonged to his great-grandfather, and although it was riddled with rot and useless, no-one was willing to burn it.

Wil hooked the halters over an old rusty nail in the stable and then he leant against the doorframe for a while. The light was already beginning to fade. Looking up into the sky, with its range of blues and violets, he noticed that a few stars were already visible. *It would be so nice to have a smoke right now*, he thought, *nicer than anything else in the whole world. Dear God, it would be great to pull on a fag and look at those stars in the night sky.* It was easier to see them nowadays, now they had no electric lights to blank them out. He knew some of them; that bright one in the West had to be Venus, because it was by far the brightest…

He began to sing an old Welsh ballad in an undertone, comparing a lovely young girl to Venus. But how did it end? Wil was just desperate for a ciggie. The stars were burning a hole in the sky above but all he wanted to do was to burn a hole in his lungs.

He walked across the yard haltingly; he was very tired now. Too much going on, and he was getting old. That pain in his belly started up again. What was it? An ulcer? Or was it hunger? No, it felt serious, slicing him like a knife in the guts. Turning to look back when he got to the farmhouse door, he saw that Venus was glittering in a pinky-blue sky. Lovely. Venus had been the goddess of love, hadn't she? Wryly, he noted that she was probably smiling on Mari and Nico. His mind wobbled around its central spindle again. Nico was the Welsh name for a goldfinch. He mouthed a famous poem: *Nico annwyl, ei di drostai, ar neges bach i Gymru lan – dear goldfinch, carry my precious message home to lovely Wales.* A war poet had tried to communicate his longing from the distant trenches. But it was the other way round now, wasn't it? People were dying in droves here in Wales. And to where would Wil send a bird as messenger? Over the sea to… Ibiza? He'd flown there once with a gang of young farmers. Incredibly hot. And as for the drinking, Jesus wept. He'd been sick more than ever before, he'd left little molehills of vomit all over the island. Little jellyfish of sick quivering in a place full of Mediterranean mystery, far from anywhere. Very far from Dolfrwynog. And he'd failed to find a girl, he'd been the only one to fail. Much too drunk. Perhaps that was why he'd never copped for a partner, he'd always been too shy, too fond of the juice.

His footloose mind wandered back to Nico. Such a strange name for a boy. He'd have a mother in Poland, probably, and she would have stood many times at her door in Warsaw or wherever shouting *Nico!* to call him home for supper. Mari was completely besotted with him already. Nobody had wanted Wil like that, greedily. Never. Perhaps Gwen from Ty Newydd farm had allowed him to experiment in the back of the Ford every Saturday night for a month or two but her eyes had never shone when she looked at him. Mari's eyes were two twinkling Venuses in the heaven of her little face. Poor little mite.

'You coming in, Wil?' asked Jack, who was standing by the farmhouse door.

'Yes.'

Jack looked at him searchingly. 'You tired?'

'Yes.'

'Want me to shut the hens in for you?'

'Dammit!' said Wil.

'You nearly forgot again, didn't you?' said Jack.

In that moment he felt rather sorry for Wil. Until then he'd felt nothing much for the old man. He was so different to the rest of them. They'd had to do everything his way, because he was the boss. But there again, he was the only one who knew what he was doing. He alone had experience of growing crops and looking after animals. Perhaps the gap between the two of them had widened because of this constant feeling of indebtedness.

Wil really had tried his best to be accommodating, it wasn't his fault that he was so old-fashioned and stubborn and strict. After all, he had no experience of the business world's slick management techniques. He'd never had to frequent countless meetings; he'd never had to tranquilise people with incomprehensible jargon and then invade their placid brains with deceitful ploys and manoeuvres. He was a farmer. He got up with the dawn, he worked all day and he went to bed exhausted, knowing that the day's work was done, or if it wasn't it would be waiting for him on the morrow. If he didn't feed and guard the animals daily they would die. The potatoes had to be in the earth in the spring and the crops had to be in the barn before winter. The alternative was simple: everyone living at Dolfrwynog would starve. Simple, yes simple, but this process called for tremendous experience and a huge store of knowledge.

Jack had watched him and tried to learn as they played chess with the weather, while different tasks and operations were fitted together to complete a huge jigsaw puzzle every week. The old man was wily and cunning. He saw things that no-one else did – weather signals, the first buds on the hawthorn, a calf starting to sicken with its head low and its legs splayed. Just as Wil was standing at this very moment. The old man was sickening, he looked out of sorts.

'You OK, Wil?'

'Yes, I'm fine.'

That old, old lie. The commonest lie in history. People could be so very brave. Old Wil had to be brave too, this was his time to be brave.

'I'll go and shut the hens in, then,' said Wil, and off he went.

Entering the hen house, he lowered his head as usual to avoid a beam.

'One, two, three, four…'

They were all there. Cluck stood proudly, a patrician figure on the highest rung of the roost.

'Are you all OK in here tonight?' said Wil to his brood, as if greeting old friends. And in all truth, that's what they were. Old friends…

Wil shut the door on them and, finished for the day, he headed towards the house. Venus, above the western horizon, was clear and cold and beautiful. There wasn't much time to admire the beauty of his surroundings nowadays, what with having to spend so many hours labouring, or worrying, or planning.

The house seemed to be boiling with life when he walked along the narrow passageway to the kitchen. People were dashing around like dancers, laughing and talking volubly. It was like a young farmers' barn dance in there. Standing in the middle was Nico, acting like one of the Magi, handing out gifts to everyone from the big canvas bag which Wil had seen on one of the horses.

Lipstick and other cosmetics for Elin – who was delighted, whimpering and giggling like a schoolgirl. In that moment, Wil felt terribly sorry for her. His poor lovely sister, once so poised and warm and funny. Tonight, both of them stood in the old homestead, their childhood dreams come to nothing, shattered and scattered to the four winds like ashes after a funeral. She was a child again, slapping on too much make-up, looking into the mirror for hours on end, talking to imaginary friends. Sulking, weeping... his big sister was little again. He felt an urge to put his arms around her, to hug her and tell her that everything would be fine, but he couldn't do that sort of thing. Not publicly, anyway. It wasn't in him, it wasn't part of the old Welsh way of life.

Mari received a handful of rings and earrings and bangles – as if Nico were a ship's captain on a remote African shore, handing out gifts to the natives. Huw was next, and he received something wonderful too – a pair of red Manchester United shorts and a smart black fishing rod with red stripes, complete with a reel and line. Huw was speechless. He walked around the kitchen in the candlelight admiring his new rod, pretending to fish, pretending to catch a whopper.

'I show you how to use that tomorrow,' said Nico like an older brother. He'd made a friend for life, till the end of time.

'Thank you,' said Huw. '*Diolch!*'

Rod at the ready, he looked up to his uncle and said shyly, almost apologetically:

'I'm going to stay here tonight, Uncle Wil.'

'OK, lad,' said Wil with a friendly grin.

But he suffered two sorts of pain when he crossed the yard towards his bed that night; one in his belly and the other in his heart. He didn't bother with the candle; he went straight to bed, in his clothes, with his big black boots still laced to his filthy feet.

I O

Dawn arrives at Dolfrwynog, spreading its pallor along the shivering highland grasses. The new light arrives in dribs and drabs, as stealthily as the foreign water seeping into the basin of the valley; it's difficult to gauge any change from minute to minute, but if Wil shuts his eyes for a while and then opens them suddenly he sees a palpable difference. Forms take shape in the shadows and insist on being noticed; Grandma and Grandad appear gradually in the loft, ghostly, beckoning… but then the strengthening light reveals them to be a couple of ragged old coats, not the old people returning from a sojourn in the past.

March arrives; spring has come early and a young family of daffodils wave their emaciated arms in the garden. They have lived at Dolfrwynog for eons; their family tree goes back further than that of the human occupants. Not a single sound can be heard in the house; everyone is in bed. In the master bedroom, Jack and Elin sleep well away from each other in the big bed, both of them almost falling off the edges. They couldn't be farther apart. A broken fan of magazines is spread out on the floor by Elin. Clothes are scattered everywhere; drawers hang open-mouthed, drunkenly, with small items of intimate underwear spewing out onto the carpet. Dirty mugs fester under the bed, green and blue algae growths blooming inside them. Disorder and anarchy have set up home together in this bedroom; Wil would be shocked if he saw it – but he's not allowed anywhere near the place. This room is a form of installation art seen once upon a time at Tate Modern; a figurative representation of the psychological state of humanity. Its title: *Desolation.*

Nearby, in her own little room, sleeps Mari. The pop posters have started to peel off the purple walls. She's a little mouse, dreaming about…

No prizes for guessing. Yes, Superman, newly flown in from Poland. She's doing delicious things with Nico, then Uncle Wil drifts across her dream with a shotgun pointing straight at them: he stands in the door of her imagination, pulling horrible faces and barking like a dog…

In the next bedroom, normally Huw's room, Nico is already awake. He hasn't been able to sleep properly since he was attacked by a gang in Liverpool. He was lucky; fear gave his legs superhuman strength and he was able to flee through the back streets, helped by darkness. But his body has retained two livid scars as mementoes; one on his back, below his right shoulder blade, and the other on his chest. These scars, already healed but quite noticeable, will be of great interest to Mari, as will his tattoo. Other women have found him attractive, he is aware of their interest.

He studies the room. There are no curtains, and the new light illuminates a landscape of dust and neglect. He decides to get up, but then changes his mind, fearful that the people around him will misunderstand him and begin to doubt him. Moving around now would seem furtive, the act of a thief.

Huw is also coming to; his light blue eyes open slowly, shut, then flicker open again. He has slept in a dirty old sleeping bag, stained and damp. Where is he? He looks around the room. Then he remembers that he has slept on two chairs pulled together by the fireplace downstairs. He rises suddenly and walks upstairs. The treads squeal like little mice. He peeks through the door to his bedroom, which is slightly ajar. Nico stares back at him, then tips him a wink and waves. First the gesture means *Hiya* and then it means *Go away*. In no time at all he joins Huw downstairs.

'Good day for fishes,' he remarks to Huw. 'We go?'

It had rained heavily overnight, and the river was running high.

'Water nice and brown, we get fishes,' said Nico with his wide smile.

'First we go get...' but he didn't know the word.

'You know, little snakes.' He enacted a little drama, fastening an imaginary worm onto an imaginary hook.

'Worms,' said Huw.

'OK worms, we get them in shit.'

Huw laughed with his eyes closed. Nico meant soil, presumably. Huw knew where to find hundreds of worms, under an old corrugated sheet in the paddock. Big worms, fat as snakes. He liked the way Nico talked; he mangled the English language comically, but Huw always knew what he meant. His manner of speaking was mysterious yet amusing.

The pair of them dressed as warmly as they could, then went out to the paddock to find earthworms, which they gathered in an old baked beans tin without a label. Huw had raised the corrugated sheet and found hundreds of fat purple-red worms, more than they could possibly need.

While walking through the paddock Nico went up to the horses, which were sheltering under one of the old damson trees in the lower corner. He greeted them and stroked them affectionately. He too was very fond of horses. Nico almost tripped over one of the graves before he realised what he'd come across. Then he stared, almost disbelievingly, from one grave to another before looking up at Huw. They gazed at each other for some time.

'What's these?' asked Nico.

'Graves,' said Huw.

'What is graves?'

'Dead people.'

Nico's face creased and his querying look intensified.

'People like you and me?'

'Yes.'

'Who they?'

Nico poked one of the graves with his left boot. Then he knelt and straightened an old jam jar containing some withered flowers.

'We get more flowers,' said Nico. 'Who these dead people?'

'Don't know,' said Huw.

He didn't, either. He hadn't a clue. He had some sort of idea that they were relatives, but he didn't know who they were. No-one had told him. Whenever he started to probe, a door was closed abruptly.

Huw shrugged and motioned that he couldn't supply any information. He looked down at the four scars on the ground; they'd always been there, ever since he was very small.

Soon they were walking down the field towards the estuary where the river poured into the new lake. The river was brown and busy, pushing against its banks.

'We go up river – always up, never down,' said Nico. He knew about such things, Polish people did. He showed Huw how to thread a hook on his line and tie a proper non-slip knot. Huw fiddled about, hooked his own thumb, but eventually got a bloodstained hook onto the line. He stared at the droplets of his own blood as they bubbled to the surface. The pain subsided and he felt braver and more manly after he'd dealt with it. Then Nico prompted him to put a worm on the hook, which was difficult and barbaric. The worm danced pitifully on its steel crucifix, then it burst open when Huw pushed too hard, exposing its innards. When they'd managed to hook a worm properly Nico showed him how to cast into the top end of the pools, where the river entered, and where the trout would be feeding.

Conditions were perfect; in a couple of hours they caught eight brown trout, three of them weighing more than half a pound each; Nico cut a hazel twig and threaded the fish through their gills so that they could be carried conveniently. As little Huw walked home with the fish-twig thrown over his shoulder, he thought that Nico was heroic. He was amazed by the beauty of the newly-caught trout, their glistening rainbow spots.

The smell of fish and damp earth was on his hands, in his hair, on the wind, it was everywhere. It was a mysterious smell, a waft from an alchemist's room. The very smell of Creation; Huw had gained an insight into the world of magic. That morning, with its primal smells and enraged river, would stay in his memory for ever, until he was an old man like Uncle Wil. On their way home Nico gathered a posy of dandelions and when they went through the paddock he put them in the jam jar.

'We get more tomorrow,' he said. 'For other graves. We give respect, yes?'

The horses gathered around them, sending misty banks of steam and horse-breath into the encircling atmosphere. Their teeth were green with grass. Huw and Nico rubbed their damp furry flanks while listening to their teeth crunching.

'Hey everybody, look what we've caught,' said Huw at the top of his squeaky voice when he opened the farmhouse door. But as usual, when he wanted an audience, there was nobody there; no-one to greet Odysseus at his homecoming.

That evening Nico made dinner for them all, using the fish

and rice he'd brought in his saddlebags when he came. It was a feast, said Elin, cooked to perfection. Mari didn't eat fish normally but she thought this meal was the nicest she'd ever tasted. Indeed it was wonderful, incredibly tasty. Nico should be on TV, said Elin, and tears started to roll down her cheeks because she'd remembered that there was no electricity at Dolfrwynog and their television had been gathering dust for many a day in Uncle Wil's stable loft.

'Please don't cry, Mum,' said Huw, who didn't want anything to impair his perfect day. It was he who had caught the fish and put food on their plates. He smiled at his family as they sat around the table and he felt a soft glow of happiness, for the first time in ages. That night he slept in the same place, by the fire, and he dreamt about the lake. At some stage he rode on the back of a dolphin, and the dolphin was talking to him, saying:

We too lived on land once upon a time, but we returned to the sea. We're happy now. The land wasn't a good place to be…

11

THAT NIGHT EVERYONE sat in a circle around the fire. Jack had been to fetch a batch of dry wood from the coal shed, as it was still called, though they hadn't seen any coal for a long time. The flames cast dancing shadows on all their faces, and their shadow-puppets danced on the wall behind them; they listened to the crackle of the wood burning and the roar of the wind in the chimney. It was just like the old days, said Wil – exactly the same as when Grandfather and Grandmother were alive. Wil looked into the heart of the fire and saw a picture of the future: he and Nico would rescue the rusty plough from the nettles in the paddock, they'd scrape away the red-brown rust from the mouldboard and the ploughshare and the coulter… the old names for each part came back to him like tiny lights twinkling on a Christmas tree – old, old words which he hadn't used for years.

'Furrow,' he said to himself, under his breath, by the fireside.

'What did you say, Uncle Wil?' asked Huw, who was sitting next to him to show that he hadn't abandoned him completely.

'Oh, nothing,' said Wil sleepily. The fire was very hot by now and he was beginning to sweat a little. He'd have to be careful or he'd catch a chill when he went back to his home in the East, across the filthy yard. His big boots would travel like slave ships across the frozen mud-waves; his big black coat would billow like a sail, and his eyes would be the eyes of a man in the crow's nest, scanning the horizon for a distant shore.

Nico was answering questions about himself, with Mari on one side and Jack on the other; Elin had stepped towards the stool which was nearest to him but had changed her mind at the last moment; she'd look silly, perhaps, if she sat too close to him. Mari asked him where he came from.

'Zakopane,' said Nico.

'Pardon?' asked Jack.

'Zakopane,' said Nico again, accentuating the last syllable.

'Zak-o-pan-e,' repeated Mari, gingerly.

'Very good,' said Nico with a supportive smile.

'Is in Poland, in South. Very pretty, lot of snow in winter,' he added. 'People ski in snow. Mountains big. Many trees.'

So it was similar to Wales, except for the skiing.

'My home in Tatra mountains, special place for Poles,' added Nico dreamily. 'Homeland. Poland think people in mountains special. They go there for holidays and listen to Tatra stories and buy Tatra…'

He didn't know the right word.

'Thing you take home…' he said lamely.

'Souvenirs?' asked Mari.

'Yes! You got it,' he said merrily. 'Souvenirs! My father he has stall in Zakopane, he sell souvenirs. Many people sell souvenirs in Zakopane. Big, big, market and many people buy,' he elaborated in his unique, attractive style.

'Here is like my home, I think,' he added. 'In old days people sit by fires and make stories, in house like this, they go from this house to other house and make stories about monsters and…'

What was the word?

Nico stood up and waved his arms around, while also saying *Wwwwww* like a cartoon ghost. A shadow ghost appeared on the wall behind him.

'Ghost!' said Huw.

'Yes, that right, Huw,' said Nico, and Huw's chest puffed out with pride.

'Meetings in house like this we call *posiady*. Women they knit. Stories about monster and ghost, and always little boy keep light burning with roots from tree, nice smell like Christmas,' said Nico. 'I was little boy who burn roots in house of my...'

The words wouldn't come to him. Nico stood again and pretended to walk with a stick, stooped over.

'Grandfather!' said Elin. 'And grandmother?'

'Yes! Right!' said Nico. 'In your language?'

'*Nain* and *Taid*,' said Huw. They tried to teach him the Welsh words, then a silence fell over the room, everyone returning to their own little world. *Who'd have thought that Polish would be spoken in this house?* thought Wil... his grandparents would have been amazed; he had fond memories of Grandmother knitting away in the corner, and Grandfather throwing bits of copper wire onto the fire so that Wil could admire the amazing colours.

Nico rose to his feet.

'I go bed now, I very tired, long day, yes?'

Everyone else got up too.

'Thank you very much,' said Nico, though he wasn't entirely sure why he was thanking them.

'Me too,' said Mari. She followed him upstairs, and when Nico trod on a squeaky plank then Mari trod on another squeaky plank to tease him, so it was squeak-squeak-squeak all the way to the top. Both were giggling like kids by the end.

Downstairs, they all listened to the squeaks and the stifled laughter.

There'll be trouble there, soon enough, thought Wil.

I'll have to keep an eye on those two, thought Jack in his black cloud.

Elin daydreamed about an unexpected encounter with Nico on the mountain, in the heather, on a lovely summer's day with a picnic spread out among the purple flowers, with lovely fresh smells in her nostrils and a playful breeze warming her naked skin…

'What does Zakopane mean,' asked Mari on the landing, in an attempt to keep Nico with her in the semi-darkness.

That look came over his face again; a look which was a trademark by now. It seemed to display pain, and confusion, and longing.

'It mean in the ground.' He pointed in the direction of the paddock. 'Like graves. Under ground.'

He searched her face, so young and intense.

'What you say when you put people in ground?'

Mari scrolled through a list of words in her mind.

'Bury?'

'Yes,' said Nico, and he put his hands on her shoulders gently. 'Under ground. Buried, yes?'

'Yes…'

'Zakopane means buried.'

Mari stood stock still, feeling the weight of his hands on her. For the first time, she noticed the tattoo on his arm. A tattoo which showed a ship on the sea, and some Polish words.

He noticed the direction of her eyes.

'You like?'

She nodded, and smiled weakly.

'The graves,' said Nico suddenly and intensely. 'Who is there?'

Mari swallowed hard and looked away, trying to avoid his eyes.

'My family,' she answered. She didn't know how to explain…

'You tell me about them?' asked Nico.

'Yes, but…'

Nico put a finger to her lips. Mari could smell earth, and flowers, and fish, all the wildness of nature – beautiful yet dangerous, a lovely but deadly world outside this house.

'You tell me again, yes? You come to me in the morning, you tell me…'

Then he moved around her and stepped into his bedroom, closing the door slowly and deliberately, watching her all the time.

When Wil sailed across the ocean of the yard to his homeland the sky had cleared, and Venus was shining as brightly as the star over the biblical manger. The Three Wise Men would receive a very warm welcome at Dolfrwynog tonight, thought Wil. But it wasn't gold or myrrh or frankincense they wished for. Food, medicine and hope were the gifts they most needed. He imagined a great silvery angel hovering in the night sky, announcing important news: Mari was expecting a child, they would have to flee…

Wil went to bed in his boots that night. He missed the little boy's company, and as he lay in his bed a dry, uncomfortable sensation permeated his body. As he tried to make himself comfortable he was overcome by a fit of anger towards the Polish lad. Then he calmed himself, saying: *The lad's OK, just give him a chance. Leave him alone, he's doing his best…*

1 2

MARI HAD A fit of the blues when she opened her eyes the following morning and looked at the posters on her walls. They were peeling away from the pitted paint, bubbling like the bellies of middle-aged men.

Mainly they were magazine models, wearing the sort of clothes Mari had never seen in any shops, and which would never be seen again either. Indeed, they looked out of date already. But that was the very essence of fashion, wasn't it? Fashion was a shooting star, replaced almost immediately by darkness, before another flash streaked across the sky. Among the models there were also males: singers and actors – the icons of her early years in high school. She appraised them, then noticed that her eyes were dusty and sore. She saw her room with different eyes altogether this morning, and noticed that it was tatty and dirty. Once, her mother had nagged at her constantly to keep it tidy, but nowadays Elin's room was messier by miles.

Mari managed to open her eyes properly and noticed something else: the paintwork was marred everywhere with Sellotape scars and furniture scrapes. What a mess. She saw her adolescence walking across the room and leaping out of the window. That period of her life had gone for ever, she realised. There wasn't even a radio in the house to keep them up to date with world events. She noticed that one of the young rock stars on her walls looked like Nico, and he too had a tattoo on his arm. She closed her eyes, and might have nodded off again, but with a determined effort she sat up and faced the day. Then she swung into action, rifled the drawers, and after picking and choosing various items she dressed as smartly as she could. Almost all her clothes were too small for her now, and looked juvenile, but she did the best she could. She brushed her hair and tied it up in a way that made her look older and more mature. She rubbed the sleep from her eyes, but left her face without any make-up. Finally, she opened a box on her bedside table and chose a particular ring. Why that one? She wasn't quite sure. It had belonged to her maternal grandmother, a fierce little woman who had also been capable of great kindness; she had seen something of herself in Mari and had given her more attention than the others, though Mari was quite scared of her.

She'd been the most giving, despite her formal and unwieldy manner. And they'd become close, in an old-fashioned way, when the slightest gesture or inflection in the voice – rather than spoken words – were used to convey feeling. It was she too who had talked to her meaningfully, and treated her like an independent person. She had entertained Mari with family stories, and made her laugh; folk tales and chit-chat had also been a bridge between them. Grandmother had been a natural story-teller, and Mari had become very attached to her weirdly antediluvian world, biblical and black, yet laced with dry humour. That was the reason, probably, why Mari wore that ring this morning; to give her strength and confidence. She had roped her finger to the anchor of the past; the ring felt safe and dependable in an ever-changing and unpredictable present.

Mari opened the door, strode onto the landing and knocked on Nico's door. She'd decided on a course of action while dressing; to hesitate would be fatal so she rushed into the day, as if she were about to sit an exam. So she shut away all doubts and braved the consequences. She stood outside his door now, playing with the ring, waiting for an answer. Nico was expecting her, but he delayed his response so as to appear nonchalant. In truth he'd been on edge for half an hour as he waited.

When Mari entered he was sitting up in bed with his back to the wall and with his legs crossed in the lotus position. Without his pullover on he revealed a red Che Guevara T-shirt peppered with holes.

'Sit down,' he said, plumping the bed alongside him. But Mari sat well away from him, at the foot of the bed, though she put her back to the wall like him. She could see him through the corner of her eye but she looked away from him, through the window, before starting to speak. She continued to fidget with her ring, and seeing that she was on tenterhooks, he tried to put her at ease by launching into a story.

'You know, young people like us do the same as this in my country too,' he said, while playing with the hem of his shabby T-shirt. He'd finger-combed his hair and rubbed the sleep from his eyes just like Mari; after all, there was no water piped to the house any longer, they had to fetch it from the well.

'In Zakopane old houses have black room and white room,' said Nico jerkily. He wasn't nervous in her company but he lacked confidence when he had to speak English.

'Black room is black because of smoke, that room is where people live, where they eat and talk,' he said. 'But white room special. If two young people like each other a lot they sleep in white room to see if it work, you understand?'

Mari turned towards him with a mixture of surprise and amusement. 'Yes, I understand.' Was he trying it on already? Did she appear as *easy* as that?

'They sleep like that till the girl make... make baby,' said Nico hesitantly, aware that he was making a mess of things. 'No good if she no make baby. But if she (he made a pregnant curve with his hand) they get marry.'

Mari thought about this for a while.

'And what if she gets pregnant but they don't want to marry by then?'

'No worry, people think baby is good... baby show she is strong woman, can have more babies,' explained Nico, who was in a hurry to finish; trying to explain something complex was so tiring.

'It was like that in Wales long ago,' said Mari. 'Boyfriends used to climb a ladder to the girl's bedroom and they slept together to make sure they liked each other before getting married. Everyone knew what was going on but everyone turned a blind eye.'

'Turn a blind eye?'

'Pretended it wasn't happening.'

'Oh, I see! So they stop doing that?' asked Nico. 'Why?'

'Religion,' said Mari. 'The chapel people said it was wrong.'

'Well,' said Nico as he freed his legs, 'I think it was better. More honest, yes?'

Mari smiled and turned away from him.

'Yes, maybe you're right,' she said. 'But don't get any funny ideas, OK?'

She said this with exaggerated virtuousness, and Nico carried on with the game, indicating with his hands and a ridiculously innocent expression that he wouldn't dream of trying it on.

At that point a heavy pair of boots arrived at the foot of the stairs. Someone had heard them.

'Are you up there, Mari?'

She lifted her eyes heavenwards and answered. 'Yes, Uncle Wil.'

'What are you doing?'

'Talking to Nico.'

'About what?'

'About our wedding, Uncle Wil. We're going to get married tomorrow in the chapel. Will you be best man?'

'Don't you be a cheeky little madam, Mari.'

'Well, what do you think we're talking about?'

'I just want a word with Nico, that's all.'

'Go on then, say what you want to.'

They could hear Wil clearing his throat.

'Nico?'

'Yes?'

Nico winked and gave her a small, intimate smile, as good as to say, *You have to treat these old fogeys like day-old chicks.*

'I wonder…' said Wil, but his voice fell off.

'You want me to help you today?'

Mari felt a warm feeling sweep through her. This Nico was a clever lad. He'd read the situation perfectly, and she liked her men clever and cunning.

'Yes,' said Wil, and he started clumping upstairs.

'There's no need for you to come up, he's coming down now,' said Mari. She didn't want the old sod inside the room with them.

'I coming down soon,' said Nico in a soothing voice. 'Ten minutes I am with you, yes?'

'*Iawn,*' said Wil, forgetting which language to use.

His boots clattered along the kitchen tiles, through the door, and out into the yard; they heard him recede towards the stable loft.

Afterwards they sat looking at each other in the weak early morning sunshine, which warmed the room and lit up their young faces. Their eyes met, and they both smiled, because they both realised that a possibility, no, many possibilities were arising, like bubbles rising to the surface of the lake below.

'I think I know why he want me,' said Nico. 'I help him today.'

'What does he want you for?' asked Mari.

'Yesterday, when I was with horses, I saw him looking at me, yes? And he has been cleaning the...'

That was another word he didn't know.

'Go behind tractor, rip earth.'

'Plough?'

'I don't know, there is one in field by graves. He want me to help.'

Mari wrinkled her face, because she'd remembered why it was that she was sitting on Nico's bed. She'd been about to tell him the story of the graves.

He remembered that too when he saw a certain look on her face.

'No matter, you tell me other time.'

'No, no,' protested Mari. She wanted to tell him now. That's why she'd dressed the way she had, that's why she'd worn that particular ring.

'I want to tell you, it's important... or you won't understand why we're living like this, with nothing. No food, no electricity, no new clothes...'

Nico allowed her time to prepare herself. He saw how she rotated the ring round and round her finger, nervously. Then she started to talk in a level, emotionless voice.

'Once I had a sister, she was called Sara. She was older than me, and prettier and cleverer.'

'Pa!' said Nico. He had to play the game.

'No, really, she was ever so pretty. And she got loads of A-levels, she was going to university. But she was always worried about us... she could see what was going to happen, I think. She became quiet, and withdrawn...'

'What is withdrawn?'

Mari thought for a moment. 'She went into her own world. She stopped talking to us, stopped taking part in family life. She spent more and more time in her bedroom, or walking the fields.'

She described how her sister had retreated to a far country, her own country.

Like her mother, Sara had become very religious; they'd go together to the chapel three times every Sunday, when it was still open. She would dress severely in black, read her Bible every evening, or she'd always be quoting from the scriptures or talking about God, and Jesus, and Paradise. The life that was to come, afterwards. Heaven was the place to be, not this Hell. She wanted to be with the angels, there would be plenty of food for everyone, and there would be peace; there would no longer be fighting, or war, or torture, or little children dying.

That's the way that Sara was for many months; dreamy, and far away, with her light blue eyes – so much like her mother's and Huw's – looking more and more towards a far horizon, an other-worldly place.

'One day we noticed how thin she was,' said Mari. 'We were so busy coping with our new life, we just didn't notice she was fading away before our eyes.'

Sara had shed every spare inch of flesh. And then she'd seen a vision. She'd seen the Virgin Mary by the well when she went there for water one day. Sara had described her in minute detail: the purple robe, the perfect hands, the porcelain face; the incredibly white skin, eggshell pure, and the supernatural light illuminating the air around her.

'Perhaps it was no food inside her, make her mad,' said Nico.

'Yes, we thought of that, but it didn't make any difference, did it? She thought she'd seen the Virgin Mary, and she wouldn't listen to reason. She was completely gone by then, we couldn't get close to her.'

They sat in silence, listening to the sounds of the farm under the window: Cluck crowing regally in the paddock, Megan singing sweetly elsewhere, the dogs barking whenever they sensed danger.

A crunching sound came towards them across the yard, through the door, across the kitchen and to the foot of the stairs. Wil was back, like a ghost, to haunt them.

Nico whispered and squeezed her hand. 'We carry on tomorrow.'

Then, loudly: 'OK, Mister Wil, I come to help you now.'

I 3

IF WIL HAD said *Dammit!* roughly ten times every day since he was eight years old, it's safe to say that he repeated his favourite word many times more during the following day, enough indeed to last a parrot's lifetime, as he was fond of saying – he had some idea in his head that parrots lived a very long time. He sounded like a parrot himself by nightfall, saying *Dammit!* over and over again in an undertone. Nico had heard the exclamation so many times he began to say it himself by the time they'd finished. They'd been at it for ages, struggling with the plough, searching for old chains which could be used to haul the implement, and trying to find bits and bobs which could be utilised to piece all the harnesses together into a working whole so that they could haul a lump of rusting metal behind the newly-acquired horses. Not that the horses were itching to take part in this pantomime; they'd neighed and stamped their way around the paddock all day, as if suspecting that something unpleasant lay ahead.

The men had patched everything into a working whole by lunchtime but there was no lunch for them so they left the farmyard like a dishevelled medieval circus, heading for The Meadow, with the cob hauling the plough and the other horses taken along for company. Wil wanted to prepare The Meadow ready to sow seedcorn, and they'd be there for ever if they went at it with the rusty old spades available to them. The plough would be a boon, said Wil, it would do the heavy work for them. It was decided that Wil should lead the cob and Nico could handle the plough. But they hadn't finished the first furrow before one of the chains had broken, and Wil had been forced to plod home in search of spanners and nuts and bolts. That first furrow was as twisted as a pig's tail, said Wil in his old fashioned lingo, but Nico had no idea what he was on about. When he finally made himself understood, Wil added that a drove of pigs would help them a lot, even pigs as mad as the Gadarene swine in the Bible. Nico wanted to know why. Because they could turf and break up the ground with their noses, said Wil.

'You want me get pigs?' asked Nico.

'Yes, you get some pigs, and diesel too, and a doctor, and anything else I think of before we reach the end of this bloody field with this stupid bloody plough,' said Wil sarcastically, since he thought Nico was poking fun at him.

'No, really now, I get you pigs,' said Nico.

Wil came to a sudden halt and the cob went straight into him, hurling him into the furrow like a sack of potatoes. He almost had a huge hoof planted on his backside. Many *Dammits!* could be heard from ground level as Wil tried to extricate himself. Finally, he squirmed to his feet and turned to face Nico, his face aflame with effort.

'You can get pigs?'

'Yes, no problem.'

Where?'

Nico tapped his nose with a finger. 'Nico get anything you like. In Poland we are very poor so we have to be clever. Polish find anything you want, yes?'

Wil laughed, and said: 'Yes, you Poles are very clever. Good at staying alive.'

'We have to be,' said Nico. 'Everybody try to kill us. No Poland at all for many years. Then Hitler kill six million Polish. It's hard to be Polish. We have to eat any food we find, yes? We have to use our brains, no? In Poland we have a saying – have trust in God but keep some cheese in your bag.'

Wil laughed again, and started to lead the cob onwards, towards the other end of the field. The plough gouged at the soil, but the end results were pretty poor. Pigs would do the trick, thought Wil. But if Nico went away, would he return? He was young and powerful, he could do so much more than anyone else on the farm. Wil looked at the tattoo bobbing up and down on Nico's muscular arm. A ship at sea. Nico had been in the navy, presumably. Wil started to believe that he too should have acquired a tattoo. A red dragon, or something like that. The Welsh had never had a navy, had they? He remembered a fine afternoon long ago at a youth camp, sailing a little boat around a lake. He'd won a cup and the boys at school had started to call him *Popeye*.

Years later he could still hear *Popeye* being whispered behind his back, whenever someone was talking about him. But unlike the cartoon sailor, with his tattoos and his dockside brawls, Wil hated spinach. Yach! He'd been given a dollop of it on his plate during an agricultural dinner with Lord So-and-So sitting next to him and he'd felt obliged to eat the stuff. Wil had nearly choked on it, it was like eating silage. He felt sorry for the cattle, how could they eat stuff like that when the natural thing was for them to have plenty of nice fresh grass?

'Whoa!' said Wil. They'd reached the end of the furrow. They both looked back along the field, and indeed the furrow reminded Nico of a skier's tracks in the snow; all over the place. An amateur skier at that, with a bottle of vodka inside him.

'Never mind,' said Wil. Turning the horse was quite a performance but they completed another furrow with Wil trying to straighten their handiwork.

'Whoa!' said Wil when they reached the headland. He wasn't

quite sure why he shouted *Whoa!* the way he did, but it sounded right. Wasn't that how they talked to the horses in the olden days?

'That one much better,' said Nico encouragingly. By nightfall they'd ploughed – maybe broken up would be a better way of putting it – about half an acre of land. At which point they released the cob and allowed him to enjoy a bit of horseplay with the other two horses.

We'll have a hell of a job catching him again in the morning, thought Wil.

They walked homewards in silence, with the darkness thickening around them. A robin warbled in the hedge as they passed by, and Wil noticed that its song had changed; the bird had dropped its winter call and was now greeting them with a lighter cadence. Spring had come very early; lambs had arrived weeks ago – that's where Jack was today, looking after the sheep. Yes, the new season had arrived a month before it should, riotously, drunkenly. The hedges were already green, nests had been built, eggs had hatched.

Wil's thoughts wandered towards his feathery friends – Cluck, and Megan, and all the other fowls exploring their little kingdom every day; the farmyard was their whole universe too, just as it was Wil's. He understood them so much better than humans. If he chatted to the hens they seemed to understand him perfectly, but people were a mystery to him. And as for women, they made him feel like a little green alien who'd just landed in a flying saucer – while this stringy lad by his side seemed to understand them perfectly. How come? Why did he have that inexplicable, magical ability to read their minds? Perhaps he ought to ask him.

Hey lad, what's the secret? Have you got a manual in your pocket, like the one for the Ford 5000 tractor which arrived in the yard on the back of a lorry, beautiful and blue and spotlessly new, with its description of the new machine: A = gear lever, B = clutch, C = brake?

Wil felt sad, suddenly. How in God's name was he going to get things in order? He was ill, and no-one knew it. They were weeks behind schedule. He needed to get the spuds planted quickly; they'd have to spread manure on last year's corn patch and turn it over as soon as possible. Tomorrow? He turned to the lad and expressed his fears.

'You want me get pigs tomorrow?' asked Nico.

Wil explained that they needed to plant the potatoes while they had decent weather.

'OK boss, you tell me what to do,' said Nico. It was almost dark by the time they got home and Wil went straight to the hen hut to count his brood. Nico heard him count *One, two, three, four,* like a child. That's what he was in many ways, Nico decided. A child who'd lived in this godforsaken place all his life, probably. He'd never had to cope with city life, dangerous and deceitful. Poor Wil. He looked terrible, he'd be lucky to see Christmas. Him and his hens… they were more like his harem than a batch of brainless birds.

Nico splashed his face with cold water and washed his hands in the bath by the house, then he turned in. It was warm there; Elin had got up today and she'd lit a fire, made them all some food. It was the same old smelly stew with chunks of turnip floating on its greasy surface. Nico didn't care, he was so hungry. While he wolfed down the stew he mentally stripped Mari of all her clothes and examined her body, in case he lost the will to live.

'Thank you, very nice,' he lied, trying to be pleasant.

Elin took his plate out to the yard to wash it, in case she made a fool of herself. She was feeling emotional, on edge. *No fool like an old fool*, she said to the stars. Which one was that one, shining high above her? Wil came down the yard towards her so she asked him.

'Venus,' he replied, adding: 'Here you are, two eggs,' and he handed them over to his sister.

'Bloody hell, Wil, I'd just washed my hands,' she said crossly. Wil had to bite his tongue. Wasn't that a perfect example of a woman's perfidy? There he was, handing over some delicious fresh eggs, without any thanks at all.

'Bloody women,' said Wil under his breath. She heard him, and turned on her heel. *Bang!* The door closed behind her with a terrific crash, shattering the silence. Wil heard her starting to cry on the other side of the door.

'There there, no matter…' he heard Nico comforting her. 'We get more eggs tomorrow, no?'

When he entered the house Wil saw a smear of dampness in the hallway and bits of shell. In slamming the door she'd squeezed one of the eggs and crushed it.

Wil said nothing. He helped himself to the stew, and he tried his best to eat it, but without any bread it was almost indigestible. He chewed laboriously, distracted by a host of thoughts. Then he returned to his squat in the stable loft, and went straight to bed. That new pain was gnawing at his insides again.

'Silly old bastard,' said Elin when she saw his dirty plate on the table. She went out again, to wash it clean. Afterwards she stared at Venus in the heavens until she started shivering violently with cold. By ten, everyone was in bed. Everyone except for Jack, who continued to sit by the fire on his own, nursing the first sick lamb of the year.

I 4

ONE DAY, IN the middle of winter, the Virgin Mary had been wandering through the snow with the baby Jesus in her arms; she was somewhere in the mountains above Zakopane, looking for somewhere to shelter for the night. But they were turned away by three wealthy families. Eventually she came to a hovel which was home to a very poor couple with ten children. They had only two sheep to call their own; all of them, including the sheep, were sheltering inside when Mary arrived. Unlike the rich people, these poor folk made her welcome; they invited her in and sat her by the fire. When Mary had warmed up, the family heated some water for her so that she could wash her baby; after she'd finished, Mary noticed that the youngest child suffered from a skin complaint, so she washed the infant in the same water. When morning came, Mary and baby Jesus had vanished, and the child who'd been afflicted had perfect skin. Outside they could see the Virgin's footsteps in the snow, and in each little hollow left by her feet there were beautiful purple flowers – that's how the crocus first arrived in Poland.

Nico finished his story and smiled at Mari.

'You see, we are very religious country, many stories about Mary and Jesus!'

She was sitting on his bed in the early morning towards the end of March, and it was already hot. No-one else had stirred yet. She'd put the ring on her third finger, left hand, because both of them knew that something was about to happen between them. Mari had started some sort of daily rite with these early calls, and a pattern was emerging. It was obvious by now that she was trying to attract his attention and his sympathy. But their quotidian ceremony involved more than that, because Mari was trying to clarify the story of her own life as well as trying to excite Nico's interest. Right now she was telling him about an ancient Welsh fable, the story of the lovers Culhwch and Olwen. Olwen had also left flowers – in her case white clover – wherever she walked. Together, Nico and Mari had noted the similarity between their flower stories; Mari had smiled innocently and said, 'Isn't it funny how the same stories are told all over the world...'

Nico looked up at the cobwebs strung across the upper corners of the windows; they shone like haloes in the morning sun. He felt like a trapped insect himself, waiting for a spider to wrap him in silk and paralyse him. Maybe that's what Mari was doing to him; spinning a web, waiting for him to become entangled. Well, he wasn't in a hurry to leave. The place seemed fairly safe for the time being. He studied her face, so open and naive... if he'd seen her in the square at Krakow he'd have passed by, he wouldn't have given her a second glance. But she was pretty, and she wanted him. After all, he was a man and she was a woman. Well, almost a woman. They were being pulled together by a very ancient magnet.

Nico noticed that his T-shirt was beginning to smell. He had a bit of a beard by now and was starting to look like the photo of Che Guevara on his chest. He began to feel sleepy again. Closing his eyes, he could hear Wil's big boots clip-clopping down the steps from his home above the stable; he followed the old man up the yard, to the hen house. As usual there followed a squeal as Wil undid the bolt to release his brood for the day, and then he greeted his feathery harem as usual. Sometimes he'd stay there for ages, talking nonsense and fussing.

Nico had almost dropped off to sleep when Mari started talking again.

She was discussing her older sister Sara.

'She'd been home for only three days when she died,' said Mari, who was resting her right hand on the rucked blanket between them. The ring felt big on her finger. What use was gold now, did it have any value? And anyway, where would you sell it? Her mind wandered around the problem.

Nico opened his eyes and watched her mouth moving. She had a full mouth, pert and red. Her teeth were even and white. He hadn't tasted a woman's lips since… it had to be almost a year, in his flat in Krakow. A one-night stand, the girl was Lithuanian. They'd stayed in bed throughout the following day, having sex, drinking wine, joking and laughing, listening to the trumpeter 'dying' as history's arrow struck him every hour in the tower of St Mary's Basilica in the corner of the square. Right now he considered taking hold of Mari's wrist and pulling her towards him. But it was too soon in the relationship for that, probably. He listened to her voice, musical and sweet, as she recited the story of Sara, though he didn't understand all the words she used. He heard the stair treads squeaking under someone's weight. Huw perhaps. The boy eavesdropped sometimes, they both knew that.

Sara, dear Sara. As yet he had no clear picture of her in his head.

'Wait a minute,' he said. 'Have you got picture?'

His question astonished her. She sat completely still, searching his face, before she was able to move. Then she rose swiftly and went to her room. In less than a minute she was back, with a picture in her hand. She sat again, before handing him the photo. At first sight there was no resemblance between the two sisters, thought Nico; Sara was tall and dark whereas Mari was quite small, with light brown hair and a flock of freckles on her young little face.

'Do you like my freckles?' she'd asked him one day. He hadn't really noticed them until then. Yes, of course he liked them... but Mari herself hated them, she made that obvious. They made her look naughty. And indeed, Nico suspected that she'd be a bit of a handful between the sheets if they started... there was a certain look in her eyes. But as for Sara: no, the picture said that she was nothing like her sister. For one thing, she'd avoided the probing eye of the lens; her eyes had risen above the picture-taker and had drifted away, as if Cluck had just crowed far away in the woods and she was looking for him; she looked as if she was responding to a distant echo, a ghostly call from far away.

Nico studied the picture for a long time; he wanted Mari to know that he was taking this very seriously. He noted Sara's white, moonish face, her straight black hair (which reminded him of Polish women) and her slenderness. Polish girls were slender too, because they were mainly poor and they hadn't caught the McDonald's disease yet. One of the first things he'd noticed when he arrived in Britain was how fat many of the women were. People called them slappers. Nico himself liked unpainted women with their own hair. He most definitely didn't like them dressed up like dolls; but many British girls walked around like fat little Barbie Dolls with their bellies bulging over their jeans. Mari was naturally thin, she was young and fresh. Too young for him, that was the truth of it. But after all he was a man, and she as a woman. Almost. Could he resist temptation? Hmm...

Mari grabbed his ankle.

'Are you listening?'

'Yes, yes, I listen.'

So Mari expanded on the story of her sister. Poor Sara, who

lay in the paddock without a cross or a headstone to mark her grave.

One day Sara had met the Virgin Mary by the well. Sara had gone there to fetch water with the red plastic bucket which had *Lloyds Animal Feeds* on its side. She had leant over the crystal-clear water to check if their frog was there, they needed it to eat all the nasties and keep their supply clean. She spotted it on the leaf-brown floor of the well, and while she was staring into the cistern she saw, not one, but two shadows leaning over the water. She turned, and by her side was a shimmering figure, a beautiful young woman with a silvery glow all over her skin. Her robe rippled like the surface of the water, it bubbled softly with movement, as smoke does, changing colour occasionally from azure to purple; Sara thought a ball of lightning had fallen to earth and was about to explode. The Virgin's skin was as white as snow and her lips were as red as the rose, exactly as she appeared in the paintings. She had a halo too, and simple sandals on her feet; she was a walking icon. The Virgin smiled at Sara and they conversed; Sara had no recollection of their actual words, except that whatever passed between them was very wonderful and uplifting. At some stage Sara swooned, and when she awoke the Virgin had gone. After that she knew there was a place in paradise for herself and her family when the day came; she no longer had to fear anything. The New Kingdom was almost ready to receive the chosen people of Earth, among them the family at Dolfrwynog.

Sara was never the same after that; she went away from them, her eyes never quite focused on the fields of Dolfrwynog from then onwards. She entered her own dimension; she stopped eating altogether, became terribly thin. She either went to her room during meals, or took her food up with her and then threw it through her window for the hens to have it. Indeed,

Wil was puzzled for a while regarding his hens' inexplicable plumpness.

Sara was probably suffering from something similar to anorexia. That wasn't a new phenomenon, said Mari. Women had starved themselves since the dawn of time, either to keep slim and attractive, or to fulfil a fantasy which took them closer to purity and divinity. They somehow believed that refusing food would sharpen the mind and enrich the soul. And for a short period Sara seemed to have tremendous energy which propelled her into a high-octane whirl of cleaning and scrubbing and cooking and mending.

She worked for hours and days on end, she never stopped moving. But when she did stop, she stopped almost entirely. She fell, suddenly, into a morass of inactivity; she became terribly depressed, lethargic, uncaring about her appearance. She became the exact obverse of the previous Sara; she stayed in bed all day with the curtains drawn, and she ate nothing at all. Everyone became concerned about her; Huw would go up to her bedroom with fresh soup and bread, when such things were still available, but Sara would smile weakly, wave him away, and turn over in bed. Elin her mother would threaten and cry and beg, but it made no difference.

'This happen to a girl I know in school,' said Nico. 'She like no food inside her, plenty of energy for a bit because food slow you down, but your mind go a bit crazy, yes?'

A rumour went round the valley that Sara could live without eating; it appeared that she'd received heavenly grace, and had reached a saintly vantage point. Neighbours came to visit her in dribs and drabs, then a torrent arrived, some of them from beyond the horizon. It seemed such a long time ago. They brought presents and offerings, even money. She was considered special – she had seen a vision of the Virgin Mary; she was on the threshold of heaven itself. At any one time there would be anything between ten and forty people kneeling around her bed, on the landing, even on the stairs. They'd pray, or sing hymns, or read from the scriptures. Some of them spoke in tongues.

'You no get doctor?' asked Nico.

'Yes, we sent for one eventually and she was taken to hospital. They did a lot of tests on her because they didn't believe she could live without food.'

No-one knew how Sara had lived for so long without eating. Her family were sure she had abstained completely. Medical people asked them if they'd kept an eye on the kitchen; had any food disappeared, particularly at night?

Yes, of course food had disappeared, but mice or the menfolk had been blamed for that.

She didn't eat in hospital either. They had given up, almost, when Sara told them she would take some food if she was allowed to return to the well, so that she could talk to the Virgin again. If she could only see her again, she would be cured.

So she was released from hospital and returned to Dolfrwynog. During that final week, without anyone knowing, she'd gone alone to the well soon after dawn one morning. It must have been a tremendous effort, she was so weak by then. Later, when they went looking for her, they found her unconscious by the well. She was carried home and a priest was called, but it became obvious that the effort had cost Sara her life and she died that same night, just before midnight.

By then more than a hundred people from the neighbourhood – men, women and children – had gathered on the farmyard to pray for her soul. Many said they saw a soft globe of light, shimmering beautifully, leaving Sara's bedroom window. It hovered in the air, they said; it shone blue and then purple, then blue again. It moved over the paddock, and fell to the ground by the damson trees, leaving a scorched circle of grass. In that spot, three days later, Sara was buried in the presence of her family and many dozens of mourners. She would have celebrated her twenty-first birthday that day. After they went, none of those people was ever seen again by the little family at Dolfrwynog.

15

MARCH KILLS YOU, April skins you.

Sitting on the top step by the stable loft door, Wil had mumbled an old Welsh proverb while Huw skinned a rabbit down below.

'What did you say Uncle Wil?' asked the boy in a faraway voice – he was concentrating on his work. By now he was fast and efficient; the rabbit was without any fur in seconds.

'March kills you, April skins you,' repeated Wil.

'What does that mean, Uncle Wil?'

He wasn't quite sure himself, though he'd said the proverb many times. Like so many other old sayings, he'd never thought about its meaning, not properly anyway.

'Well, I suppose March is a bad month for old people because their bodies are weak after the winter and they've no resilience if the cold keeps battering them,' said Wil in a voice which sounded lamer and lamer with every word…

'And then, if they're weak, April can finish them off.'

Was that the real meaning? What did the English say? *Ne'er cast a clout till May is out…* did that mean the same thing?

'God knows,' said Wil, addressing the slate step below his feet. The slab had pretty patterns, which reminded him of white waves breaking on a beach. *Sweet Jesus*, he said to himself, *I wouldn't mind seeing the sea again before I go*. And yes, he'd love to go sailing again. Popeye… he imagined himself at the helm of a boat with a pipe in his mouth just like Popeye, with an empty spinach tin in his hand and huge muscles like Nico. He sang a song which his grandfather had taught him as a toddler:

I'm Popeye the sailor man,
I'm Popeye the sailor man,
I'm strong to the finich
Cause I eats me spinach
I'm Popeye the sailor man.

And there would be a girl like Olive Oil, Popeye's sweetheart, waiting for him on the shore at the Isle of Man, ready to welcome him and love him whatever he was like. But there again, Olive was terribly skinny and he himself had a tendency to like them ample, like his mum…

'What are you singing, Uncle Wil?'

'Oh, just something I used to sing when I was a lad like you.'

'Will you teach me the words, Uncle Wil?'

March had been mild and warm, unnaturally hot in fact. Wil and Nico had been able to sow the seedcorn in The Meadow and they'd also been able to plant all the seed potatoes in last year's plot.

Wil had sown in the old-fashioned way, by hand.

'We'll get some nice flour now for our bread,' he said to the Pole after they'd finished. They'd stood together on the headland, admiring their handiwork. Heavy clods were scattered all over the surface, but the two of them had done their best.

As they stood on the newly-harrowed earth, Nico had told him a story.

'Hey old man,' said Nico, since that was the way he greeted him nowadays; Wil had been forced to bite his tongue at first, but now he was secretly pleased. It was warm and honest, and he'd grown to like this young man.

'Hey old man,' said Nico, 'Men from Zakopane in old days make quick food out of flour.'

'Bread?' asked Wil.

'No, they take flour in bag with them when they go hunting for many days, then they make special food. They make fire and put stones in it to get hot. They put flour in cap off their heads, mix in salt and water, put hot stone from fire in it.'

'What, inside their caps?' gasped Wil.

'Yes, inside cap,' said Nico.

Wil was astonished. The old people at Dolfrwynog had lived a hard life, but making food inside your own cap was beyond belief.

In addition to planting the maincrop, Nico had planted individual spuds in places far enough from each other, all over the farm, to prevent disease spreading from one to another. It was an exigency against the possible failure of their main food supply; Wil had applauded him for his foresight.

'Well done, Nico,' he said sincerely. 'Good work, lad. There's two of us with our thinking caps on now, isn't it?' Wil was trying to joke about caps.

Nico had no idea what he was talking about… the old man was really beginning to lose it.

One of the hens, Mimi, had hatched ten little chicks and Wil had moved them all to the stable loft so that he could keep an eye on them, since he feared the rats might eat them. He'd spend hours talking to his little brood, and every morning he'd take them all down to the paddock and put them in a hutch of his own making; he'd move them around, day by day, to give them new pasture. They seemed to occupy his whole mind, he was like a father worrying about a thirteen-year-old daughter who'd gone to the school disco.

Huw had also returned to live in the stable loft. After the initial excitement surrounding Nico's arrival it had all gone a bit flat, since Mari commanded all his attention now. Elin had also abandoned hope again, after moping around him for a while. After all, she was an old boiler now, like one of Wil's scrawny hens, good for nothing except the pot. Who would want to touch her? She'd run out of eyeliner and her eyes seemed to stand out like a toad's. She thought she looked dreadful nowadays, though that hadn't prevented Jack from edging towards her in bed. Dirty sod. She was scared of responding to his advances, without contraceptives; she couldn't risk having another. That would be terrible. Who in their right mind would bring a child into the world nowadays?

But another part of her longed desperately for the warmth of his body, indeed *any* body.

It came at a heavy price, being human; one minute you'd need to be alone, you'd want a bit of peace to get your head straight, and then you'd feel the rest of mankind aiming their magnets at you; there would be a powerful force dragging you towards them as if you were an old baked beans tin being sucked up by one of those magnetic devices at the recycling centre. And what about Mari? What if she was up the duff... it didn't bear thinking about, what with no hospital now, not even a doctor, and no medicine either. They lived like wild animals, there was no cushion to protect them; no M&S food to console them, no ebay, no fashions to follow, no gold card, no life-affirming trips to the heavenly glass and steel shopping centre with its eternal promise of warmth and plenitude...

There was another worry too – the lake was still growing. She'd watched it through her bedroom window. And she'd seen strange sights, which she couldn't explain. Were they fish, those hulking great shapes in the water, big and dark and menacing? Was it a seal she saw poking its dark, glistening head out of the water as she wobbled towards the potty in the corner one Sunday morning? She and Jack had started using one of her mother's old chamber pots to save them from the cold and the wet on dark nights.

So was it a seal? If so, what was it doing in the lake, because seals were saltwater creatures, and it really shouldn't be living here in an inland valley.

Every morning Elin lay in bed, trying to be brave, listening to Huw and Wil talking rubbish on the yard, feeling alienated, listening to the filthy farmyard dogs in their filthy hut snarling and barking and whimpering, or she'd be overwhelmed by the sadness in the hens' monotonous, senile song as they scratched feebly at the ever-present dirt below her window.

Worse, it got worse; she was forced to listen to her own daughter as she chattered and giggled just a few feet away, as if she were a new bride in the first flush of marriage. Elin's blood simmered when she heard them fooling around, having pillow fights – and doing something else too more than likely, judging by the meaningful silences which came over the place on occasions. Today, she'd heard Mari discussing her natural father, Gwydion, and it had set her teeth on edge.

She pictured her first husband as he arrived home in his uniform one autumnal evening, his face ashen and his hands shaking. A huge riot had broken out in the city; he'd sat in the kitchen, telling her about the destruction and looting which had taken place not so very far from them. Feral gangs with knives and guns had taken control of whole districts. He said the family would have to leave before one of them was injured or killed.

Nonsense, replied Elin. He was being too dramatic. Surely it couldn't be that bad.

He'd taken her to the window and pointed to the East, where an orange glow lit up the night sky. *Fire*, he said. The gangs had set fire to the industrial estate. The police had been beaten back, at least three fire engines had been destroyed.

In that moment she'd seen paradise dwindle and recede. Would she have to leave all those lovely shops, so nice and warm and clean?

Elin had refused to countenance such a thing. Leave? Abandon all that was precious to her? Say goodbye to their sumptuous lives, their monthly wages, their hopes for the future? Where would they go, anyway?

Back to the farm, said Gwydion. That was their only choice. Listen to me Elin, listen. We have to go away from here.

Elin heard his voice echoing from the past. And she heard her own voice echoing back. *Don't be so bloody stupid*, she'd replied that evening in the kitchen.

The rows. That's what she remembered most. The terrible rows, violent and loud, after the kids had gone to bed. And then the city had made the decision for them.

Through her window, Elin could hear a song drifting up from the farmyard below…

I'm Popeye the sailor man,
I'm Popeye the sailor man…

16

MARI AND NICO were standing close together in the paddock, picking young nettle leaves to make soup.

'Ow!' said Mari. She'd been stung on her leg again, and this last *Ow!* was her loudest yet. The truth was that Mari had shut her eyes tight and walked purposefully into a clump of nettles. She'd been stung worse than she intended, and it really hurt. It was a ruse to get attention, and now she looked pathetically in Nico's direction, knowing that she was being childish. Soon he was kneeling in front of her, rubbing her legs with dock leaves and turning her skin green.

'You look like alien now,' joked Nico, who had an idea what was going on.

'So you've known lots of aliens, have you?' countered Mari sarcastically. She was irritated with herself, because she was too old to play games. Suddenly, she felt much older.

Mari felt his right hand tighten around the soft skin on the back of her knee; with her hands resting on his sunburnt shoulders, she could feel his muscles moving around below the skin. Pretending that something was caught in his dark hair, she ran her fingers through the warm curls. That was the moment, probably. The moment when possibility swivelled on its gleaming skate, came to a stop, and became probability. For her, anyway; as if a soundless click in her head had marked a new beginning. She'd felt a current running up from her fingertips as they moved through his hair; it had raced up her arms like an electric shock and passed through her shoulders, into her neck. After resting there for a millisecond, as if trying to decide whether to go up to her head or down to her heart, the frisson had raced downwards, electrifying the silky hairs on her breasts; her skin had tautened as it passed down, down...

'OK now?'

'Yes, thanks.'

He was standing in front of her, above her, all around her with a dock leaf in his hand. That look in his eyes – was it different to his usual look? Mari studied the tiny green flecks in his light brown eyes. Emerald atolls in a sea muddied by churning sharks. Nameless little islands, remote and undiscovered in a faraway ocean somewhere in paradise. Was there a coconut tree on each of those tiny islands in his eyes, was there a miniature Mari sitting with her back against each of those trees, a castaway with a shipwrecked heart? And did that other her, micro Mari, have a bottle in her hand, containing the most important message she would ever send out to the distant world?

'I'll finish the nettles – you start on the trees up there,' said Nico.

He meant the hawthorn bushes; he'd shown her how to pluck their delicate little leaves without catching her fingers on the thorns. Mari went up the paddock and began to collect the soft greenery. The bumps on her legs were painful and itchy, and she had to stop frequently to scratch them. After filling an old plastic sack with nettles, Nico joined her among the blackthorns. He started picking at the leaves, though half of them went into his belly rather than the red bucket in his left hand. Mari stopped working to reproach him, but he carried on doing it, and to mock her further he pretended to prick his fingers on the thorns, saying *Ow!* melodramatically in a girlish voice and dancing about theatrically. Mari thumped him on the back fiercely, so he stopped messing around and concentrated on the work in hand.

After a long silence he said: 'I go soon.'

A grey mist came down on her and the world around her swayed.

'I go and get pigs for old man Wil. He want pigs.'

Then the sun came out again; her sight cleared, the ground steadied. Tiny hot tears pierced her eyes like needles.

'You're coming back, then?'

'Yes, I come back with pigs.'

Where on earth would he find pigs? Or was he planning to slink off somewhere else? Mari reminded herself that he'd have gone already if he wanted to. Before dawn, like a thief. A host of fears and dark thoughts took flight in her imagination, like balloons, some flying high in the sky and others falling flat on the ground. She noticed a figure coming towards them from the lower fields; it was Jack, her step-father or whatever he was, returning from his morning walk around the sheep and their newborn lambs. He had a sheep on his back, and it was clear that she was dead. A lamb bleated from one of his coat pockets.

Jack was obviously very tired; he looked like a soldier carrying a wounded comrade away from the battlefield after a heavy defeat. Tramp tramp tramp tramp… the man looked beaten, he was waving a white flag in the air. For the first time ever, she felt sorry for him. She knew almost nothing about him; no-one else did either for that matter – he was that sort of man. Jack had come with them to the farm when they fled from the city. She had been puzzled by his presence in the car, a strange man who smelt completely different to her father. She'd been small then and no-one would tell her what was going on. She was still in the dark, no-one had explained anything to her. Mari had been left to guess about his relationship with her mother. Had he been a secret lover who had surfaced during those last desperate days in the city? There wasn't much evidence of love between them. At first, Mari had hated him. He had taken over from her father without a word being said. But she soon realised that her new cosmos was too small to contain hatred; there wasn't enough time for such luxury. The effort of changing their lives completely had shocked them into silence and drained their strength. Their energy was completely used up by the daily effort of staying alive, there weren't enough volts left for love or hate. The first few months had been miserable and terrifying. They'd all seen poverty on TV, in India or Africa, but they had no real conception of what it was really like. The shock of it had almost driven them mad. Silence day after day, a screaming silence; their ears had barely been able to cope with it. They'd longed for the comforting noise of a car, or a radio, or a TV, or an iPod. It was the sort of silence which must have caressed the first creatures to struggle onto land; a silence which stretched way, way back to the Ethiopian savannah three million years ago when Lucy and the first hominids had walked on the Earth. Their ears were oppressed by the throbbing silence at Dolfrwynog; their hearing was overcome by it as it whispered its message, day and night: *I am the echo of Creation… I am here, I am everywhere… I was the hiss in the ears of the first mastodon and I will hiss in the ears of your children, and their children's children…*

Mari listened to the whisper of Jack's feet as he struggled through the wet grass; she looked up and saw a thread of bloody mucus streaming from the sheep's nostrils. She looked away again. That was another awful thing about being here: death was all around them, always, every minute of the day. Some creature or other was dying every second. That didn't happen in the city, except occasionally. Death came sentimentally to the childhood hamster, and death came entertainingly on television, but it didn't come like this, bloated and putrid. You could turn off the TV but you couldn't pull the plug on death, not here. Death was actually alive, it crept around you like a reptile, always watching you, its long sticky tongue ready to whisk you away, into the void. And maybe you would be next...

Jack passed them without saying a word. He'd been quiet for weeks, though Nico had heard him screaming as loud as he could when he was alone with the sheep in the fields. He also waved his arms around like a madman. The animals feared him and they'd start running whenever they saw him approaching.

Mari and Nico went along the hedge slowly, picking leaves and chatting. Nico asked her to finish the story about Gwydion; he'd looked down at the graves below and he'd remembered her description of the city unravelling and then melting in the heat of social breakdown.

But how could she tell him about her father, when she herself knew so little? Just thinking about it made her feel hot and uncomfortable inside. And who knew the truth, anyway? She didn't, for sure. The only story she had was her mother's tearful version; no-one else had told her anything. She saw a picture of her mother sitting on her bed one night. Mari was six or seven, and she wanted a bedtime story, but her mother had been weeping; she had blue streaks of mascara on her cheeks. Then she'd pulled herself together and told Mari two stories, one about the fairies and the other about her father. But somehow the two stories had fused in Mari's young mind.

One day, a long long time ago, a very brave man went to work...

Was it her father who had gone to work, or the king of the fairies? There was a school in one of the stories, and frightened children... was it her father who had been very brave and saved them all, or was it the king of the fairies? She couldn't remember, her memories were muddled. And she couldn't ask her mother, it would upset her so.

One thing she knew for sure: her father had been a policeman. She had a picture of him in the same drawer as the photo of Sara.

Standing side by side with Nico, surrounded by sweet hawthorn scents, she started to tell him a story.

17

Nico was in the kitchen, sitting at the long white table in the centre of the room. He was leaning over something in front of him, concentrating on a delicate task.

'What are you doing?' asked Mari when she'd found him after half an hour of searching; she'd been everywhere except the fields. She stood as still as a cat about to pounce, a few yards away from him, a small dark silhouette with her hand on the door frame. Idly, she picked at the paint with her fingernails and sent a small shower of old gloss onto the floor by her feet; the flakes lay there like bits of confetti at a fairy wedding.

'Nico?'

He remained silent; by now his nose almost touched the object of his attention. Mari could see his tongue playing at the corner of his mouth, rippling like a crimson snake leaving a cave. But tired of pretending to be stand-offish, she joined him at the table; she put an arm around his shoulder and lowered her head to see what he was up to.

Nico had an empty eggshell balanced on the tip of his finger, which explained why he'd been so careful when he'd sliced the top off his egg that morning, and now he was decorating it with paint.

'This called *pisanki* in my country,' said Nico. 'You like?'

Mari admired his work; he'd created a delightful picture of two fat little lovers holding hands, in bright colours: red and yellow and green and blue.

'Huw give me paint,' he added. 'This egg for you, yes?'

He blew on the shell to dry the paint.

'Easter soon, yes? Easter eggs are good magic… we have good harvest now,' he said, explaining that this custom was important in his homeland.

His eyes shone, Mari could see dampness around his lashes. Perhaps he longed to see his homeland again, though he didn't mention it very often. Krakow: he'd described the great central square, and he'd talked about going for walks on the banks of the Vistula. She had been told about the mountains around Zakopane, with snow on them all the year round; dense spruce forests, remote lakes. Bears. Auschwitz. He had been to Auschwitz, on a school outing, and he'd seen the infamous words above the main gateway: *Arbeit Macht Frei* – work sets you free. Explaining its meaning to her, he'd laughed cynically.

'Look at us here,' he said. 'Does work make us free? Not bloody true! Hard work kill you if you're poor, kill you if you don't know how to get food. Bad words!'

So what kind of work had he himself done? He wasn't forthcoming. 'Many things,' he said after a while.

And the tattoo?

He shrugged his shoulders, as if he wasn't quite sure why it was there.

'Why did you…' Mari started quizzing him. But Nico raised a finger to his lips and pointed to the world outside their window.

'Listen,' he said. 'Getting worse now, wind getting strong all morning. Bad storm coming maybe.'

They both stayed like that, Nico sitting and Mari standing close to him, listening to the wind. She looked out through the grimy glass and saw the apple trees at the bottom of the garden being whipped to and fro. The room had gone dark; the light was failing, even though it was still morning. Yes, he was right, the wind had grown stronger since breakfast. Breakfast? One solitary boiled egg and as much cold water as she could drink had failed to calm the gnawing hunger in her stomach. She was losing weight, too; he could feel her ribs beginning to emerge from her flesh. Perhaps they were all starving to death, slowly. They'd have to get food from somewhere, but where?

Mari heard something shattering outside the window. Glass? A slate from the roof? She noticed now that the bedroom doors were banging against their frames. Where was everyone? The house was like a ghost ship. In the dwindling light, Mari felt like the first mate on the bridge of the *Marie Celeste*, looking over the captain's shoulder as he studied his charts, a few moments before tragedy struck. But what exactly had happened to the ship, and everyone on her? Mari had always wondered about that. What had been the fate of the captain's wife, and her baby? Had it been something quick and unexpected which bore them away, or had it been something like this? Hunger gnawing at their insides, then a sudden storm? Mari imagined the waves almost engulfing the ship; she saw Nico tying her to the mast, the wind tearing at her clothes. She tasted salt on her lips, and she licked them in the gloom of the kitchen; but it wasn't salt she tasted. It was blood. Running her finger along her mouth, she discovered that she'd bitten her lower lip.

Nico asked her where the others were. Elin was probably in bed, she replied. Huw? With his uncle, hopefully. Mari began to worry about them. She went upstairs on tiptoe and discovered that her mother was sitting up in bed, looking out through the window.

'Storm,' she said needlessly. 'Look at those trees. Can you hear the wind?'

The two of them listened to the gale groaning and hissing in the chimney. Heavy rain splattered against the window; hailstones clattered against the glass like bullets.

'Where's Huw?' asked Elin.

'I don't know.'

Elin turned towards her.

'Can you find him for me?'

Mari looked crossly at her mother, and lost her cool.

'Go and look for him yourself. You're his mother, you go and find him instead of lying in that bed all day like a…'

Mari held her tongue.

'Like what?' asked her mother, with a fiery look in her eyes. 'You'd be in bed yourself if you had half a chance, and not alone, either.'

Mari stomped out of the room and went downstairs. Huw was standing in the kitchen, soaked to the skin.

'Bloody hell, Huw,' said Mari. 'Where the hell have you been? Mum's nearly out of her mind worrying about you.'

Huw stood absolutely still, looking at her.

'Well, don't just stand there, go upstairs and get changed.'

'I haven't got any clothes to change into,' he answered squeakily.

'Dammit!' said a voice by the door. Uncle Wil had arrived. He appeared in the doorframe, a wet yeti dressed in sackcloth. His big black boots were coal ships floating in their own polluted estuaries.

'Terrible weather,' said Wil. He stayed in the doorway, like a soggy scarecrow.

'Go and change, for God's sake, or you'll catch pneumonia,' he urged Huw.

'I haven't got any clothes except for these,' said Huw again.

'Come upstairs *now*,' said Mari, extending a hand towards

him as if she were a schoolmistress who'd just discovered that a pupil had wet himself.

The two of them disappeared up the stairs, and the two men listened to them banging about above their heads.

'Storm,' said Wil. Nico turned towards him, looking like a cow in a stall, watching the farmer arriving with a milking stool.

'Yes.'

Nico put the finished egg in an eggcup and admired his own artwork.

'You like?'

Wil started to smile, but the expression on his face suddenly froze.

'Dammit!' he said yet again. He turned on his heel and ran towards the paddock, because the eggshell had reminded him of something.

The little chicks were in the paddock, still in their hutch.

18

THE STORM LASTED for two weeks. Five of Wil's little chicks were killed on the first day, because he'd forgotten all about them. The wind grabbed their hutch and threw it into the air; some of the chicks survived, others were swallowed by seagulls. Wil searched for survivors among the nettles and the rusting farm implements. Of those he rescued, another two died in the night – from shock, probably. It nearly broke Wil's heart. On his knees in the paddock, with a half-dead chick in his hands and cold rain streaming down his back, all the despair which had dammed up inside him broke free and he cried like a child. His emotions had been building up for months, growing gradually like the lake below Dolfrwynog, and on the first day of the storm he almost drowned in his own feelings. He went up to the stable loft and he was silent for days. Three of the chicks he managed to keep alive, but there was a blackness inside him which he'd never felt before; it spread though his brain, through his whole being, to the tips of his filthy toes. The wind roared and the rain fell without pity; trees were uprooted and fences were smashed. Windows were blown out and slates were smashed to bits. Wil had never seen anything like it, throughout his long life. The weather had gone mad, it was truly frightening.

Huw visited him now and then, with some food if there was any available. Although he slept in the loft with Wil, he sheltered in the house with the others during the day, while the storm continued to rage; they would huddle around the fire, as Wil's chicks huddled together in their box. Whenever Huw went to see his uncle he would wrestle the door shut and then stand by the foot of Wil's bed, a regulation stream of snot abseiling from his little red nose.

'Are you OK, Uncle Wil?'

'Yes, lad.'

'How are the chicks, Uncle Wil?'

'Still alive, y'know.'

'Can I hold one?'

'Yes of course, but be careful.'

Huw would kneel by the crumpled cardboard box which housed the hen and her brood. Wil spent ages every morning rooting around the paddock, looking for something they could eat. If the storm didn't pass over soon the chicks would die. To make matters worse, the pain in Wil's guts was getting worse, or maybe he had more time to notice it now that he was shut in all day.

Kneeling on the dusty floor, with a little bundle of yellow fluff cheeping in his hand, Huw recited the day's news as if he were a TV presenter.

Jack had been to check on the sheep every day and x number of lambs had died of cold, or y number of sheep had lost an eye to the crows. One of the dogs had died in the doghouse. Jack had started to carry his gun with him at all times, for some reason which he wouldn't reveal. Elin stayed in bed all day, as usual. Nico had been scribbling notes and reading Huw's old books, asking for an explanation every so often. He'd ask:

'What *pilgrimage* mean Huw? What is *shrine*?'

It was clear that he was formulating a plan, though Huw was no wiser because Nico wrote in Polish.

And Mari... Mari had been busy in her bedroom, ripping down the old posters and repainting the walls. She'd mixed the remains of several pots of emulsion and the resulting colour had given them some light relief; it was a strange yellowy pink.

'Well, it'll look better than it used to,' said Mari proudly. She'd scrubbed it clean and tidied up. She wasn't sure what made her do it. Something had happened inside her and a little voice in her head had said, *That's enough of living in filth, look to the future, make a nice little nest for yourself or you'll go under, you'll drown in dirt and despair…*

Looking out from her pink-with-a-bit-of-yellow palace she saw a landscape that was changing rapidly; a world that was behaving like a once-kind parent who had suffered a head injury in a car crash and was now acting in a completely different way: brutal and moody, despotic and unpredictable.

Every morning now she followed the same routine; after waking she'd look out of the window, clutching her duvet around her to keep warm. Then the same routine: she'd dress, wash her face with water scooped from the outside panes of her window. She'd put her grandmother's ring on her left hand, tidy up, make her bed, and then she'd stride out on the landing. Next stop was Nico's room, which she entered like a mouse, making sure she didn't step on the squeaky bits. She'd sit on his bed, waiting for him to wake, she'd look at his eyes flutter open, search for her, close again. She'd wait for his hand to find hers and she'd listen to the never-ending rain streaming along the gutters outside. She'd listen to his breathing, the wind, her heart beating. She'd wait for him to sit up in bed. She'd wait for him today, tomorrow, for ever. But she wasn't aware of that yet…

It's early in the morning. Mari is in Nico's room, waiting. The wall feels hard and cool against her back. But she likes this sensation – the solid stone-cold feel of the old farmhouse against her warm skin, reaching right to her backbone. It's an old feeling; she's aware that her grandmother and her great-grandmother rested their backs against the same mortar and shared this experience. As usual, she looks at Nico who's still asleep in his bed. He's not a snorer, which is important to her: it would be harder, she suspects, to love a man who sounded like a pig turfing in soil when he was sleeping. He looks so innocent. After all, he's only a lad. He doesn't look much older than Huw when he's asleep like this. Such eyelashes. He looks a little like that photo of Che Guevara's body, taken after he was shot in Bolivia. The silky fluff on his cheeks suggests a trace of auburn, as if he were a colt changing hue in the spring. She watches the bedclothes move up and down fractionally as he breathes in and out; they smell of the earth, because the weather has been so atrocious she hasn't been able to do any washing for a while, though the bed hasn't begun to stink yet, like Elin's. While she's watching, Mari rehearses her story. She fidgets with the ring and recites the first sentence to herself; indeed, she has the first four sentences off pat, ready to be told.

I remember my father's face, and his smell. I remember going with him to play on the swings in the park. I remember the stubble on his chin tickling my cheek. I remember him sitting at the table with a pink paper hat from a Christmas cracker on his head...

But she doesn't remember anything else, nothing at all. What will she tell Nico when he wakes? The truth? But what *was* the truth? Her mother's version? The version with two mixed-up stories, one about the king of the fairies and the other about a policeman who went out of the door one morning to face a mob baying for blood, anyone's blood?

Nico stirs and searches for her hand, or her knee, in his sleep. Soon his light brown eyes are searching for her face.

She's there. He goes back to sleep for ten minutes, then wakes suddenly and stares at her. His eyes are big with sleep.

'Hiya.'

'Hiya.'

Small talk for a few minutes. I dreamt about… is it still raining? … come closer… you feel nice…

His long white body feels like nothing else she's ever felt or touched in her whole life.

With her cheek in his hair, she tells him the story of her father. At last. It's the story of the first grave in the paddock, under Wil's grimy window. A grave without a single plastic flower on it, swimming in a stew of cold mud. Light brown soil, the colour of a sick calf's excrement.

She tells Nico about the arson attacks on the industrial estate, the petrol bombs, the chanting crowd. She tells him about an emergency call from one of the primary schools on the outskirts of the city, in one of those endless, soulless suburbs which flesh out every big city. A gang of four or five men have entered the school and the children, more than a hundred of them, are being held hostage. The men demand money and a helicopter. A huge amount of money. Suddenly, Mari recalls a picture of her father on the television. Is it a real memory, or is it made up? She has no way of knowing. But she sees her father on TV, walking through a cordon towards the school. The whole world has fallen silent by now – the negotiator with a microphone, the crowd and the sirens have all gone quiet.

She sees her father walking slowly, slowly towards the school entrance and then he stops, with his hands in the air. She sees him talking to someone through a window. This all happens in slow motion. After five minutes… ten minutes… who knows how long? … he steps inside the building, and in a few minutes a small child steps into the doorway. It's a little girl, she's black and her coat is askew, the buttons done up wrongly. In her right hand she holds her lunchbox: it's green with a picture of a frog on it. The frog has a pink mouth, wide open. The girl starts walking away from the door, slowly at first and then quickly, she starts running towards the crowd. She sprints for the last ten yards, straight into her mother's arms. *Isn't it wonderful*, says Mari, *how a little kid can spot a parent in a big crowd?*

On the six o'clock news they hear that Mari's father persuaded the gang to exchange him for a child. Then, the screen shows a stream of parents walking across the yard, exchanging themselves. A parent goes in, a child comes out. They hug each other, comfort each other at the door. This stratagem works. About fifty parents go in and the same number of children come out; parents of every shape and size swap themselves for children of every shape and size. One little kid refuses to let go of his mother, he won't leave her there. And then things go badly wrong. Instead of a parent, a soldier from the SAS crosses the yard with a hidden gun. He hurries past a released child and enters the building. Then, shots are heard. Is that how she remembers it?

Later, on the ten o'clock news, they hear the last bulletin before they flee their home for the last time. A number of people, including children, have been killed or injured at the school, among them Mari's father. He's been shot in the shoulder and the stomach. It's too dangerous right now to visit him in hospital, but they go at first light. He's very ill, but he's famous now. 'HERO COP SAVES SCHOOLKIDS' says the only newspaper that's left. His face can be seen on every TV screen, all day.

The trouble in the city spreads, it engulfs the hospital while they're inside. They have to escape, an adjoining street is already ablaze… and then the hospital is on fire. Somehow they manage to carry Mari's dad out of the building, with the drips still attached. But who is that man waiting for them by the main entrance? Who is that stranger who carries him into a car and then drives like a madman through the streets, through red lights, through the fires and the looting gangs? They reach open country and drive for hours through the night. When she wakes they're at the farm. They've all been asleep, except for the driver. Now they all wake up, everyone except her father. With her head against his arm, she senses that something has changed.

The driver's name is Jack. A quiet man, who drives through the darkness and brings them to this farmyard. Keeping the main lights on, he goes to a rear passenger door, opens it, and shakes her father's shoulder. Then he shakes it again, harder this time. Jack stares into two lifeless eyes. Then he orders everyone except Elin into the house. Afterwards he stays with them at Dolfrwynog, but he doesn't say very much. He screams in the fields. He sleeps with Elin but they never touch. And slowly, in the wind and the rain and the mud, he goes mad. Jack, the quiet man, the stranger who comes into their lives like a ghost from the future, gradually loses the will to live.

19

After a fortnight of roaring and smashing and threshing about, the storm ceased suddenly one night. A serene blue sky and a big yellow sun greeted them the next day. After getting up slowly and warily – he could hardly believe his ears at first – Wil went out to the middle of the farmyard and stood there with a circle of hens around his boots; they'd somehow survived by scratching around inside the farm buildings. As he surveyed his little kingdom the sun burned his scalp; the mud around him dried and cracked. White steam shrouded the manure heap as the rainwater evaporated, and the hills around him were plumed with mist as the earth warmed up suddenly.

He tried to evaluate the storm damage. Roof slates were scattered all over the yard and broken objects were strewn everywhere. The storm had been the worst he'd ever experienced in springtime: its hurricane force had battered the farm for two whole weeks, day after day. At last, he was able to stand in his favourite spot, looking at his feathery friends as they bowed and paid homage to him. A long time ago, when Wil was a child, he'd seen the world as a gigantic tree, shading him like an umbrella; on it grew countless apples and in each apple lay a secret or a priceless piece of knowledge. With each bite he learnt something new about the world. Every minute brought new opportunities, ripe and lush. But by now not a single apple remained. The tree was diseased and about to fall. He saw no beauty left in his kingdom, no matter how long he looked to the North or the South, to the East or the West.

Only a happy man with food in his belly and plenty of spare time could enjoy beauty. Not even his own family looked beautiful when they were hungry, when their bones were showing through their skins. Neither was nature lovely when trees were dying and smelly carcasses lay all over the meadows. Not even the sunny blue sky above could give him pleasure that morning because he knew it might sear and kill his potato crop, or destroy most of his corn, like last year. Nature seemed to be exacting revenge on mankind for the harm done over centuries; it was payback time after many a drubbing at the hands of a bullying and uncaring species.

Wil studied the farmyard, centre of his universe. He felt like a little earthworm which had been caught in a torrent and left twitching, pallid and weak, on the sodden ground. He knew by now that something unpleasant was happening in his insides; he had a rattlesnake in there, biting him frequently with its poisonous tongue. At that very moment a wave of pain spread out from the centre of his being. He clutched at his stomach with his left hand, dropped his head and closed his eyes. And while he stood like that on the yard in his big black boots, stooped with pain, he heard a little voice calling to him from one of the bedrooms. It was Mari, and she was also suffering.

'Uncle Wil!'

Still racked with pain, he was unable to respond.

'Uncle Wil!'

He stayed still, paralysed with agony.

When May comes, so graceful in green…

Another little voice, inside his head, was reciting an old poem. But why?

When—May—comes—so—graceful—in—green… said the inner voice again, and he felt like a child standing before a class, enunciating every syllable carefully and clearly. Perhaps it was his own voice, coming from the past. Perhaps his brain was trying to help him by deflecting his attention away from the pain.

When May comes, so graceful in green,
She brings verdancy and dignity…

At last, the pain was receding. He straightened slowly and turned towards Mari, who was in the window of the room in which Nico normally slept. She'd discovered that he'd gone, then.

'Yes, little Mari?'

His mind raced around the farm. May had arrived but Jack still hadn't moved the sheep from the lower fields, which were needed as hayfields.

'He's gone, Uncle Wil,' said a faraway voice.

He stared up at her. She looked so small in the window, framed in black, with her hair stuffed into a colourful red bandana as if she were a gypsy girl. He recalled her standing there as a little girl on holiday, in better times, shouting, *Uncle Wil, can I come to collect the eggs with you please?* or, *Uncle Wil, can I feed the pet lamb please?*

Poor little mite. Wil didn't know much about love, but any fool could see that Mari had fallen head over heels in love with the young Pole, and that he'd break her heart into a thousand pieces if he didn't return to Dolfrwynog.

'Uncle Wil… do you know where Nico is this morning?'

Her pained voice sliced the air, at the same time as another pang of pain sliced him in two. He flinched again, and clutched his belly. But Mari failed to notice. Her eyes had left him, they'd climbed up the hill and gone towards the mountain; she'd guessed already.

'Where is he, Uncle Wil?'

She wasn't looking at him though, she couldn't see his pain.

Then she ran downstairs, through the house, and out to the yard. By then the pain had abated and Wil had straightened.

'He's gone to get some pigs.'

She was astonished, even though Nico had warned her. Pigs? Why pigs? What was the point of bloody pigs? Surely it was an excuse to leave her, to escape from the farm.

'Don't worry Mari, he'll be back,' said Wil. But she detected the uncertainty in his voice and laughed sardonically.

'Come back? Of course he won't come back. Why the hell would he come back here? To a shit-hole like this? Have you gone mad? We'll never see him again, Uncle Wil. He's gone for ever.'

She moved away from him slowly, keeping her eyes on him all the while, and started walking up the hill away from him.

'No Mari, please don't. We've got enough problems already without having to worry about you. It's too dangerous up there on the mountain, and he's been gone for hours. You'll never catch up...'

She stopped by the gate, with her hand on the latch. What should she do? Follow him... yes, she'd go after him, no matter what the consequences. There would be no point in living here without him. She opened the gate and went through it. But then, as she started walking, Wil shouted after her.

'Mari! Mari!'

She stopped, and turned towards him. She looked like the smallest doll in a Russian *matryoshka*, a little doll which had been inside a slightly bigger doll, which had been inside a still bigger doll. But that's what children were, really, thought Wil. Dolls which came from inside other dolls of the same shape and colour...

Was he beginning to ramble? Had pain and hunger begun to distort his mind? And there was something else bothering him too. He'd lent his gun to the Pole, just like that, without thinking it through. Had he done the right thing? Would the door to the stable loft squeal open in the middle of the night, would there be a terrible roar and a flash, followed by the eternal darkness of death?

'Yes, Uncle Wil?'

Mari was looking down at him, waiting.

'Huw,' said Wil. 'He's not well. He hasn't got out of bed today and he's very white. Will you come to help me?'

He hadn't intended to ask her, but now he saw an opportunity to keep her there. His ruse worked.

'What's wrong with him?'

'I don't know. You're better with him than I am, will you come to the loft and have a look at him?'

Slowly, she descended down the yard and went towards the loft, past Wil, without looking at him.

'I hope you're telling the truth,' she said as she passed.

Soon the farmyard was a seething hive of activity as people came and went between the stable loft and the house. Mari ran to the house; Elin ran from the house to the loft; Elin walked slowly from the loft to the house with her son motionless in her arms; Mari ran from the house to the well, with the bucket inscribed with *Lloyds Animal Feeds*, empty on the way there but slopping water into her falling-apart trainers on the way back, drenching her feet. Then Mari ran to the river with an armful of washing; when she returned the sheets were cleaner but they were no whiter as they went on the line to dry.

By the afternoon Huw was sleeping in his mother's bed, on clean-ish sheets, after Elin had washed him as carefully as she could; he was too sleepy to object when she reached his willy. His face was paper-white and he had deep shadows under his eyes. His mother noticed, for the first time, how thin he was.

She started weeping quietly as she ministered to him. How in God's name had she failed to notice before today? His little body was skeletal. And she, his own mother, hadn't noticed. She felt a hot wave of guilt and self-reproach sweep over her, reddening her face. Her own son in such a state, and she had just lain there in bed all day. She felt his forehead, and it was hot under her fingers. She stayed at his bedside for the rest of the day, damping down his fever and spooning cold water into his mouth. By nine in the evening he'd turned the corner, and he slept quietly for the rest of the night.

When daybreak arrived, Elin believed the worst was over, but realised that she'd been lucky on this occasion. Huw's sudden sickness gave her such a fright she promised herself that she would never neglect her children from then on. That morning the red bucket went to and from the well many times; Elin scrubbed her bedroom from top to bottom and she went to fetch wild flowers from the hedgerows to adorn the bedside cabinet and the windows. Slowly, over the next few days, she became re-acquainted with her son. She realised how unhappy he was as she lay by his side on the bed. Time after time she said to him:

I'll never let that happen again, Huw. Never…

It wasn't possible to ascertain the cause of the fever. She asked him what he'd been eating. The answer was: very little. Where had he been? *Fishing by the lake.* The lake? Were there fish in it? Yes, there were huge fish in the lake, and many other things too. Big black shapes, moving around slowly. The lake had grown, it was still growing. Had she noticed? By now it had moved beyond the trees where Nico had first been spotted and it was creeping up their trunks; the trees stood like children playing in the sea, waiting for the tide to gobble up their legs.

Had he drank from the lake?

Yes.

Was it that which had made him ill?

Perhaps... he'd also tried to gnaw at one of the fish he'd caught.

He'd gnawed at a fish? What the hell had come over him?

I wanted food, Mum, I was so hungry. That awful feeling in my tum.

Elin wept silently on the bed, with her arms around him. Her own son chewing raw fish.

Downstairs, in the hot silence which descended on the farmhouse every day, Mari made scrambled egg for her brother every morning and then sat down at the table, reflecting on the fact that there was nothing else she could do. There were no medicines left in the house, not a single tablet. And she had no idea about the old remedies, the wild herbs and potions of her ancestors.

Every eggshell which was left over she used to paint an Easter egg for Nico, to mark his absence; at the end of a week there were seven painted eggs in a row on the shelf by the window, each one cradled in green moss, with chains of little wild flowers around each egg cup. On the first egg she'd painted herself and Nico back-to-back on opposite sides of the egg, both of them snarling. But by the seventh egg they were close up and smiling, with their arms around each other.

20

I T WAS MAY. Fluffy, innocent lambs frolicked on the lower
meadows. Sparrows chattered and treated themselves to dust
baths near the hen hut. Cloudless blue skies blessed every day.
The fields shimmered under the sun, covered in a scintillating
blanket of daisies and buttercups. The new moon shone big and
silvery when night fell.

Mari was in the kitchen, musing. When was Easter? Perhaps
it had already passed by. April seemed to ring a bell. But without
a radio or TV in the house there was nothing she could consult
except an old calendar. When was Easter Friday? No-one had a
clue at Dolfrwynog. What did it matter, anyway? Elin was the only
one left who had any time for religion. But despite everything,
there were eight Easter eggs on a shelf in the kitchen, with a
stream of golden sunshine falling in a shaft on Nico's handsome
likeness. In addition to the egg which Nico had painted, Mari
had created another seven, one for each day her beloved had
been absent. All of them featured two tiny figures, getting closer
and closer to each other. On Mari's first egg they started back-
to-back, on opposite sides. In keeping with her memory of
him, Mari had given Nico curly hair and a tattoo on his left
arm: a little blue ship sailing on little blue waves. She'd painted
the tattoo with one of her own eyelashes. Today, in the early
morning, she was at the table again, with a new eggshell, which
she'd washed carefully. She was trying to decide what sort of
picture she'd paint on it, now Huw had eaten its insides. Mari
and Nico could be seen shoulder-to-shoulder on yesterday's

egg; so what about today's? Should she separate the two figures and send them away from each other, parting them yet again? Since a whole week had passed, she was caught in a dilemma. One simple fact sustained her; the man who was her acting stepfather, Jack the screaming stranger, had followed Nico to the mountain, with his shotgun, and he wouldn't come back, he said, until he knew one way or another what had happened to the young Pole.

Mari sat in a beam of sunshine in the kitchen, worrying about Nico and worrying about the egg in her hand. Perhaps she should change key, paint a picture of Huw and Uncle Wil on the yard, discussing the hens. Painting a hen on the shell would be ironic and a little sad. Huw was much better, and his mother had been at it adapting and washing his clothes. He looked happier and cleaner than he had for months. He smiled quite often now, and sometimes he laughed his old tinkly laugh, even when he was doing things he wasn't very fond of doing, like skinning rabbits or gutting fish ready for the pan. His mother had changed, too. She busied herself around the house these days, and she'd help her brother Wil whenever she was needed on the farm. She saw, at last, that he was a sick man and needed some care and attention himself.

And so it was that change came to Dolfrwynog during those hot, dry days of early May. The four of them worked hard to keep the potatoes alive by carrying water to them in every available receptacle, including the red bucket. The four of them went down to the lake and stared into its murky depths. One of them thought he'd seen a huge fish swimming slowly in its shadows; another saw a shape creeping along the bottom like a huge, sinister octopus; Mari thought she saw a mermaid with a cascade of golden hair. None of them ventured into the water, though it seemed to tempt them. They feared it in a primal, aboriginal way. It seemed to have enormous power over them, as if its shadows were a foretaste of death itself.

In the overpowering silence of the cwm they seemed to hear nothing but the insistent slop of the waves as they ate into the farmland; occasionally a raptor circled overhead, in the searing blue, rasping a pitiful, pitiless scream.

'Shhh…' said Wil, when they were down there one day. He tapped his ear and motioned towards the rocky cliff at the far end of the valley. 'Did you hear it?'

The four of them stood very still at the water's edge.

'What was it, Uncle Wil?' asked Huw.

'A fox,' said Wil. They all listened avidly, and continued staring towards the crag. And yes, they heard the echo of a fox barking somewhere up in the scree.

'Or someone is trying to send a message, perhaps,' said Huw, who was thinking about a tribe of native American Indians pictured in the ancient family books back home. He hadn't looked at them for ages. Perhaps Big Chief Sitting Bull was crouching at the end of the valley, mimicking a coyote to indicate that a war party was about to descend on them…

Huw saw them first – the band of Arapaho or Cheyenne, making their way down the mountain in the distance: there were about twelve of them, moving in an undulating line, like swarming bees on the move.

'Look!' said Huw, lifting his finger towards the mountain. He was overjoyed at having seen them before anyone else. He listened hard, in a bid to hear the ululation of the braves as they prepared to spur their horses to a gallop. Huw felt fear rising up his spindly legs like cold water. With the lake on one side ready to swallow him, and a band of Indians on the other, he felt that things were going from bad to worse. Could he expect a quick death at the hands of these approaching warriors – the zip of an arrow as it splintered in his body, or might he suffer something worse still: a slow painful dismemberment, ending with his scalp swinging from the belt of a half-crazed brave…?

'But what's that over there?' asked Wil. He was pointing above the Indians, towards the ridge crowning the mountain. It was a giant, surely, descending the hillside and trailing the war band. He seemed to behave like a sheepdog, moving from one flank to the other, shepherding the warriors down towards them. Behind him he was dragging a huge black sack.

'Ye gods,' said Wil. 'That's Nico… he's found us some pigs. Yes! Those are bloody pigs, or I'm a Dutchman…'

Everyone listened, moving their heads slightly, trying to catch any noise on the wind. And yes indeed, in his overheated imagination Huw heard a distant *Ia-ia-iaaaa* noise, exactly the same as a Sioux warrior might make. Nico was on horseback, leading a smaller packhorse behind him.

'Nico!' said Mari, who'd run halfway up the field before anyone noticed what was happening.

'Nico!' she repeated, at the top of her voice. They heard her calling again and again, until her voice was a dim echo somewhere near the farmyard.

'Look at her,' said Elin with a wobbly, indulgent smile. A few weeks ago she'd have murmured *'Pathetic, Mari'* under her breath, but things had changed. Her daughter had fallen in love. And why not? He was handsome and strong. She'd have fallen for him too, probably. And here he was, back among them, coming down the mountain with a herd of pigs, and bringing them all a supply of food. Elin heard her daughter's voice growing fainter every time she shouted *Nico!* on her way through the farmyard, up the steep hill, and through the high meadows on her way to the mountain gate where Nico was enjoying a bit of a rest after he'd ushered his pigs through the opening. They were already grunting and turfing through the pasture, as if they owned the farm. Mari finally reached him and ran straight into his arms; he looked more like a man defending himself than someone greeting his lover. He almost fell backwards, such was the impact of her arrival; he was forced to hold his gun in the air above them, in case it went off.

'Hey now, you be careful!' said Nico. He smelt the warmth of her hair below his chin, and despite everything he felt glad to be back with her, up against her hard little body again, close to her fertile mind...

'You like my pigs?'

She looked at them. What could she say about a group of dirty, smelly animals?

'They're beautiful, Nico,' answered Mari as she took in the scene: there were about a dozen black and white pigs, plus the big black stallion which had carried Nico; and a light brown packhorse with a mustard mane and a large pack on its back. All the animals had taken this opportunity to feed on the banks around the gate.

Then Mari noticed that Nico had bruises in several places; there were blue-black rings on his cheek, on his neck, on his arm. He also held himself like a man who'd been injured, slightly cowed.

'Ow!' he said when Mari thrust her head between his shoulder and his head.

'You OK, Nico? What happened?'

He looked at her with his brown and green-flecked eyes. How much of the truth should he tell her? Then again, how much of the truth had she told him? How important was the truth, anyway?

'I fall off horse.'

He realised that she didn't believe him.

'Horse fall crossing river, I fall into stones.'

She stayed silent. How important was the truth by now? She herself had been economical with it. He was there in front of her, he was back at Dolfrwynog, and that was all that mattered. So what if they'd lived like actors in a Spaghetti Western? He was alive. Their hearts were beating, the blood was still coursing through their veins. That was the sole meaning of their existence now. Just being alive.

'I bring you food, yes?'

Nico gestured towards the pack on the second horse.

'I bring flour for bread, other things too.'

Mari put her arms around him and squeezed him as hard as she could. He flinched.

'Sorry, Nico. Thank you, Nico. Thank you for bringing us food. Thank you for coming back.'

'You not expect me to come back?'

'No.'

'Hey, you silly girl! Nico always come back!'

She sank her face in his shirt, the same shirt he'd worn when he left them over a week ago. That smell... what was it? Her mind raced through all the possibilities she could think of, but two particular smells made her pause and think. One was the nitrous smell of a discharged shotgun. And the other?

What was that other smell? Her freckly little nose was trying to tell her that it was the smell of blood. But how come? There was no stain. And yet, the odour was unmistakeable, it clung to her nostrils. No, she decided, it had to be in her imagination. She relaxed into his arms, and gave him a long, passionate kiss. *Welcome home*, said her body. *Welcome back to your home in Wales.*

2 1

THE PIGS WERE rolling in clover – but where on Earth was Jack? He was the subject of every conversation till late that night at Dolfrwynog. His mysterious departure caused unhappiness to Elin alone; he didn't mean much to anyone else there. They discussed his behaviour during the last few weeks before his disappearance. He'd fallen silent, they'd been lucky to hear a word from him. He'd lost his glasses and he'd been unable to see things; he'd stalked around the place like an owl, slowly rotating his head from side to side, looking for objects which were clearly visible to everyone else. Had he gone mad? Was he ranging across the mountain like a wild animal? After all, they'd seen him running around the meadows screaming and chasing the sheep like a crazy wolf. *Poor soul*, thought Wil. Maybe he'd fallen into one of the bogs up there. He imagined two dirty wellingtons floating on the surface of a bubbling morass. But Huw had never liked him, mainly because he'd supplanted his real father without a word of explanation.

Unfortunately, Jack had taken one of the guns with him. To counterbalance this, Nico had brought another firearm, and a heap of cartridges, when he returned with the pigs. In addition, he'd brought flour and salt and yeast and tinned food. 'Yes, *tins*,' said Wil – which of them had last seen a tin of peaches?

After firing up the stove to see if it still worked, Elin knocked up some dough. Then everyone sat around the two bowls she'd used, waiting for the dough to rise, like a family in the old days watching TV together; someone would get to their feet every so often and peek under the teacloths to see if anything was happening. Yes, it was coming along champion, said Wil. Thank God that Elin still remembered how to make it, he added. It was amazing how many things like that were a mystery to them; they'd taken so much for granted because everyone had relied completely on supermarkets. They'd never had to learn how to make bread; they'd forgotten all that basic stuff during the long years of plenty.

Nico laughed when he saw the Easter eggs – so he painted another that evening, to finish the collection; the final egg was put at the end, so that Nico's two contributions framed Mari's efforts. The new egg raised many a smile, since it showed Nico and Mari with two pigs, all of them holding 'hands' and dancing in a circle. Nico had painted a pig's snout on his own face and on Mari's too, plus curly little tails sticking out of their bums. After the bread had baked – and by then it was close to midnight – they enjoyed a simple feast together, with fresh bread and tinned pears.

Pieces of bread went down one gullet or another as soon as a chunk could be torn from a loaf. The room fell silent, except for the sound of many people chewing; Wil said they sounded like the dogs in their hut, slavering over the remains of a family dinner. But Huw thought they sounded like cannibals tucking into a freshly cooked missionary, far far away in the southern seas. He imagined drums beating and a large pile of bones gleaming in the moonlight. Had things like that ever happened, really? Or was it all made up? The way things were, it was more than possible it was happening again that very day, somewhere or other – if people went without food for a long time they were driven to desperation, even normal people, and they'd do anything to get some food inside them. They'd even eat other people. It had happened in the past; he remembered seeing a film about a group of South American schoolboys who ended up eating their playmates after their plane had come down in the Andes, or somewhere like that. Huw looked at Nico across the table, in the candlelight, and indeed he did look like a cannibal gnawing on a bone. He'd caught the sun while he was away and he was dark brown now; it was easy to imagine him with a bone in his nose, and it was easy to imagine Uncle Wil crouched over a drum, whipping them into a frenzy…

'Music!' said Wil suddenly.

'Pardon?' said Elin.

'What about a bit of music,' said Wil again. 'Like the old days.'

He got up and walked over to the piano in the parlour next door. It was covered in all sorts of odds and ends, but Wil was in determined mood and he moved everything off it. Then he lifted the lid and banged out a few notes with one of his dirty, cracked fingers.

'Come on, Elin, give us a tune,' he said through the doorway.

'Yes, come on, Mum, Nico can hear some Welsh tunes,' said Mari, in an attempt to encourage Elin. Nico was treated to a rather half-hearted concert, since it was late and they were all tired.

Wil started with 'I Asked Her for a Kiss, Down on the Sandy Shore', but soon lost his way. Song after song went the same way, he couldn't get past the first verse because he hadn't sung them for years and he'd forgotten the words.

Elin got up from the piano and began to close the lid, but Wil begged her: 'Come on, at least we'll all remember *Hen Wlad fy Nhadau*.'

He was determined to impress Nico with the national anthem and they all rose to the occasion, since they all remembered the words. They went through it twice, getting louder every time.

'This is our national song,' said Wil proudly through the door in Nico's direction, but Nico had fallen asleep, so they woke him up and sent him to bed. Mari went after him and stayed with him. There was no point in pretending now – everyone knew about them anyway. Even her mother was in on the act, she wasn't blind. Mari lay with her lover in the narrow bed, though he was already dead to the world. In moving his boots, she noticed that some of the stitching along the sole had changed colour, from dark yellow to crimson. While she folded his clothes away she noticed a stain on his jeans. And lying alongside him in bed, she saw nail marks along his right arm. He'd been in a fight with someone, that was obvious.

And who had owned the flour and the tinned food? Who had owned the gun, the pigs and the horses? Mari was highly suspicious. She closed her eyes, but she was too excited to go to sleep.

Nico. His name travelled through her mind like a ghost train going through a dark tunnel; she imagined them both sitting at the front of the train, screaming. He had his arm around her, holding her tight, because she was scared. She imagined a cobweb brushing her nose, and a skeleton with luminous red eyes leaping out in front of them, then a creepy ghost cackling from a dark hideyhole.

What an imagination she had. What love she felt for this man by her side; she felt the surf of her feelings break on the strand of his body. He'd come back to her. He loved her, despite the fact that living at Dolfrwynog was like being on an eternal ghost train which they couldn't get off. Uncle Wil was the skeleton, he'd lost so much weight. Jack was the ghost, disappearing into the darkness and then screaming suddenly.

Something else lay heavy on her mind as she looked at the moon silvering the sky and listened to the dogs baying into the night. The third grave. Should she go on with the pantomime – the stories, the ring, the morning ritual? Was there any point in all that? Wasn't he always going to be with her, anyway? But maybe he'd returned only because he knew she'd be there, sitting on his bed in the early quietude, telling him weird and wonderful stories.

She turned over on her side to face him and studied the tattoo. Close up, it seemed big and ghostly in the moonlight; at this angle the ship was about to sink below the waves, with her stern in the air. Mari stayed like that for ages, smelling his sunburnt skin and fantasising about the shipwreck on his arm. Finally, she folded the coverlet back and let Nico's ship sink slowly below waves of bedclothes. There would be explosions and smoke; boiling seawater and lights disappearing one by one. She heard people screaming, calling out to their children or their loved ones… followed by the silence of the night, and a huge moon like the one over Dolfrwynog tonight, turning the sea into a vast, limitless mirror. Her vivid imagination conjured up a small lifeboat with a girl and a young man on it. The girl had a baby in her arms. Who were they, this little family alone on the ocean?

She napped for a while, then turned her back to him, forming a bow within a bow. The third grave: she would start that story in the morning. It would be the story of Rhiannon from across the valley. Only half-awake by now, Mari had decided that the show must go on.

2 2

Nico was sitting up in bed, looking at Mari. He wasn't quite sure if she'd slept with him last night. Had it been a dream, that lovely warm feeling? Her hot little body next to him, her breath on his arm? Today she was sitting in a chair in the corner, and she was in her storytelling frock. He looked for the ring on her finger, and it was there. But she hadn't started her morning rite in the usual way; she'd been telling him about her week on the farm, while he'd been away hunting for pigs. Huw had fallen ill after chewing on a raw fish, or drinking dirty water, and he'd had to stay in bed for a few days. Uncle Wil had discovered a new nest in the hay barn, with an egg in it, and he'd put another X on his chart in the stable loft. He'd hidden himself away in the barn and kept watch, so that he could find out which one of his harem had been deceiving him. The chicks were doing nicely but Cluck the cock had lost some of the fine feathers in his tail, thanks to one of the dogs. Jess would be having pups soon. Having recovered a bit, Huw had gone for a walk along the lower meadows and had come home in a froth of excitement; although he couldn't be totally sure, he was convinced he'd seen Jack sitting in the topmost branches of a sycamore tree at the far end of the farm. On the other hand, it could have been an old black plastic bag. One way or another, he'd nearly messed his pants.

As she chatted away, Nico had time to appraise Mari in her storytime frock, her hair stuffed into a multi-coloured scarf, trying to look older than she was. He saw her in a new light this morning. True, she was too young for him, by quite a few years. But she was more mature than many older girls. And there were other factors. The awful state of the world had thrown young people together in unexpected ways. There was less choice available, now that human society had snarled to a halt. And many social mores had also been abandoned, there was a new morality – the morality of necessity. This young girl had offered her heart, but she hadn't told him she loved him. In a short spell of silence, he asked her:

'How you say I love you in Welsh?'

She blushed immediately and dropped her eyes to the floor.

'We don't say that sort of thing in Welsh. It sounds… a bit strange.'

'Strange?'

'Not right… you don't feel quite right when you say it.'

'Well say it, anyway.'

'No.'

'Don't be crazy,' said Nico, his mood darkening. 'I don't want you to love me, just say the words, then I know what they sound like.'

Mari became even more embarrassed. He'd told her the truth at last – he didn't want her love. So that's how the land lay. She wasn't good enough for him. Mari rose from the chair in one quick movement.

'Where you going?'

'Mind your own business.'

'Hey now, don't get mad. I was only asking you question. I don't know anything about your language – you talk it all day to each other, how am I supposed to know what's going on?'

They both stayed very still, watching each other.

'Come on now, please sit down and talk to me. I can't read

your mind. I only want to know what words sound like in your language.'

Mari hesitated, then sat down again, nervously. She looked straight into his eyes, challengingly.

'*Rwy'n dy garu di.*'

'Is that what you say?'

'We don't say it, but it means I love you.'

'Why you not say it?'

'Because it sounds… we're too shy to say it.'

'I understand now,' said Nico. 'Same in Tatra mountains, we don't say *I love you* either. No words like that. We say, *I'm glad to see you…* that's all we say, it's enough. Like signal.'

Nico explained that Poland's mountain folk were much too shy by nature to boldly say *I love you* to a member of the opposite sex. Instead, a subtle little drama was enacted; the couple would dance in a way which conveyed symbolic meaning. The angle of an arm, or the way someone was held, could convey more than an hour's conversation.

'The old people were the same round here too, apparently,' said Mari. 'They'd talk for ages about all sorts of things like the weather and the price of sheep before they got round to what they really wanted to talk about. Quite nice really, it showed respect for other people and it was kinda dignified, if you know what I mean.'

'Yes,' said Nico. 'I like listening to them too – talking is like a nice game to them, they have all sorts of rules… in the end they say more by saying nothing much!'

And that's how they chatted together that morning. Mari really couldn't decide if she should start her story, but maybe tomorrow would be better. Nico saw the consternation on her face.

'Hey you, some time soon now I want to hear about the

other graves, you promise me,' he said, in an attempt to soothe her. Mari realised how sensitive he was being, how quickly he saw things.

'Perhaps this afternoon we go for walk to see lambs together,' said Nico as he rose. When the bedclothes fell away from him, Mari looked at his nakedness without any embarrassment or self-consciousness. This was how they would live from now on, there was need for pretence. Life itself was naked by now. They were living, almost, as Adam and Eve had lived, presumably. Fashion and morality meant nothing. All they wanted was food in their bellies and a warm place to sleep. They were living in a primitive society again; nakedness and simplicity would be the norm, plain and natural. Despite that, they had two black clouds tethered permanently overhead, even on sunny days – and that's because famine and sickness were always there as a looming darkness, always threatening them. They almost lived like animals in the wild now, always close to the edge of existence.

While messing about in the river together that afternoon, both naked, after swimming in the pool by the big oak tree which had been there since Uncle Wil was a child, Mari started the story of the third grave in the paddock. Water was the key to the tale, since Rhiannon from Pant yr Haul had used it to escape after a long period of neglect and cruelty.

'We came out of the water a long time ago, and Rhiannon went back into it,' said Mari.

'She said something to me one day. She said that everything would go back to the water eventually. Maybe she was a bit unhinged by then…'

'What is unhinged?'

'Mad, I suppose. A bit mad. She thought that all living things would return to the water eventually – like dolphins. She'd read somewhere that dolphins had lived on the land for a while, and then they'd gone back to the sea, as if they'd got fed up of walking around, or whatever they did, and went back.'

'You think that's true?'

'God knows.'

The two of them were lying in the grass below the oak tree, holding hands. Mari's mind had gone off on a lazy wander, while Nico had dropped off to sleep by her side.

This was how Adam and Eve must have lived in Paradise, thought Mari. Lying on the earth in the hot silence of summer, enjoying the sensuous touch of the grass on their naked flesh, enjoying the soft play of the breezes through the fine hair on their bodies. And the man beside her, sleeping; his body was a mirror, reflecting the green of the grass, the yellows and the blues of the flowers. The river murmured, the bees hummed. This was the happiest moment of her life. She'd try to capture it, frame it, and put it on the wall of her favourite room inside her head. She'd keep it for ever, she'd go back to that room repeatedly – on fine days and on rainy days – to consult it and to admire it. It would prove to her that she'd *lived* at least once in her life, that she'd tasted purity of emotion, that she'd loved with absolute clarity for at least one whole day.

They arose, they dressed, and they left that place. They went to watch the young lambs gambolling in the fields. They walked through the pastures bare-footed, sometimes whispering to each other, sometimes going in complete silence. Sometimes far apart, sometimes together, looking at each other or stooping to admire a beautiful feather on the ground, or searching for nests in the trees, or plucking and presenting an immaculate flower from a hedgerow.

On the way home, Mari finished the story of Rhiannon

from Pant yr Haul. Nico listened carefully, asking a question now and again, or making a discreet comparison.

Rhiannon had come to the valley from a faraway place, no-one knew where exactly. She belonged to a very rich family, and as was customary with rich families her parents had intended her to marry into another rich family; they wanted her to pick a comparable partner with excellent academic qualifications and a good job. But one summer, when she was waiting for her A-level results, she'd met Alun from Pant yr Haul farm at a party. She fell for him almost immediately, with the passion of first love. She refused to listen to her parents or her friends, who were worried about Alun from the beginning. Yes, he was tall, handsome, and physically very fit; Rhiannon had met him in town one Saturday night when the local rugby club was having its annual shindig, and Alun was a star player. That was the type she liked, a rugger bugger, and who could blame her? What do they say about girls – that they tend to go for men similar to their fathers but without all the faults? Because Rhiannon's father had also been a well-known rugby player.

Rhiannon fell in love with Alun. Her love was simple and huge. But alarm bells sounded from the start; for instance, she didn't know how to deal with his moods when he'd been drinking. There was a sober Alun and there was a six-pint Alun, who was completely different – a bad-tempered man, unpleasant and cruel. The next day he'd bring flowers and chocolates, he'd lower his head and apologise. Every time, Rhiannon forgave him.

Rhiannon married him despite her parents' opposition and came to live in the valley, at Pant yr Haul farm. *Haul* means sun, but she didn't experience much warmth in her new home. The honeymoon was over in days; by the year's ending Rhiannon live in such oppressive conditions that she became almost mute for the rest of her life. On some nights, when he was at his worst, she was forced to sleep with the dogs in their filthy kennel. Alun had plenty of excuses at the ready; he blamed the failure of his farm on the state of the world, he blamed everything on everyone else. He made her carry him on her back whenever he was in his black moods; he beat her until she was a mass of bruises.

Rhiannon tried many times to escape. But her husband was a cunning man as well as a sick man; he'd lock her away at night and keep her with him all day. This went on for many years and Rhiannon lost all hope. No-one knew about her oppression because her husband turned every visitor away at the gate. Her own brother was driven away.

Then the water came to rescue her. She too had watched the lake forming below her home, creating a small sea between Pant yr Haul and Dolfrwynog. She waited patiently until it reached the bottom of the field below the farmhouse. Then, one day, while her husband slept in a drunken stupor, she dragged an old door to the rim of the lake and rowed her flimsy little raft across the water, using a bit of old planking. Fortunately for her, Alun saw nothing, and since his dogs couldn't follow her spoor across the water she was able to take refuge in Mari's bedroom. This had happened many years previously, when it was still possible to communicate with the outside world. Many messages were sent to her family, but answers came there none. They couldn't establish if anyone had received the messages, but the result was devastating; from that day on, Rhiannon went into a steep decline. Like Sara, she refused food; she even made attempts to join the dogs in their hut at Dolfrwynog.

Rhiannon was discovered one morning, floating in the lake, drowned. She'd simply walked into the water, it appeared, so she was buried with the others in the paddock.

'She died of a broken heart, I think,' said Mari to Nico. 'She used to stand at the top of the farmyard and look towards the road coming down into the valley, as if she expected someone to take her home. But no-one ever came, and she just gave up. She'd made a terrible mistake and she paid a terrible price.'

Nico remained silent after Mari had ended her story. 'I hate men like that,' he said. 'Men who beat their wives are scum, yes?'

Mari smiled at him. 'You're never going to beat me then, Nico?'

'Never,' he answered. And their hands met as they reached the paddock.

'But how you know this story if she never speak to anybody?'

Mari turned to face him.

'Because she did talk in the end, but only to one person. Herself. We heard her say the story to a ghost in front of her eyes as she walked about. She told it as if it were someone else's story – as if she couldn't believe it was her own story.'

Nico nodded slowly, to signal that her story had moved him.

They went to stand by her grave, and Nico said: 'We must get flowers for her, yes?'

'I'll do it tomorrow,' said Mari. 'Come on – I'm hungry. Let's go to the house for some food.'

They crossed the paddock and headed for the house. When they reached the door, Nico pulled her towards him so that they were both facing the upper meadows, above them. With his hands on her shoulders, she sank her back into his chest and relaxed, but then he lifted a finger upwards.

'You see something?'

Mari looked carefully in all directions.

'No'.

'You see those clouds beginning to come in?'

'Yes, I see them. So?'

'Rain tomorrow. No more sun like today. Also something else. You see bushes on top of hill?'

'Yes of course,' she answered – there were dozens of gorse bushes in the direction he was indicating.

'That small one near tree, you see it? The one with no yellow on it?'

'Yes I see it,' said Mari, though she still wasn't quite sure where he meant.

'That no bush. That one move about all the time we walk here from the fields.'

'What do you mean?' said Mari.

'That bush not a bush. That bush a man.'

23

M ARI WAS PICKING flowers in the rain. Wild flowers, from the hedgerows; she had no idea what their names were, most of them anyway, but their wonderful colours weren't dulled by her ignorance. Knowing such things as the names of flowers was probably unimportant now, she thought. There were no teachers to quiz her on such things. Red flowers, pink flowers, blue flowers. Wasn't that enough? Foxgloves… what an odd name, anyway. She imagined a fox slinking slyly along the meadows with red gloves on each paw and a dinky little black hat on its head, like a model on a catwalk.

That was the sort of thing going through Mari's mind, little fluffy cloud-thoughts, as she collected posies to go on the graves in the paddock. Rain was falling lightly, almost imperceptibly, all around her while a posse of dark clouds assembled far away in the West. The rain hadn't bothered her up to now, since it strengthened the scent of the flowers and created an air of luxury. But then her T-shirt became sodden and her jeans began to stick to her legs. She'd already collected a nice big posy and secreted it in the hedge; now she had another to match it, so she set off for home. Far away – on the edge of her consciousness – she heard two shots, so she stopped in her tracks, as a fox might on smelling danger. They had come from somewhere above her, in the high meadows. Nico – where was he? She started running towards home; hadn't she seen him cleaning the new gun that morning? It had to be him – shooting rabbits, perhaps. But she knew that Nico didn't shoot rabbits as a rule, to save on cartridges – he used traps. She became agitated: hadn't Nico seen someone moving on the hill above them yesterday?

She made a real effort to calm herself as she walked towards the paddock. She split the flowers into four posies and put them on the graves, ready for their receptacles. She'd already asked Huw to prepare some jars or pots, but there was no sign of them so she went looking for him, and found him sitting on the upper step of the stable loft. He said *Dammit!* as soon as he saw her.

'Sorry Mari, I forgot…'

Huw ran around the sheds looking for jars or vases to add to the one that was already there, and eventually he found another old jam jar and two flowery vases which had adorned the farmhouse in better times – they'd probably belonged to Uncle Wil's grandmother. All three receptacles were extremely dirty, so Huw said:

'I'm off to the well to give these a good clean,' and he started to move away with the crockery dangling from his fingertips.

But Mari stopped him in his tracks.

'Better not. Didn't you hear the shooting?'

'Shooting?' said Huw, coolly. 'No, where?'

But he gave the game away by raising his eyes towards the hill above, and Mari realised immediately that he knew something she didn't.

'What do you know, Huw?'

'Nothing.'

'Don't fib. You know something…'

Mari jabbed him repeatedly with a forefinger and hassled him; it didn't take long. Huw divulged that Nico had left the farmyard with his gun immediately after she had left to gather flowers. He'd seen him slink up the hill towards the gorse bushes above them, on the skyline.

In the next hour Nico returned to Dolfrwynog with his gun cradled under his right arm. He was walking slower than usual, head down, and he had a rabbit in his left hand, stiff and cold. Anyone looking at him closely would have noticed he was paler than usual, and very subdued. Nico went with them to the paddock, helping Huw with the red bucket which was slopping water all over the place. They also took the three flower-holders and Uncle Wil's spade, which normally rested against the wall of the hen house. Nico tidied around the graves while the others put the flowers into jars and vases. Everyone was wet through by now, but after finishing they all stood for a while, looking at the scene. Mari felt very sad because the rain added an element of mournfulness; it all seemed more poignant than if they'd done it on a sunny day. It was a meaningful occasion, like a Remembrance Day service in the old days. The village ceremony every November had meant very little to her of course, but her grandfather had treated each occasion as a major event. She understood why, now. That was the way of the world. One generation's tragedy meant very little to the next, and pretty well nothing to the following generation. That was how the collective consciousness worked, wasn't it? The national memory. Only a few big events remained in the public eye, and some of those were mythological, like the story of Noah and the Flood, or the history of Cantre'r Gwaelod which was drowned by the sea off west Wales. Mari looked up into the sky; the clouds were thickening, and by now they were flowing into the cwm on a strong westerly wind. She started to tremble, and she could hear Huw's teeth chattering. Had the fine weather ended? She looked towards Nico, who was standing with his head stooped low, as if they were at a funeral. He was staring at the grave nearest to him, which was smaller than the others.

He realised, for the first time, that it was a child's grave and he looked up suddenly, catching Mari's eye. Then he walked off hurriedly with the spade in his hand.

'I'll catch you later,' he said as he turned away from her.

'Where are you going, Nico?'

He took no notice, and walked through the paddock towards the hill, with his head right down.

'Nico!' shouted Mari.

Away he went, up the hill, without a backward glance. Then he vanished.

Mari and Huw went into the house to dry themselves, and Mari knew that something terrible had happened up there earlier. Something nightmarish, if the epilogue involved a spade. She changed and put her wet clothes to dry on a clothes horse. Then she went to bed, for no particular reason; it seemed her best option. She watched the clouds racing across the sky and listened to the wind strengthening, beginning to moan in the eaves. It was a familiar sound by now. Rivers of rain swept down the windows. She saw deltas in places; she imagined the faraway Amazon, or the Mississippi, then she thought of the beautiful little rivers of Wales: the Teifi and the Tawe and the Dwyryd and the Conwy. A terrible loneliness came over her as she lay in her little bedroom at Dolfrwynog that afternoon; the wind sounded like an ancient wind coming from the far reaches of the world, from the far reaches of time itself... a wind which had been heard by her ancestors, whistling and grating in the cromlechs of the Stone Age. It was a wind which had travelled through deep time to frighten her. She felt it had witnessed every small pain which had afflicted mankind throughout history, every act of torture and every death. It linked every physical ache that had ever been suffered, like a toadstool's filaments spread out in a gigantic fan of connections underground. A huge black dog settled on her bed and started to whimper.

She napped for a while, then felt someone's weight settle on the foot of the bed; was the black dog moving? But she knew it was Nico. Blood and gunpowder again. What had she done? Why on earth had she decided to love this one? *Ha!* said a little voice in her head. *Decided?* There had been no choice at all in the matter. He had sawn Mari in half and torn her heart from her body.

'Had a nice time killing someone?' she said sleepily. 'Think I don't know what's going on?'

There was no movement from the weight on the end of her bed, so eventually she lifted her head to look at him. Yes, it was Nico, still in his coat. She looked at him again. He looked awful – covered in mud, reddish-brown earth smeared all over his arms, dirt on his face too.

'So you want them to kill us first?' said Nico.

Mari sat up quickly and looked at him properly.

He was right.

'It's us or them now, Mari. We kill them or they kill us. Understand?'

Mari swallowed hard, and then nodded. She understood very well what he meant. If Nico wasn't there they'd all be dead by now probably. Or they'd have starved.

'I do this for you, Mari. I do this for you and me. For us.'

Mari found it hard to reconcile herself with what was happening.

'But we spared you, Nico. Uncle Wil could have killed you too.'

'Bad mistake, Mari. He should have killed me. You were lucky with me. But those two men out there would have killed us all. You believe me?'

He hadn't moved an inch throughout their conversation. The room darkened around them, and by the end she could see only his profile.

After a while, Nico rose and went to the door. He turned, and stared at her.

'Tomorrow you tell me another story. That is how we live now. That is how we survive. I shoot the men, I get the food, you tell the stories. OK?'

She nodded, then shrank back into the bed.

Nico had delivered a grim warning. Only the strongest, the most cunning and the most resolute would live from now on. She listened again to the wind, and during the night a fourth story took shape in her mind, like a dream; like an event which happened a very long time ago, in someone else's imagination.

2 4

THOSE BLACK CLOUDS continued to roll over them for another three days, dropping one watery cargo after another, as if they were huge dredgers unloading holdfuls of harbour sludge into the depths. In the farmhouse, hope faded slowly. They'd been through this before; the constant cloudscape, the inquisitorial wind. It was as if the farm had been moved to a new postcode in purgatory or hell. The weather was set for another miserable period, and they knew it, but their resilience was weakening.

Uncle Wil was also weakening and losing hope. It was Huw who released the hens every morning now, and shut them in every night; his uncle stayed in bed throughout the day sometimes, except for his visits to the nettles. He wasn't eating, and he was unsteady on his feet. At the beginning of the month he'd asked Huw to report to him on the state of the hens every evening; he'd wanted to know where they'd wandered to, how many eggs they'd laid, how the chicks were progressing. But by the end of July he fell silent and lay there on his filthy old bed, under his greatcoats, with just his head showing. Poor Huw was torn in two by the experience; the conscientious part of him wanted to help his uncle and keep him company in the loft, while the other, childish half, wanted to escape back to the house. Fair play to the lad, he kept vigil in the loft, over there in the Far East, though sometimes he felt like a hostage who'd been captured by pirates, rotting away in an island prison, waiting for his relatives to pay his ransom; he imagined a pile of gold coins rattling on the long white table at Dolfrwynog, or a leather pouch full of valuable rings and jewellery. Occasionally someone else would come over from the house to chat with the old man. But Huw was still his favourite.

Nico listened to his own little storyteller, Mari, every day. They slept together now without comment from anyone, though Mari went back to her room every morning to put on her special dress and to fetch her special ring. There was no real reason for her to do this any longer, and she was puzzled by her own actions. She was observing some sort of inner ceremony, presumably. Or maybe she'd entered a fantasy sequence, as if she'd gone back to her childhood and was trying to create a chain of interconnecting dreams. She'd enjoyed dressing up as a child; she'd been a fairy for a long time, wandering through the house with her silvery wings, her sparkly crown and her wand. The very thought of that time brought burning meteorite tears to her eyes. Perhaps she was trying to reclaim some of the innocence and naivety of her childhood. There was no fear then, no suffering or famine. *Once upon a time, in the land of the fairies…*

She would sit on Nico's bed – or rather, their conjugal bed as it was by now – with her back to the wall, sensing the ancient chill of the mortar, looking out through the window towards the top of the yard. Sometimes she'd see Huw walk up there to free the hens. Once she saw him kick Megan like a football, and she'd shouted at her brother through the window. Cruelty was trickling down the chain; the time had come for someone to kick the cat. But the grey clouds continued on their course, and the month dwindled away into darkness.

She started her final tale with a detailed description of Dylan, her younger brother. He had been completely different to the others, with long blond hair and Scandinavian eyes, as blue as blue could be; he'd have looked at home on a street in Norway or Denmark, no-one would have spared him a second glance. But there were two distinct features which drew everyone's attention to him: he was very small, though not a dwarf, and he behaved differently to other children. In being tiny he wasn't deformed; everything was in the right place and in the right proportion. He was merely on a miniature scale.

Some had suspected that he was autistic, or maybe had Asperger's, but this had been discounted by the docs. Though he had never spoken a word in his short life – he was seven when he died – there was nothing wrong with his brain. Indeed, he was exceptionally intelligent; Dylan had complete understanding in his eyes and he was also funny and easily amused. He was always fun to be with. Yes, Dylan was an exceptional child, and Mari painted a marvellous portrait of him: the way he blew the hair from his eyes, producing a funny whirring sound with his lips; the way he danced along the lower meadows with his arms out, floating in the air like a merry-go-round, or sometimes he'd mimic a whirligig, his hands like two birds flying in the air around him. And then he'd come back from the far meadows with moss and lichen and leaves, he'd make a magical house for Mari's dolls, and light it with shards of green and red glass strategically placed to catch the light.

But although Dylan was a sweetheart to everyone, there was one special person in his life – his great-grandfather. No-one paid much attention to Great-grandfather by then because he was so old and sleepy he had almost gone already; he had forgotten everything, even his own name. Dylan did everything for the old man; it was Dylan who took him his breakfast, dinner and supper; he'd even chew the meat for his great-grandfather if it was tough. It was the little lad who dressed him in the morning, and took him for a slow amble around the farmyard if it was sunny.

'The old man refused to eat any more food when he reached his hundredth birthday,' said Mari to Nico on the bed. 'We were living in poverty even then, and he could see that there wasn't enough food to go round. So he said to us all one day by the fire that he wouldn't eat any more food after that day. He said: *I will not take any more food from the mouths of these children, I will not see my own family starve away in front of my own eyes… I am an old man now and I have served my purpose. It is time I went, I am of no further use to this world.* That's what he said, in Welsh of course,' said Mari.

'So what happened – did he starve to death?' asked Nico.

'No, he didn't starve to death, and Dylan was the reason for that. Because Dylan also refused to eat any food if the old man refused. He let it be known that if his great-grandfather refused to eat then so would he. For two weeks the old man refused food. He watched Dylan refuse his food also, and then on the fifteenth day he relented because he saw that Dylan was as stubborn and pig-headed as he was. So he said: *Yes, I will eat some food then, or this scamp will die in front of my eyes.* And everyone cried – even Dylan and the old man. Then the boy chewed a piece of meat and took it over to his great-grandfather, who had no teeth, and the old man took it. They sat together by the fireside that night, eating together, and they were laughing and crying every other moment too.'

Mari told the story about the little boy and the old man eating together and walking around the yard together, with Dylan leading his half-blind relative between the hens and the geese and the dogs and the cats. Then, when night came along, it was Dylan who took the old man up to his room; he'd undress him, and he'd end the day by winding up an old musical box which played the same piece of music over and over again every night, until Great-grandfather went to sleep.

That was how Mari started the story of her brother Dylan.

25

MARI STOOD IN the parlour, looking at the last calendar which had been put on the nail by the piano. It was old and faded, and it was covered in biro notes: someone's sports day, another's dental appointment. Family birthdays were noted in red; Mari thumbed through the months, looking at her mother's writing. Elin had given up again after Jack's disappearance and had taken to her bed. She spent nearly every day reading old romance novels.

'What month is it?' asked Mari. She turned around, but there was nobody there to answer her.

She went upstairs to her mother's loft.

'What month is it, Mum?'

'No idea. It's summer, isn't it? Who knows, it's so hard to tell.'

Right now they were going through a grey patch with clouds racing down the valley every day, driven by strong westerlies. After a fortnight of this everyone was down in the dumps again. Huw stood like a wounded bird by the window, looking out every day on a hostile world. He hated playing in the house.

Mari walked across the yard to the stable loft to visit her uncle. Usually these days he could be found napping or daydreaming, and when her eyes had grown accustomed to the light she saw his boots poking out from under the greatcoats.

'How are you today, Uncle Wil?' she asked from the doorway. Then she approached him and continued: 'Are you better this morning?'

'Absolutely champion, love,' he replied in a weak voice. This was his usual response.

'Want any breakfast, Uncle Wil?'

'Not quite yet love, I'll wait till later,' he answered.

Mari fiddled about for a while, tidying up after Huw, then she asked:

'What month is it, Uncle Wil?'

'It's July, love,' answered Wil without hesitation. He'd kept a tally of the days in his diary, though he wasn't as conscientious as he'd been in the old days: with the weather behaving so oddly it didn't matter much which month of the year it was. The potatoes would be rotting in the earth by now. Someone should go and check. He'd ask Nico that evening when he called.

'Taters,' he said over-loudly. 'Mr Tattoo needs to check his taters.'

He chuckled at his own pathetic joke but the laugh turned into a groan.

Mari noticed tears in his eyes, because of the pain, presumably.

'It's close to the middle of the month,' he said. 'About the fourteenth, I'd say.'

He laughed again, but this time his rasping breath turned into a hacking cough. He raised himself on an elbow and said:

'Do you know what? It must be my birthday. Yes indeed, it's my birthday, or as near as dammit anyway!'

He fell back onto the bed, sending off a small cloud of dust into the atmosphere.

'Blinking heck, Uncle Wil, we'd all forgotten,' said Mari. 'Happy birthday!'

She went over to the bed and lowered her head to give him a kiss. He smelt awful, but she shut her eyes and dropped a smacker on his cheek. He'd grown a beard and the experience was a bit like kissing an old billy goat. Poor Uncle Wil. Turning to look at her, he grasped her arm.

'Don't leave me, Mari, stay for a bit, will you?'

He was looking at her like a puppy who'd lost its mother.

'Of course I will,' said Mari, who sat on a milking stool by his bed. 'Are you in pain?'

'Let's not talk about that. I don't get much company these days, so I'm not going to go on about my health. There are more important things…'

He turned away from her to look at the wall, while his tears subsided. He had so many things on his mind. The potatoes, and the corn, and the livestock – what was going to happen to them? He himself was useless by now, he couldn't even look after the hens. His own little world was about to disappear into deep space. His little Welsh entity, so shy and old-fashioned. Once upon a time, when he was young, he'd seen a big magical world beyond the mouth of the valley; a huge world containing numberless nations and fascinating civilisations; amazing geographical phenomena, and countless opportunities. But one day he returned to the yard after mowing a field of hay and the whole world had disappeared; after forty years at Dolfrwynog he realised that the fabulous world he'd glimpsed through the cwm's narrow mouth had rushed by in a hurry, leaving nothing but the sweet scent of its own promise.

Then, with the arrival of old age, and the disappearance of that world which had so mesmerised him when he was young, he was forced to shuffle around on a small impromptu stage – a tiny Welsh farmyard with a few scrawny hens in the North and a muck-heap in the South. But by today even that world had gone – his whole universe had been stuffed into this loft above a hut where horses used to chomp their hay and oats, so many years ago. There was no longer a North or a South, an

East or a West; no more adventures would come his way again. Neither love nor children would illuminate the scroll of his life. The little Popeye who had navigated his boat around the youth camp lake had vanished into the void a long time ago – that little child had sailed beyond the moon, further than Mars and Saturn and Pluto…

'Mari, I don't want to live in this room, on my own. What can I do? Where can I go? I'm not going to last long in this place, you know that. I don't want to stay here…'

Mari knew what he was trying to say, she understood. Uncle Wil was dying; his life was coming to an end, and the stable loft wasn't the right place for that to happen.

'We'll move you back into the house,' said Mari. 'You can have my room.'

'No, no, I couldn't…'

'Shhh, Uncle Wil, don't waste your breath. I'll go and prepare things straight away. There's no point in making a fuss, I've decided and that's it, OK?'

Uncle Wil turned his face to the wall again. He was relieved. Mari had heard his plea and she had responded to his hopes. He wanted to return to his home, that was the right place to be, not among piles of rubbish in this dirty old room.

Mari looked at him and began to cry. Today she'd witnessed something important – the impending death of old Wales. Yes, that's what was happening, in front of her eyes. The death of an ancient tradition, the old Welsh way of life.

'Please don't cry little Mari, or I'll start too.'

Mari smiled and wiped away her tears.

'There's one small thing.' She didn't know how to tackle the issue. Uncle Wil would need a bath before returning to the house, because he smelt like a corpse. How should she broach the subject?

'Don't worry, Mari love, I'll go up to the well before coming over,' said Wil. He'd seen the question in her eyes; perhaps he understood women better than he thought. No, he'd never understood them and he never would.

He was merely seeing what needed to be done. Perhaps that was the greatest difference between his generation and this one; the old people had an innate ability to spot work that had to be done, whereas this lot had to be led to it. But perhaps he wasn't being fair to them; after all, hadn't Mari just seen his need and succoured him? Fair play to the girl. Tears sprang to his eyes once more, and he turned to the wall.

Wil laboured to the well, and removed every rag from his scrawny body, then washed himself. By God, the water was cold! He'd taken along a very old pair of flannel pyjamas in a faded candy stripe, but he was almost too weak to put them on by the end. He had to sit for a while on the slab by the well, recovering. But by nightfall he'd reached Mari's loft at Dolfrwynog. He was back in the room he'd slept in as a child. Wil had returned there to die.

26

MARI POPPED TO the pantry to fetch some flour. Yes, there was just enough left to make a cake. Huw was ordered to fire up the stove and Nico was sent to get wood from the store. Mari wasn't completely sure how to make a cake, but she did the best she could. She put some flour in a bowl and broke one of Megan's lovely brown eggs on the rim; then she mixed it all up with some water. She felt sure that this was the way it was done; she was too proud to ask her mother, who probably knew better. Mari eventually tired of mixing the ingredients and asked Nico to complete the task. To tease her he went at it like a maniac, pulling silly faces as he pounded the mix melodramatically; his tomfoolery worked, and everyone in the room ended up laughing or grinning. The endless rain and greyness had created an element of mania in everyone by now. Nico spent the rest of the day rescuing as many of the spuds as he could before they rotted away; he placed them in rows to dry in the stable loft – on the table, on Wil's bed and along the floor. There were enough to last for a while, but there wouldn't be enough to last the winter. *God knows what we'll do then*, thought Nico.

The cake went into the oven when the stove had heated up and everyone sat in silence around it, warming up. After a while Mari asked what they'd do for candles when the birthday cake was ready. Everyone scuttled around looking in every drawer and cupboard, but they drew a blank. Determined not to give up, Mari went up to Elin's room and started rifling through the drawers without saying anything, since she wasn't feeling particularly reverential towards her mother.

'What are you doing?' asked Elin.

'I'm looking for candles to go on Uncle Wil's birthday cake.'

'What?'

'It's Uncle Wil's birthday, we're making a cake.'

'Oh.' She pointed to a tall cupboard in the corner. 'Over there, third drawer up on the right.'

Mari went over to the cupboard, and saw that her mother was right.

'How did you know these were here, when the room's in such a hell of a mess?' asked Mari.

'I know where everything is in this room,' said Elin, 'so what would be the point of putting them in a place where I'd never find them if I tidied up?'

The reply astonished Mari; her mother's response had been that of a teenage girl, not a middle-aged woman. So she bit her tongue and descended the stairs with seven tiny pink candles in her hand. She remembered them clearly because they'd been used on her birthday cakes when she was little.

The oven wasn't hot enough to bake the cake properly and its middle was soft and soggy when it was put on a plate in the kitchen. Huw stuffed the candles into the sponge and then they all climbed the stairs in a long line with the treads squeaking a whole symphony of sounds below their feet.

'Come on, Mum, come to Uncle Wil's room,' said Mari when she reached the landing.

But Elin continued with her reading, as if she were afraid that Fate would suddenly catch up with her if she stopped – by now she'd retreated completely into a fantasy world.

When Huw opened the door, Uncle Wil was fast asleep. What should they do now?

Down the stairs they all went, in a ghostly line, as quietly as they could.

But in an hour or so they heard a knock from Wil's bedroom and Huw went up to see how he was.

'Bring me a drink of water, will you, lad?' asked Wil.

Huw returned downstairs and announced that his uncle was ready to receive them now.

For a second time they trooped upstairs, and this time Wil was sat up in bed, looking a little better.

Happy birthday to you,
Happy birthday to you...

They all sang as best they could, huddled together by the door – there wasn't enough room for all their faces to be seen by Wil.

Sto lat, sto lat,
Niech zyje, zyje nam...

Nico chimed in with the Polish version, and everyone laughed, everyone, that is, except for Uncle Wil, who had started to weep silently – they could see boulder-tears careering down his feverish cheeks, like an avalanche in the uplands.

Mari and Huw sat on his bed to console him, and it was Huw who blew out the candles.

'Happy birthday!' said everyone except for Nico.

'*Sto lat!*' said Nico, and everyone laughed again.

Then they went in a line downstairs again, and sat around the fire. There was relative silence till supper; Huw crashed around on the piano for a while, playing Chopsticks badly with two fingers, until everyone shouted, *Shut up, Huw,* in a chorus.

Later, upstairs, Nico and Mari held each other as tight as they could, while listening to the wind seething in the eaves.

'This weather no good, we have no food for the winter,'

said Nico. 'We have to do something different now Jack and Wil not working. Perhaps move away.'

Mari tightened her arms around him even harder, until he could barely breathe.

'But where can we go? There's nowhere left…'

'We have to think of something, or we starve this winter.'

Silence. Then Nico asked her to tell him more about Dylan, her little mute brother. He'd been thinking about Dylan all day.

'You tell me more about little boy and old man. This story useful for us some day.'

'What do you mean, useful?'

'Never you mind – you tell me story, I like it.'

Mari played with his curly hair as she recounted the story of Dylan, her little brother, and his unusual relationship with his great-grandfather. The little lad would grasp the tip of his relative's walking stick and lead him around the farmyard, as if they were a miniature train and he was the engine. He fed the old man and dressed him. But when the lake came to drown the belly of the valley, the old man was stricken. His old home, the house where he was born, was still there in the dip and he couldn't cope with the thought of it disappearing below the waves. Every morning he asked Dylan to take him down there, to his ancestral home, half a mile below them in the valley's cleft, and he'd stand there in the centre of the old homestead watching the water as it closed in on the buildings and lapped at the gate which led to the outside world. The water worked its way towards the house slowly but surely; then it invaded the kitchen and the pantry and the rest of the ground floor. The two of them would wade through the building with water sucking at their legs and snapping at their toes with cold, hostile teeth. Every day they'd go together to watch the rise of the water; gradually it went up the walls, up the stairs and into the bedrooms. Soon enough the old homestead had almost disappeared altogether.

They'd stand at the rim of the all-conquering water, and the old man would recite the old epics of Wales, or he'd sing the old songs in a reedy voice. Then, one day, a great storm arrived in the valley. Despite this, the old man insisted on going down to the water's edge, as he did every day. *Don't be crazy old man, you'll die*, said everyone around him. But he refused to listen. He started to walk downwards, on his own, towards his childhood home and the wind whipped him from side to side, the rain covered him in a mantle of grey. His voice could be heard for a long time, railing against the wind and the rain. Then he disappeared from view. An hour went by, but no-one knew what to do. The little boy, his constant companion, was locked in the pantry to prevent him from escaping and following his great-grandfather into the storm. But at some stage, nobody knew when, he managed to slip the latch and run down the fields towards the water.

Mari stopped, and listened to her lover's breathing. It was deep and steady. He had gone to sleep.

27

HE'D WOKEN UP at last. After stirring, then snuggling up to her, he said *Hiya* softly.

For one reason or another, Mari had slept only fitfully. She'd lain on her side for a long time, listening to the wind wolfing around the house, and trying to picture the face of the tiny baby floating inside the fluid depths of her womb, swimming around like a very small fish in a big ocean. Because she knew by now that she had a child forming inside her. She wondered if the little thing would have curly hair like Nico eventually. Or light brown hair, like a mouse, and freckles all over its face. A trace of a microscopic ship floating on its developing right arm? Of course, Mari would speak Welsh to it and Nico could teach it Polish. Should the baby have a Welsh name or a Polish name? Both, surely, a name from each language. Gareth Gustaw Evans. Huw Jozef Evans. Her lips moved as she said the names.

'Mari?'

'Yes, Nico?'

'You say something?'

His voice was sleepy and velvety.

Mari turned over and studied her lover's drowsy face. How could he sleep so easily when the world was so topsy-turvy? He'd already stated the obvious, that they wouldn't have enough food for the winter. But in all truth, what could they do? The fact was that only Nico could rescue them now. Jack had vanished, and Wil would be gone before Christmas, by the look of things. Mari could feel Nico's heart beating below his warm brown skin. Its throb felt far away, like a ship's engine. The little sod had gone off to sleep halfway through her story last night, after making all that fuss too. But there was no point in saying anything. She smiled and kissed the ship on his arm.

'Bad boy, you went to sleep when I was telling you about Dylan.'

'Sorry, Mari. Very tired.'

Another ten minutes went by while he woke properly. Then, in a while, he said:

'You give haircut for me today, OK?'

She lost her tongue for a while.

'Haircut? But why? I love your hair like that.'

'No, I have haircut today and I kill a pig for food. How much salt left?'

How the hell should she know?

'No idea,' she answered crossly. What the hell was going on? Haircut? Salt? Kill a pig? She was confused and angry.

'Now you finish Dylan story please,' said Nico. 'Important for me to know the end. Important for future, yes?'

Once again she found herself struggling to understand him.

She went into a sulk and started to get up, but Nico put an arm around her and pulled her back into the bed. It wasn't altogether unpleasant for her.

'No, this very important. I need to know about Dylan or maybe we won't be able to live this winter. You understand?'

'No.'

'Don't worry Mari, I explain everything soon. I make plan. Only way out. No food for winter, we must think of something. Maybe this idea I have will save us, I don't know.'

'What is it?'

'Tell you tonight, now tell me about Dylan.'

Mari completed the story, looking at the cracked ceiling

above her. Dylan had escaped from Dolfrwynog and followed his great-grandfather through the flooded fields. At one stage his wellingtons became stuck in the muddy soil and he left them where they were. For a whole month they stood there, bodiless, because no-one could bear to touch them. Dylan ran barefoot through the mud, almost blinded by the rain, until he reached the old farmstead. Somehow, through a superhuman final effort, his aged relative had swum out to the house and climbed onto the ridge of the roof. He sat there, shouting defiance at the storm, shaking his fists, and still declaiming ancient and revered Welsh texts in his shaky, high-pitched voice. His white beard streamed with rainwater as he summoned the heroes of old to his aid.

Dylan realised that the water was rising; it was creeping up the roof, and all that remained in a while was the ridge itself, two chimneys, and the old man astride the coping tiles, riding his phantom horse into the tempest. Without thought for his own life, Dylan leapt into the foaming lake and swam out to his great-grandfather; then he stood on the ridge, grasping the old man's shoulders, with their heads and torsos alone showing above the surface of the water. He urged his great-grandfather, in their private but unspoken language, to swim back to the shore with him or they'd die.

The old man gave a terrible cry when he realised that the little boy had joined him on the roof. Gesticulating, he begged him to swim back to the shore. But Dylan stayed; he wouldn't let his great-grandfather die alone.

And that was the last time they were seen alive. When the family at Dolfrwynog realised that Dylan had gone, they put two and two together and followed him, all of them, down to the water's edge. They were just in time to see the final few minutes, before their two relatives were sucked down below the waves. The old man was never seen again, his body still lay in the lake somewhere. But Dylan they found, and he was buried in the paddock.

When Uncle Wil arrived at the lake he gave a terrible cry, said Mari, who was afraid in case she'd over-egged her story. Wil shouted *Dylan!* at the top of his voice, time after time. He ripped off his coat and boots, he leapt into the water and swam into the house. Twice he entered the waterlogged building, but he saw not a trace of his relatives. At the third attempt he seemed to stay down for many minutes, and the rest of them were beginning to panic in case he too had succumbed. But then his face bobbed to the surface, and this time he had a lifeless body in his arms. It was Dylan, the little boy, with his wet blond hair swept over his light blue eyes, his mouth full of water. He would never again make that enchanting sound with his lips, never again dance like a whirligig along the lower meadows through the spring flowers with his hands flying in the air around him, like the two doves returning to Noah's Ark.

Mari finished the story and they lay completely still in each other's arms for a while, until they heard Huw's feet strike a squeaky tread on the stairs; he'd been listening to them.

'Huw!'

But there was no reply. He probably felt guilty for eavesdropping near their door. His eyes were full of tears because the story had moved him. Mari and Nico rose; they dressed and went downstairs to the kitchen. And then, at Nico's insistence, Mari cut off every hair on his head, as close to his skull as she could. When she finished he looked like an escaped convict.

'Perfect,' said Nico when he saw himself in a mirror. 'That's just how I want to look. Dangerous.'

He kissed her cheek, without knowing that she was pregnant, and without knowing how much she loved him during the moment when she gathered his hair from the floor and stuffed it into her pocket. Neither did he know that in that second as she stooped, Mari had felt the first movement inside her; and Mari was mercifully unaware that the act of cutting off his hair would herald a completely new chapter in their lives.

2 8

NICO WAS INSISTENT. He was going to kill one of the pigs. 'I must get food ready for you,' he said to her in the kitchen, holding one of the family carving knives. He'd been sharpening it for ten minutes, and now its glinting blade made Mari feel afraid.

'But why now, Nico? What's got into you?'

'Things are happening, we must get ready,' he replied quietly. The haircut had changed his looks completely; he appeared mercenary and dangerous. Mari didn't like the new look at all, she didn't like the new Nico.

'You look like a bloody convict,' she said crossly. 'Frightening. A couple of scars on your face and you'd look like a terrorist. What's up with you?'

'Scars… maybe good idea,' said Nico, looking down at the blade.

'Maybe I get some scars too, eh?'

'You dare and I'll never touch you again,' said Mari. 'At least your hair'll grow back.'

'No chance of a kiss then?' said Nico with a silly smile.

'You can sod off,' said Mari.

'Anyway, you come for a walk this morning, look at animals?'

She took her time answering, but Mari knew she'd have to tell him about the baby soon, so she said: 'OK, but you put that knife away now, you're making me nervous.'

Nico laughed at her and went out to the yard. He noticed

that Huw had forgotten to release the hens, so he went up to their hut. When he opened the door he discovered that only three hens were still alive, and Cluck was among those dead or missing. He called on Huw as loudly as he could, but there was no response. He went over to the doghouse and looked at Jess and Pero through the grating, wondering if he should take them with him. He'd take one of them perhaps, as company and as a guard dog at night; Jess was about to whelp, so he'd leave her behind. His mind wandered around all the possibilities. His plans would have to be meticulous, or everyone would die. He'd already decided that he couldn't let them perish in these terrible conditions, though he'd had to agonise long and hard before coming to a resolution. It was a fifty-fifty decision in the end, because his natural inclination was to walk out on them, to escape into the darkness of the night like Cluck.

Conscience... that was his greatest burden. Pity and sympathy were hurdles in his way; they were weaknesses rather than strengths now that he had to fight for his life. He'd felt pity for this little family as they awaited their fate in the Welsh foothills, benighted on a moor in the middle of nowhere. And the girl, Mari... yes, she'd been a comfort to him in the dark days, when he'd been lost in a strange and hostile country. Her willing little body had succoured him and warmed him like a hot water bottle in the middle of winter. She loved him, that was obvious. And if a girl loved a man in that way, wasn't there some sort of duty, an onus on him to return some of that love, to pay back some of the debt? He wasn't sure of his feelings towards her; he hadn't thought about it much. She'd been there for him, and that was enough, somehow. He didn't want to think about it too deeply.

'Nico!'

Her girlish voice called to him from across the yard.

He straightened and turned towards her. Standing there by the door she looked like a schoolgirl, slender and very young in her ragged jeans and her daft headscarf, jammed on her head like a wedge of pita bread holding a kebab. In his getting-to-know-the-world days he'd been addicted to kebabs and had eaten one every night as he returned home from the tavern. Now he was looking at a scene from old Russia, from somewhere in the vast flatlands of the steppes, with a young female commissar, in her red scarf, greeting her soldier boy as he returned from the war...

'Yes?' answered Nico.

'You ready to go?'

'Come on then.'

It had stopped raining at last and the air was suffused with a damp, tropical warmth. They went down into the field below the house and meandered through the lower meadows. Mari dropped her guard and suddenly they were both completely comfortable with each other again, something which had given their relationship an increasingly assured depth. Neither of them felt any particular urgency right then; time had a new meaning now, it had clotted into a few moments of urgency dotted like little fishing boats on the endless sea of uneventfulness which surrounded them. Everyone at Dolfrwynog had abandoned GMT, which meant nothing now, and they had all stopped pretending that they could hold it together and sustain themselves. The illusion was over. Even Huw had realised they couldn't grow enough food to live on, that they couldn't carry on living like that for ever. And in the brief caesura between the past and the future they'd started wandering around in a dream, almost relaxed, knowing that nothing they did was going to change the future; it was bearing down on them now, inexorably. They were resigned, like trench soldiers waiting for the whistle.

They had no idea what would happen to them of course, but they knew that everything was about to change again, finally and decisively. They ate anything that came to hand, as if they were aborigines wandering through the landscape; Huw had started to eat leaves and wild raspberries, even the occasional caterpillar. Their clothes were in rags and their shoes worn out. Huw walked barefoot among the rabbit traps, he hadn't washed for months and he rarely spoke to anyone. The family at Dolfrwynog were regressing, they were sliding back into the ancient past.

Mari and Nico stood by the lake, hand-in-hand, staring into its depths. Both of them were thinking about Great-grandfather's homestead below the water, and Dylan's vain attempt to rescue the old man. A heart-breaking story, thought Nico. But was it true?

He looked at Mari through the corner of his eye. He rather thought that Mari's marvellous tale had been a fable and no more, a means to keep him there with her. A bedtime story for a child... or for Nico in this case.

'Nico,' said Mari hesitantly. 'I've got something to tell you.'

'Too right,' said Nico. 'I think maybe you got a whole heap of things to tell me.'

'No, listen to me, Nico. It's important.'

He turned to look at her, face-to-face.

'No, you listen to me now, Mari. All this load of shit. All your stories about Virgin Mary and little boy Dylan, bullshit yes? And you know what? This no lake. Look at it. Trees under water yesterday, out of water today. Water move up and down, yes? This is sea. This no lake, Mari – this is sea. You understand, Mari? This is the big sea.'

Mari looked at the water. Was he telling the truth? Had the

sea really reached their valley? She stooped and put a finger in the water, and was just about to put it in her mouth when she had second thoughts. What about her little baby?

'Now it's my turn,' she said. 'You ready for this? Because I've got something really big to tell you.' She fell silent for a moment, then smiled. 'Well, it's something really small, actually.' She laughed lightly. Because her baby was very, very tiny, while it was going to have a huge effect on her life. Quite ironic, really.

'Yes?' said Nico, who was beginning to lose patience. 'What is it?'

She grasped his hands and looked into his eyes.

'Nico,' she said quietly, 'I'm going to have a baby.'

A long silence… then Nico sat down on a damp tussock – he felt the dampness invade his bottom.

'That's all we need,' he said in a tired voice. 'That's all we bloody need, Mari. A baby.'

He sighed heavily, and continued to sit on the damp tussock, saying over and over again: *that's all I need… that's all I bloody need…*

29

M ARI'S SALTY TEARS tumbled into the lake. No, it was bigger than a lake. It was part of a sea, according to Nico. She walked into the water slowly, up to her knees. It was horribly cold, but she stood in it and wept. Looking through a shimmering film, she felt her hot little droplets falling down into the water. She'd completed the circle now: water rose from the sea and formed clouds, then it fell to earth as rain, which became the water in Dolfrwynog's well, from which Mari drank her daily water. And here she was, transferring it back to the sea to start the process all over again. The baby inside her also lived in a little sea of its own, because the amniotic fluid in her womb contained exactly the same ratio of salt as the interminable sea which was sucking at her jeans. Men and women and children were merely fish who could walk; their arms and legs were the remains of fins, and their throats contained the shadowy remains of gills.

Mari felt a strong magnet pulling her into the water; the time had come to end her stay on dry land, she must take to the water now. No-one would grieve for her if she vanished below the waves. Billions had perished already, what did it matter if she and her baby joined them? Nico had no wish to be a father, he'd made that obvious; neither did he love her, or he'd run into the water and drag her back to land.

She took another step into the water, and then another, until the water reached her hips. *Go on then*, said a little voice in her head, *go in as far as your freckly little nose.*

But Mari stayed where she was, crying. Then she stopped. What was the point? She wasn't going to walk any farther into the water, she didn't want to drown like Dylan. But there had never been a great-grandfather like the one she'd described. Nor an old homestead below the waves. All that stuff had poured out of her fertile little mind, a bedside story in the same league as fables about fairies and giants. But it was she who had created it all, it was her own magical imagination which had conjured up that enticing tale. She could be proud of that, at least. A story like that would have brought her plaudits in a creative writing class, in the days when there were such things as schools and universities. Before the end of the world.

'I know you won't do it, so come back here Mari,' said Nico. He hadn't moved an inch from the tussock, and a big wet stain had moved along his jeans, almost to his knees. 'Come on. Don't be silly. I know you won't do it.'

Mari turned and returned to land. She stood in front of him, with her hands on her hips. She'd stopped crying by now, but her eyes were red and sore. She looked at him accusingly.

'So you don't want our baby?'

'I didn't say that.'

'*That's the last thing I need* – that's what you said.'

'It was a big shock, Mari. I didn't expect it.'

'What did you expect, the way we carry on? It was bound to happen sooner or later, wasn't it?'

'Yes, I know. But it's still a shock. And now is a bad time, Mari. We are fighting to stay alive. No food. No doctors. How you going to cope?'

'Oh, so it's me who's going to cope, is it?'

'No, I help you.'

'So you're going to help?'

'Yes, of course I help. My baby, I help. I am Polish, I am Catholic.'

Mari squeezed herself next to him on the tussock.

'So you're not going to run away?'

'No, I help you with baby, Mari. But I have to go away for a bit.'

'How long? Where?'

'A couple of weeks, maybe a month. Don't worry, I kill pig before I go.'

Kill a pig? What the hell did that have to do with her baby?

'One thing I must know, Mari, these stories – what is truth about them? I know there are people in graves, but who are they really?'

'Nico, they are the people I told you about.'

'But the stories about the way they died – all true, Mari?'

She rested her elbows on her knees and put her head in her hands, just like Nico. She was cornered, she'd have to tell him the truth. So why not now? She'd hoped to delay it for as long as possible, to keep him there with her in her fantasy world. And her ruse had worked: he was still with her, by her side on this tussock, she'd kept him for long enough to…

But she hadn't intended to trap him, not really, not in the way he set wire nooses for the rabbits. No, that hadn't been her original intention. She'd wanted his company, and his raw love. All hope had left her in that awful period before his arrival. There had been no-one she could be happy with, no-one within a hundred miles who could give her what Nico had given her. Some fun, some pleasure. Sighting him on the moors, leading the horses, had been like an answer to a prayer. Surely she couldn't be blamed for behaving the way she did. Mother Nature was a very powerful force, how else should a young woman behave? What else would a girl like her do except flirt with him, hold hands with him, and let his warm brown hands cup her breasts in the shadow of the oak tree? Wasn't that the reason for her existence on the planet?

'What do you want to know?' she said to him, eventually.

'OK. Let's start with the first one, the Virgin Mary story. What is truth?'

Mari told him the truth. Yes, it was Sara her sister who was buried in the first grave, and yes she'd died of hunger in the first famine which swept through Britain when order broke down. They'd witnessed the end of society as they knew it. Only a fraction of the population had survived the first few months; the bloody chaos which descended on the land had killed nine in every ten. Lack of food was the main reason, with milling hordes fighting for every remaining scrap in the cities after the supply chain broke down. First to die were the old and the sick. Young people, mainly males, were almost the sole survivors after six months, marauding gangs who fought over dwindling resources in increasingly violent encounters, in scenes which mirrored the action in *Blade Runner* and *Mad Max*. Indeed, the monitory films of the twentieth century had foreseen the future quite accurately. And then another factor kicked in – a universal lack of hope. Thousands and thousands had gone mad because they couldn't cope with the silence. The fourth iPod and iPhone generation had become so accustomed to a reassuring man-made noise in their ears they couldn't live in a completely natural environment. Yet more went mad after losing every bit of hope. Nico was aware of this; he'd been among the street mob in Liverpool when the balloon went up. He'd been one of the lucky ones, strong enough to save himself. Many others, thousands of them, were butchered as he watched from his hiding place. That sort of trauma had sent many off their heads.

'Sara never saw the Virgin Mary at the well,' said Mari. 'I made that all up. Sara just gave up hope, really. She couldn't cope with the world when it changed. She didn't want to do anything, she just sat there, day after day, looking into space. We tried to make her eat, tried to force it down her even, but it was no use. She got thinner and thinner, and then she just died in her bed. There was nothing we could do. She just gave up hope and stopped living.'

Emotionally, she told him about the others. She hadn't discussed the true scenario before, and it was almost too much for her, the sudden outpouring.

The story of Gwydion her father had been closer to the truth. Yes, he'd been a city policeman but he hadn't been killed in the way she'd described. He'd been healthy when they arrived at Dolfrwynog, with his family and Jack, whose role had been ambivalent. He may have been Elin's lover or he may have been Gwydion's friend, no-one was prepared to divulge the truth. One day, a gang of hoodlums from a nearby town had arrived in the area around Dolfrwynog and the family had heard shooting as the marauders fought with neighbouring farmers over food and livestock. Some of them attacked Dolfrwynog one night but the men were ready for them, guns loaded at the ready; four attackers were killed before the rest fled. Their bodies were flung into the ravine by The Meadow, their skeletons were still there in the undergrowth. But one of Dolfrwynog's inhabitants was mortally wounded. Gwydion had been shot in the leg, and it became septic. With no doctors at hand to treat him, and no hospital, he was dead within a fortnight. He'd been buried in the paddock, next to his daughter. By then, no-one had been able to grieve; one shock after another had numbed them all. She herself had felt nothing until now…

And as for Rhiannon – most of her story was true also. Rhiannon had indeed died on the farm, of a broken heart. But there had never been an Alun, and Pant yr Haul had never existed. No, Rhiannon had been Mari's sister and she had married a wonderful man, indeed the whole family had fallen in love with him – Mari herself had a huge crush on him. He'd been a doctor at the city hospital, and he'd been killed when a gang raided the pharmacy for drugs. When Rhiannon came to live on the farm with them she'd done her best to cope and adapt, to take part in the life of the farm and to start afresh. But slowly, almost imperceptibly, she'd gone downhill. Perhaps Sara's fate had also affected her. And in the end she went the same way. An empty sedatives bottle was found by her bedside, but they couldn't be sure that she'd intended to kill herself. No-one wanted to believe it anyway.

And then Dylan… her best story. There had never been an old man nor a drowned homestead. Quite simply, Dylan had drowned while swimming in the new lake. That was the awful truth. He'd been used to the city swimming pool with its rails and its guards, so he'd gone beyond his limits. Mari was the one who'd found him, late one evening while the rest were out hunting for him. She had shed every drop of water in her body while they buried him in the paddock.

When she ended her explanation she put her cheek on his shoulder and stayed silent. That silence stayed with them all the way home. But at some stage, while they were crossing the field under the house, their hands met and they realised without saying anything that their lives would be bound together inextricably from that moment onwards, till the end of time.

30

AUGUST MARKED A turning point. After high summer they made no attempt to farm or to grow their own food. They simply gave up on the old conventional ways of living; now and then they'd kill a lamb, or they'd eat wild fruit and pignut roots. The weather changed again and the clouds disappeared completely, to be replaced by a searing, stultifying heat which dried and baked the earth into a hard terracotta pottery. They were forced to take shelter during the mid-day period as if they were in Morocco or the Sudan. This deadening heat sent all the animals to the shade of the trees and hedges, and drew a curtain of silent somnolence over the whole land. Without Uncle Wil knowing, all the remaining hens went into the pot. Although he'd noticed the absence of poultry sounds – cock-crows in the early dawn, and celebratory cluckings after egg-laying – he didn't say a word. What was the point? It was their world now, he'd let go of the reins and his own existence had started to gallop away from him in an uncontrollable direction. He ate very little, and his will to live was diminishing day by day; indeed, he had only one ambition left – more than anything, he wanted to be as brave as possible in his final days. Every hour was a battle now; he wondered, with awe, how all those soldiers in history had been able to run towards death on the field of battle. Wil learnt to steel himself by freezing his features and gripping the side of his bed whenever someone came up for a chat, as if he were grasping a shield to protect himself during a military affray.

They all lived in a dream. The lower meadows shimmered

in a hot green and yellow dream; voices sounded diffused and muted; reality itself had become a sepia copy of the real thing. They were children again, tired and over-extended, waiting for their parents to pick them up after an end-of-term party. Huw wandered around half-naked, without shoes, brown as a Bengali in his little red football shorts. No-one had tried to cut his hair for months, so he looked like Mowgli or a mini-Tarzan swinging among the animals of the jungle. He told the grown-ups that he'd seen dolphins in the water, and he went down there every day to look for them. He'd call to them with his own special whistling sound. And then, one day, it really happened – a school of dolphins appeared suddenly out of nowhere, frolicking around him as he stood up to his waist in water. Elin witnessed the scene from her bedroom window, watched her son among his new friends, splashing water onto them, calling out to them, trying to ride on their backs. By the middle of the month Huw was a feral animal-child, living wild in his own world; he'd stay away from the farm for days on end, sleeping in a copse by the water's edge so that he could keep a look-out for his new playmates.

Then he disappeared completely for days, and Mari and Nico went looking for him. Their voices, calling out to him, weakened as they moved away from the farmhouse, towards the boundary of the Dolfrwynog territory, shouting *Huuuwwww* in bursts, as loudly as they could. Eventually they found him in the upper branches of a massive sycamore tree at the far end of the lower meadows: he'd been stuck there since the previous day, clinging to the bole of the tree.

'What on earth are you doing up there, Huw?' said Mari crossly. 'Come down at once, your poor mother has almost gone crazy worrying about you again.'

'She's mad anyway,' said Huw. The words seemed big and

clumsy in his mouth, because he hadn't said anything much for weeks and his speech was beginning to go rusty.

'Come on Huw, we worry about you,' said Nico in a kinder voice.

But the fact was that Huw couldn't get down; he'd managed to get up there easily enough, but he'd failed to descend to safety: he was stuck, and he'd spent the night shaking and crying and shouting for help.

Nico climbed the tree and led him to the ground, branch by branch until the boy's dirty little feet were back on terra firma. He wept pitifully in Mari's arms, his bony little body convulsing with relief. Then he ran away from them, towards the lake, towards his new family.

Nico and Mari went down to the pool to bathe together. They were in the water for more than an hour, swimming about lazily and meeting up for fleeting kisses. When they emerged, Nico suggested they should shade under the giant oak tree because it was incredibly hot in the open.

'People with…' (he pointed to her freckles) '… get sunburn bad,' he said. 'And we got to think of the baby…'

'So, suddenly you're worried about the baby,' said Mari provocatively, though she was also grinning slyly.

They lay down under the tree, and he put his ear against her belly, listening.

'Don't be silly, it's much too early for that,' said Mari. But was it? What did she know about such things? After all, this was her first time…

They lay on the green grass, naked, and again she admired the dance of the colours on his skin; green from the sward, yellow from the buttercups, blue from the speedwell. He too was thinner, and she could see the framework of his ribs under his skin, reminding her of the skeleton of a ship. She took hold of his hand, then rolled towards him and went to sleep for a while with her head on his arm and with her own arm curled across his chest. As she meandered slowly towards sleep she could feel her skin drying in a breeze which caressed her skin, bringing with it all the sensuous demi-sounds and fragile floral smells of summer. An occasional bleat stirred her inner consciousness, and she could hear a buzzard mewing in the sky.

When she woke she came to with a start. Her skin had cooled; she must have slept for quite a while. A large bird was drifting above, flying in a slow circle, mewing harshly. Nico was still asleep, but he too woke with a start, as if responding to danger. And so they lay together, listening to the bird, enjoying this slow time together. It was probably the closest they'd ever been.

'Mari,' he said in a whisper.

'Eh?'

'You awake?'

'Yes...'

'Warm?'

'Yes, I'm fine.'

'Mari, I got a plan. Maybe stupid, I don't know. But we got to do something. All right now in summer, but when baby come... what we do then?'

'Don't know.'

'Maybe baby come in winter. We need food for winter.'

'Yes, I know that – so what's the plan?'

Nico sighed heavily. 'This is only thing I can think of. Crazy idea, I don't know. Your stories... maybe they help us now, maybe not. You want to hear my plan?'

'Yes Nico, of course. Get on with it.'

Then she sat on him in a quick movement, riding him like a horse, facing him and playing with the fine auburn down on his chest.

'Many days from here, about a week by horse, there is a town made from huts,' said Nico. 'I saw it when I get pigs. Many huts, I think you call them shitty town, yes?'

It took her a while to translate *shitty town*.

'You mean shanty town?'

'Yes, that's it, shanty town. Hundreds of people live there, refugees, yes?'

He continued with his description. 'Most people there very poor, starving like us. But some rich and fat, you know how people are – always some make good living in bad times, no?'

Mari murmured and nodded.

'I go to that place, bring rich ones here. Maybe I will tell them about Virgin Mary at well and Dylan drowning to save old man. Tell them great big lies to make them come here. They bring food and gold and things like that. Then you tell them stories, they like them very much. Like pilgrims in old days, they believe any old rubbish but they feed us and pay us, yes?'

Once again this man had managed to surprise her. Mari moved off him and lay on her back in the grass again, playing with a stem, chewing at it. His plan, gleaned from Huw's books, was audacious and a bit frightening. A shiver of anticipation went through her. But what choice did they have, anyway?

She rolled onto her side and faced him again, her eyes level with the tattoo on his arm. She traced its pattern with the grass stem, then replied:

'OK Nico. We'll give it a try. I can't think of anything better. Let's go for it.'

3 1

THEY WERE ALL sitting around the long white table at Dolfrwynog, and the setting sun was colouring the window with yellows and reds and purples. Today it was Huw's turn to sit at the end of the table, in his red shorts. As he played around with the talking stick, he looked like a child actor waiting for the cameras to roll in a budget version of *George of the Jungle*. His mouth and fingers were bright red from the wild raspberries and strawberries he'd eaten during the day. And he looked feral by now, wild and animalistic; he could have featured in one of the *National Geographic* magazines on his bedroom window-shelf. One of Dolfrwynog's fusty old books was the main reason for their meeting that evening because it had given Nico an idea – and a flash of insight had sparked a daring plan of action. The book lay open on the table as he began to unfold his vision, and as he spoke he tapped the pages to emphasise each point he made. It was in that book, many months previously, that Nico had first read a chapter on the pilgrims of the Middle Ages. He'd been struck by the fact that the monks and clergymen in those days were businessmen as well as Christians; yes, there were honourable reasons for all the holy ceremonies and services, but there were other forces at play too. Sanctifying a holy person might have genuine and authentic roots, but the act also drew thousands of pilgrims to their graves in the hope of salvation, merely by association or by touching the saint's sarcophagus. Indeed, the saints' mortal remains were often moved from one site to another to attract pilgrims. Holy relics were sold at these sites, bones or artefacts which were said to belong to the saint, though as often as not they were bogus. A new souvenir industry flourished, and although it was partly sincere it made the monks a lot of money. The system became corrupt and the monks became fat. The whole process fascinated Nico, and while reading about it he detected an opportunity to help his new family at Dolfrwynog. Sitting at the table, with the book in front of him, he outlined his plan. In the next week he would leave the farm on one of the horses. He'd travel over the mountain, since that was the only route open to him now – the new lake had surrounded the farm on three sides and had almost created an island. He would take a gun and a dog. He would be away for about a fortnight, perhaps longer – he couldn't be sure. It would take at least a week to find the shanty town he'd noticed while he was stealing the pigs. Then it would take at least a week for him to identify the king rats there and persuade them to go on a pilgrimage to visit the 'saints' at Dolfrwynog. In the meantime everyone would have to prepare the house for them by cleaning it properly, since the visitors would be staying there. Everyone except for Uncle Wil would have to move over to the stable loft, and Mari would have to 'sanctify' Wil by creating another of her amazing tales; perhaps she could suggest that he was a heroic figure who was dying after performing a miraculous feat. Mari's role was to entertain the visitors with her stories when they arrived; and as payment for their visit the pilgrims would be asked to provide food and presents which could be bartered later. It was a long shot, but they were desperate now and Nico surmised that life in the shanty town could be difficult and dangerous; the king rats and their women would welcome some sort of diversion to take their minds off the constant day-to-day hassle of life in a hostile environment. Elin could play the piano and Huw could ride the dolphins. Everyone would have a part to play. That was Nico's plan, he couldn't see any other way to save the family seated around him at the table.

In the lull which followed Nico's address, Mari took the opportunity to announce she was expecting a child. Her mother and Wil were the only ones who hadn't heard – Huw had learnt the usual way, by sticking his ear to their bedroom door. As expected, Elin started to cry and then she threatened Nico. They all listened, watching her with tired eyes.

'Be quiet, Mum!' said Mari hotly. She couldn't put up with her mother's foolishness any longer. 'How many children did you have? And how did that happen – the Angel Gabriel again? Don't be so bloody stupid. It's happened, that's it. What did you think we were doing in the bedroom together – playing with our dollies? Get used to it, Nico and I are going to have a child.'

Elin rose and went upstairs, sniffing and mumbling all the way. She knocked on her brother's door and entered his room without waiting for the usual *Come in!* Wil had heard the commotion downstairs and was waiting for her.

'Don't upset yourself, my dear,' he said in a kind voice. 'These things happen, you know.'

'But I was the last to know, as usual,' said Elin miserably. Her nose was red and her eyes were brimming with tears.

Wil turned towards the sunset and asked her to open the window; although it was late, his room was stiflingly hot. They'd all realised that Dolfrwynog was about to experience another extreme heatwave like the one in 2089, when many hundreds of thousands died all over the world. He felt increasingly like a fish thrown up on a riverbank, fighting for his life.

He wondered idly how many people were left in the world. There were entire countries in the tropics, probably, without a living soul left standing. Wave after human wave had fled Africa during the fifties and sixties. But there wasn't enough land for everyone and resources had dwindled. Nato had started bombing boats – and their desperate human cargoes – as they crossed the Mediterranean. The sea level had risen considerably by then and a substantial part of Britain had disappeared under seawater by 2080: the UK had become an archipelago of islands, thousands of them. Wales was an island too by then, with a smattering of farms and coastal shanty towns; they were populated by refugees mainly, scavenging survivors who had killed and pillaged their way across Europe, or who had managed to escape from the violence and destruction which had decimated the cities. They were a peculiar mob, the survivors; people of every race and creed, from all parts of the world. Of course, under such circumstances religion had prospered and many millions had died in sectarian battles, many of them won by a new millenarian sect which predicted the end of the world on various dates in the near future. Most of the shanty towns were ruled by pirates, living not unlike the Vikings of old. They'd sail off for weeks on end in their stolen boats and return with holds full of stolen booty, and slaves too sometimes. Nobody at Dolfrwynog had any idea what was going on, but they knew what had caused most of the trouble: climate change and the collapse of capitalism.

A heap of nonsense had been promulgated by the chattering classes about carbon footprints and green living at the beginning of the century, but nothing of substance had been done to combat the growing crisis; years of vacuous doublespeak by a generation of stupid and ineffectual politicians had led to nothing. And then, suddenly, it was too late. They looked back on half a century of posturing and empty talk, only to realise that the answer had been very simple all along. Every final answer in the history of man had actually been very simple, as nakedly simple as Einstein's famous equation. But by then it was too late.

Elin sat on Wil's bed and held his bony old hand.

'What a pity we spoilt everything,' she said regretfully. She sounded like a little girl whose birthday party had run out of control, with everyone standing around awkwardly, waiting for their parents to take them home. In a way, that's what had happened. They had lived in an earthly paradise, but the party which had been the industrial revolution and its capitalist aftermath had developed into a bender, leaving almost everyone drunk or sick.

'Never mind,' said Wil. 'It's too late to do anything now. We weren't to blame, were we?' But then he remembered how they all used to live, and he fell silent.

'What are we going to do, Wil?'

He squeezed her hand.

'We must help them as much as we can. They're young, they still have some hope left.'

'Pah!' said Elin. 'Hope? What use is that…?'

'They can't lie down and die you know,' countered Wil. 'They'll fight for survival, somehow or other. Come on now, we really must help them.'

Elin dried her tears and returned to her own bedroom, shutting the door much too firmly. Huw raised his eyes when he registered the clap of her door, then he ran out into the night, across the farmyard, down the field below the house, towards his new family.

3 2

Nico ARRIVED BACK at the house looking sweaty and flustered.

'Damn those horses,' he said to Mari as he stormed past her.

No-one had tried to catch the horses for ages and they'd reverted to being almost wild again. He raged around the house looking for something sweet, so that he could entice them, but of course the cupboard was bare. He'd have to use deceit, as usual. He put a handful of gravel in the red bucket and shook it in front of the horses, trying to fool them into thinking there was food inside. After all sorts of gambits involving the help of Mari and Huw, they managed to ensnare one of the ponies. Nico was in a raging temper by the end; he lost all control and gave the bucket – their last precious bucket – a hefty kick, splitting it down the side.

'Dammit!' he said… and then he grinned slyly, because he was using the old man's favourite word pretty often himself these days.

Huw enjoyed himself for a while, throwing stones at the bucket, laughing and generally behaving like an idiot. But Nico's travails continued for another hour as he searched for a saddle and other necessities. Then he had a fit of self-doubt and almost released the horse again – was he really doing the right thing? What would happen if an urban gang arrived when he was away? So he went up to Wil's room and had a chat with the old man, with the end result that he left the spare gun and a box of cartridges by the old man's bedside. Wil was left in charge; Nico pointed to his eyes and said:

'You are guard for house now, you listen all night, yes?'

Wil nodded agreement. He'd heard many a *Dammit!* from the direction of the paddock earlier and he'd been able to smile for the first time in ages.

Nico then went to visit Elin.

'You get up every day now, lady, you walk through fields and up mountain every morning to look for men.'

'Men? I wish,' said Elin. But she agreed to help Wil with the guard duties.

Out in the yard again, Nico stood in the centre – as Wil had done many times – and surveyed the scene. So much had changed in so little time, and he started to feel quite low. Old Wil would never again stand at the centre of his little kingdom, looking North and South, East and West, chatting to his feathery harem, and muttering *Dammit!* as he was wont to do so often. They would never again hear Cluck crowing on the summit of the midden, as so many other cockerels had done during the long life of the farm. One of civilisation's earliest sounds had ceased to be heard at Dolfrwynog. The old world was about to disappear before their very eyes. Nico felt a surge of nostalgia for all that was lost; generations of simple, quiet people who had loved and laboured, and then vanished into the mists of time – who had been alive for but a few short years in the history of the world, and who had then reverted to dust again. He felt sad for all the little languages and charming customs which went with them; he longed to meet those shy, peaceable people who had laboured in Dolfrwynog's fields and folds – they would never see the bitter fruits of their labour, and that, in a way, was a blessing. He also thought of the beautiful, fresh-faced girls who had carried their milk pails across this yard over many centuries, and who would never again flash a smile at a handsome new plough boy. They would never be seen again, nor their type. They had gone, and the beautiful world they had inhabited had been destroyed by the human race itself. So many lovely countries had been ravaged. All the seas had been poisoned. So many species of animals and birds and fish had been hunted to extinction. And all because man believed he was a god who could do what he willed with the living world.

Nico called Mari, grasped her hand and took her down to the lake. A host of large pinky-black jellyfish had been beached on the shoreline during the night, and they looked like a flight of sinister flying saucers which had fallen to Earth. Mari stared into their jelly-like interiors and detected electrical pulses and beats. But it was so hot that they were withering and dying quickly.

'I don't want to leave you like this,' said Nico dejectedly. 'It's not safe – what happens if another gang come?'

'No, it's our only chance,' answered Mari. 'We've got to try this plan. Otherwise we'll starve to death this winter, and what about the baby?'

Nico's face betrayed the uncertainty within him.

'You come with me?'

'No, that's even more dangerous,' said Mari. 'But come back soon, I can't live without you for long.'

Her eyes welled up, and they hugged each other tightly.

'If I'm not back in a month something has happened,' said Nico. 'You make other plan then. OK?'

'You'll be back, I know you will,' she replied.

They continued holding each other for many minutes by the edge of the water, then Nico said:

'I go and kill pig now.'

'You what?'

'Make place to keep meat, then kill pig. You have enough food then – potatoes in Wil's room, meat in safe place. Don't worry, I know what I'm doing.'

They returned to the house, then Nico departed with an old spade slung over his shoulder. Huw followed him to see what he was up to. When they arrived at the well he saw Nico removing his Che Guevara T-shirt and starting to dig a hole on the lower side of the water cistern, about a metre square. Then he covered the hole with slabs of slate which acted as a lid, so that the water ran over without entering the newly-dug chamber. In a while he'd finished the task.

'Place to keep meat, nice and cold,' said Nico. 'You come with me now, get pig.'

They returned to the house to find a cleaver, then they walked through the lower meadows, towards the pigs, which they found digging around the great oak tree near Nico and Mari's swimming spot. Nico reflected on the possibility that the two of them would never sunbathe there again, and his mind dwelled on an inner picture of her naked body. After standing still in the shade of the tree for a while, Nico made a dash for one of the younger pigs and caught it by a hind leg. The piglet squealed pitifully and struggled convulsively in Nico's grasp.

'Get me stone, big one,' said Nico, so Huw ran to the river bank and returned with a rock. In no time at all Nico had dispatched the pig with a flurry of heavy blows to the head.

After slinging the poor animal over his back he started the journey homewards, Huw following like a dog. In the next couple of hours he chopped up the pork into half a dozen sections and then stored most of it in the new cell by the well. Some of it he took to the house where he put it in their biggest saucepan, so that a stew could be made which would last for many days. It was too late by then for him to start his journey, so he decided to stay another night with the little family at Dolfrwynog. After stabling the horse and having a bite to eat, he and Mari retired early to their bedroom, but they both found it hard to settle. The loose horses in the paddock were restless and noisy; Nico went there twice with his gun to check in case strangers had arrived. Perhaps the heatwave had seared the sward and there wasn't enough food for them, he suggested to Mari. And indeed the night was so hot they could hardly touch each other, each brief meeting of flesh brought an eruption of sweat or heat spots. To exacerbate matters, Uncle Wil took to snoring like a pig and Huw shouted out in his sleep, calling out to the dolphins in the sea of his sleep. All in all they had a terrible night's rest before Nico's departure.

In the end he went swiftly and unexpectedly. As soon as a glimmer of light appeared in the window he rose silently and went downstairs with his clothes over his arm, then dressed hurriedly in the kitchen. After retrieving his pack from the parlour he went over to the stable and soon he was off up the hill, in the direction of the mountain gate. By the time Mari woke he was on a hill overlooking the farm, looking at the great orange orb of the sun easing itself over the horizon. Near her head, on Nico's vacant pillow, Mari found a note containing a terse message:

Gone, love you. Back in a month. Look after you and baby.
Nico XX.

He'd been unable to say farewell because of the fear inside him and the storm in his head; he felt sure he'd be unable to control his emotions. Mari noticed that he'd left two kisses: one for her and another for their baby.

33

I T WAS THE sun which ruled their lives now. Day after day it crawled at a snail's pace across the cloudless sky, from early morning till sunset, in a tortuous arc. Mari felt compelled to visit Uncle Wil at regular intervals with cold water from the well to cool his body; he was a little embarrassed by her ministrations, but grateful. From mid-day till four they were all forced to take cover in the coolest place they could find; Mari had found a nest in the shade of the trees which overhung the well, and she'd lie there for hours reading one of Huw's musty old books or sleeping. Huw preferred to go down to the water so that he could swim or play with the dolphins if they were in the vicinity. He'd cut a tattoo on his arm, in the same area as Nico's, showing a dolphin leaping above three crinkly waves; he'd made this image with an old dart and some ink. The pain had been excruciating, and he'd bayed like one of the hounds whenever he pricked his skin. But pain was an inescapable part of life now, and his bravery was meant to be seen as a childish sign that he had taken over as man of the house in the dog days that followed Nico's departure. He'd stopped talking, or had forgotten how to, since he merely shook his head or nodded or signalled with his hands whenever someone asked him something; perhaps his muteness was another form of tattoo, signifying the trauma which had scarred him for life.

After two days of pork stew, Mari was sick of the stuff and she gave the remains to Jess and her pups. Only two of the litter remained, and since Mari had let them out of the dog house so that they could partially fend for themselves, they wandered around the yard looking for food; or she'd come across them in the paddock, with the pups whimpering or hanging from a teat. Mari developed a craving; her mind was flooded with images of a chocolate bar with its sumptuous wrapper and its sacred skin of silvery paper; the image blurred her eyes with longing throughout the day. Sometimes she'd imagine that she really had some chocolate in her mouth, she could taste its exotic luxury and she would actually start to chew on its chimera. And at other times she'd long for red jam, for anything except stew. Since the demise of the hens there were no eggs to eat, so she lived on potatoes, which were dwindling fast, and wild fruit. An almost imperceptible swelling showed where her baby was lodged, and she'd talk frequently to her little son (she was convinced it was a boy) as if he were already there by her side.

'What should I do about Uncle Wil?' she asked her unborn baby one day as she rested under the trees. 'I'll have to make up a story about him too, won't I?'

One of Nico's Polish tales had been playing on her mind – a story about a group of horsemen in a cave below a mountain; a detachment of soldiers who'd been in a deep sleep for a long time. One day, when a young smith was working in his smithy, a man had arrived at the door: an unexpected caller dressed in old-fashioned but expensive attire, dignified and regal in bearing. This visitor asked the smith to accompany him to the cave so that the soldiers' horses could be shod ready for their reawakening. But when he'd finished the smith wasn't paid in the normal way, with money. Much to his astonishment the stranger scooped up handfuls of hoof clippings and presented them by way of payment. On his way homewards the disgruntled smith opened his bag and hurled the shavings onto the ground; but when he arrived home he realised that the few shards of horse-hoof remaining in his work-bag had turned to gold. He rushed back and searched everywhere for the discarded shavings but he couldn't find them; he searched throughout his life for them, wandering through the mountains like a madman, but he never found them and he died insane.

Nico's story had reawakened a faint memory in Mari; it echoed a tale she'd heard from her mother at bedtime many years previously. She surmised that some form of the story might serve to entertain the shanty town rats if and when they arrived at Dolfrwynog, especially since she needed to create an alias for Uncle Wil. She'd need to convince the 'pilgrims' that Wil was heroic with a great story to tell. Mari knew there was a cave of sorts among the gorse bushes which covered the hill above her home, though it wasn't really a cave but an old mine left by prospectors looking for lead many centuries previously.

As she started to clean the house, ready for Nico's pilgrims, when the heat of the day had subsided, she began to play about with the story in her head.

'Come on, Mum,' she said on the landing, 'we've got to get this place ready for the people when they come.'

'What's the point,' answered Elin. 'What's the use of cleaning the place, Mari? He won't come back, you know there's no hope of that. We'll never see him again.'

Mari went into the bedroom and sat on the smelly bed. Tears were coursing down her mother's blotched face, and Mari realised that her mother looked as ill as Uncle Wil.

'What's up, Mum? Don't you think we should give it a go?'

'Why bother, Mari. We're starving to death in this place and there's not a hope in hell he'll come back. Even if he does, what sort of people will he bring with him? Will they bring food for us, and presents? Don't be daft. They'll kill us more likely.'

Mari studied her mother's face and realised just how low

she'd sunk. She really had no hope left in her, none. But she'd lost her husband and three of her children, was it surprising that she was in this sort of state?

'Listen, Mum, we've got to be brave. I've got a baby on the way and I've got to try my best to stay alive. And anyway, you promised Nico you'd help me.'

But she pleaded in vain. Elin turned on her side and looked silently through the window. Things had gone too far; she'd lost almost everything, and even her little son Huw was beyond salvation, living as he did – like a wild thing in the fields.

'Mum, I understand how you feel, I really do. But I'm begging you from the bottom of my heart now to help us. Just this one last time, Mum. Or Nico's effort will mean nothing, we might as well shoot ourselves this second. Do you hear?'

Elin continued to look through the window, watching the sun set; the whole window became a large red mural as she lay there.

Mari returned downstairs, prepared a saucepanful of potatoes and scoffed most of them, while at the same time imagining a huge pile of chocolate bars on the table in front of her, cascading onto the floor, filling the parlour until they snuffed out the light coming through the window.

34

WHEN MARI WOKE the following morning she heard strange sounds coming from the next room – her mother had started cleaning her bedroom. Mari heard drawers opening and doors creaking, then the sound of water cascading into a bowl. In between the sounds she could hear her mother's chesty, uneven breathing. Without mechanical sounds from fridges, CD players and TVs, or the occasional crowing of the farmyard rooster, a deathly silence had fallen on Dolfrwynog. Mari rose quickly and joined her mother in the big bedroom.

'Thanks, Mum, thanks ever so much,' said Mari as she hugged her mother. A jolt went through her when she realised how frail and thin Elin had become. She felt all bone, like a skeleton. Her mother realised what was going through her mind and gave her a weak smile.

'Don't worry, Mari love,' she said. 'I couldn't eat even when there was food available.'

They both looked through the window, at the sun rising over the hill above them. It was already a mustardy red, huge and hot, ready to attack them mercilessly. The pastures had been badly affected by the heatwave and they were turning a sandy yellow; the traditional greens of Wales had been blowtorched, and the family could be living in the scrublands of Mexico or Africa.

'Would you eat a little soup if I made some?' asked Mari.

Elin shook her head. 'No, it's too late now,' she said passively. Gesturing towards the paddock, she added: 'I'll be with them before long.'

A spurt of tears came into Mari's eyes as she moved towards her mother.

'No Mari, I'm ready to go.' She put her hand to her heart. 'The pain's been too much for me, love. One after the other they left me, I can't take any more.'

She pointed to Mari's belly.

'You'll know yourself soon enough what it's like to be a mother. Nobody really knows until they've a child of their own. The pain's awful, Mari. The pain of losing them. The pain of losing hope. No, I want to be with them now, in the paddock. That's the best place to be now, the world is just too terrible…'

Mari took a step towards her but she raised her hands and said:

'Come on, let's get the place tidy. Will you help me with these bedclothes? They're too heavy for me.'

Mari took all the bedclothes to the river and stayed there until dinner time, washing them. The river was low, and she realised that she and Nico would never again sunbathe in the shade of the great oak tree because the pigs were sleeping there now on a bed of dried mud.

She went home and put the sheets on the line, then went to rest in her lair by the well. A thousand problems buzzed around her head like blowflies; what could she use for bedding in the stable loft? She would have to stuff old sacks with wool.

And what about a story to suit Uncle Wil? An idea had taken root while she was washing the sheets earlier. Bones… surely there were some bones left in the ravine, the remains of those four lads whom Jack and Wil had shot dead during the raid on Dolfrwynog. After resting for the whole of the afternoon she went down to the ravine and started looking for the remains of the gang, among the briars. She wondered how Jack had been able to throw them there, without a second thought seemingly.

Such cruelty, such uncaringness. He'd chucked them down there as if they'd been dead sheep. That was the spirit of the age they lived in: sympathy and kindness had gone by the board, they all behaved like wild animals now, killing and being killed without a thought. Those lads had been like ants being crushed underfoot.

In a while she came across the remains of the bodies among the wild flowers, under some blackthorn bushes. All the flesh and clothing had long since rotted away and four white skeletons were perfectly discernible, bleached white by the sun. She stood looking at them for a few minutes and imagined them as they'd been when they'd arrived in the valley – young, powerful and vital, just as Nico had been when he arrived in her bed; they had been missed terribly, probably, by mothers and girls like her, though they too were probably dead by now. Life was so cheap, she reflected. Only for a short time in the history of man, in the latter half of the twentieth century, had human life been given a sense of value. Only then had body and soul been given a chance to exist in harmony, and it was only a small minority of well-off countries which had enjoyed such a boon. Nowadays, people scuttled about like woodlice, and no-one worried if thousands went down the drain every day.

Mari's mind flew to Nico; she loved him. Losing him would be unbearable. Her body tensed at the thought; an awful wave of fear swept through her, as if acidic water had entered her mouth and had poured through the caverns of her body, burning her insides. What if one of those skeletons had been Nico's? Her eyes filled with hot tears for the second time that day. She was feeling emotional. Perhaps it was the baby. Perhaps a host of accumulated fears had built up inside her and were pressing on the dam of her sanity. She decided to return the following day to fetch the bones; she'd need a bag and tools. Huw could help her; he'd like that – messing around with bones, and visiting the cave.

Mari returned home to face another problem; she needed to find a receptacle to ferry water to the house, since Nico had destroyed the red bucket. She cursed him, because the only thing that came to hand was an old tin bucket, rusty and pitted; she managed to fill in the worst holes with small bolts from the tool shed. Then she went to fetch some water from the well for Uncle Wil, only to notice yet another problem: the water supply had dwindled to a trickle, and it took some time for the cistern to fill up again after she'd taken some water out. God, it was one thing after another. Would there be enough water to go round if Nico brought a large group to the farm?

Back in the house, Mari washed her uncle's body with a cool rag and forced him to drink a glassful of water which she'd brought back in a big white jug. While washing her uncle she felt a tiny little movement, the first proper evidence that he was there. The little bugger was saying *I'm here!* inside her. She put her hand to her tum and rested it there for a moment, imagining Nico at her bedside when it came to the birth – holding her hand, whispering in the new baby's ear and kissing him…

When she eventually got to bed she made plans for the morrow. She'd failed to find Huw – he'd disappeared into the wilds again. During the night she heard Wil moving around the house, from window to window, taking a stool with him so that he could sit and look out on the surrounding countryside. When she awoke in the night she could see his profile against the landing window. He was sitting on his stool, as still as a statue, with his gun pointing out into the night.

35

A FORTNIGHT WENT by. Every morning, when Mari opened her eyes, she saw Uncle Wil sitting on his stool, looking out on the world with his gun poking out of the landing window. Occasionally he coughed into his sleeve, in an attempt to keep the noise down. As soon as she woke, Mari started to worry about Nico – it was like a headache, arriving with the first rays of light. Even though each day crawled by at snail-speed, the end of the month was fast approaching. Anxiety grew inside her like a twin to the new baby, gnawing at her insides in the same way as constant hunger clawed at her, a daily background noise in her life. But what could she do? The pork by the well had finally gone off and had been eaten by the dogs, who seemed to be in better condition that the humans. Elin and Wil were two living skeletons dressed in charity clothes.

And Huw surfed the wilderness Mowgli-style, talking to the animals and roasting rabbits over fires he lit somehow on the lake's shoreline. He looked more and more like a cannibal in the old comics, and he slept in the wild because his old bedroom had been commandeered and cleaned ready for the visitors, if they ever came.

Every day followed the same pattern. Mari opened her eyes, saw Wil, then worries descended on her like a flight of sinister crows landing on her windowsill. She'd suffer hunger pangs, the sun would arrive, the heat would become unbearable, everything alive would wilt and cower. On some days it became so hot she would moan or even cry; each breath became a trial of will. She thought of Huw's newly-caught fish, trapped in a slow dance of death as they waited for him to smack them on the head with a stone. And a picture came to her mind, something she saw a few days ago: her little brother squatting on his haunches by the river, lifting a stone to despatch a fish, and then losing control – he'd hit the trout time and time again, so many times that the fish disintegrated and spread all over his hands and face and hair in gobbets of fish-flesh. He'd made a terrible noise with each blow, a primitive grunt which electrified the hairs on the back of her neck. She'd stared at the scales gleaming on his skin, and she'd been frightened by the look in his eyes... an inhuman look, as dead as the look in the pulped fish eyes.

Every hour crawled by like a patient shuffling down a hospital corridor. Every day without Nico was a day lost, a day without purpose. No Nico, no food. No Nico, no hope. Every hour without his smile seemed as long as a year. She talked to him by the well, she dreamt about him every night. She composed songs about him in her head. She made love to him, she had intense sex with him, she caressed him tenderly, all in her imagination; she lay with him underneath the great oak tree, naked, where they'd been the happiest young lovers the Earth had ever seen. For an hour in the vast history of the universe, they had been the happiest people ever to live and to love.

One morning, early on, Mari came across Huw on his haunches, beginning to dig with his hands into one of the graves in the paddock. It was Dylan's grave, and Mari was shocked to the core when she saw him there, scrabbling in the dry soil like a hungry animal.

'What are you doing, Huw?'

He didn't answer, other than to grunt and bare his teeth. Poor Huw. He'd probably gone mad.

'Come on, I need your help to fetch the bones from the ravine,' she said to him.

A strange light came into his eyes when she said *bones*. He followed Mari to the farmyard and waited around for her while she searched for a sack. In the end she had to settle for a smelly old fertiliser bag, and then they made their way towards The Meadow; in no time at all they were standing above the four white skeletons. Huw immediately started to play with the bones, picking them up and putting them down again in a ritualistic manner.

'Try to remember their shapes, will you?' said Mari. She looked into his eyes, to see if he understood her. But there was no clear indication that he comprehended what she was saying. Between them they put as many bones as they could in the bag, and Huw cradled the four skulls in his arms. He looked vampiric, like the son of a witch doctor taking decapitated heads home to the village after a tribal altercation. Mari laboured up the side of the hill, and having found the cave, they both paused for a while in the opening, resting after the long haul up in the searing heat. They'd had to take turns, one dragging the sack and the other carrying the skulls, then changing roles every so often. After resting, Huw stood up and held one of the skulls in front of him. Staring into the dead man's eyes, he manipulated the jaw-bone to make it look as though the skull was talking to them. At the same time he made monkey noises.

'Three more days,' said Mari to her brother. 'One, two, three. Today, tomorrow, the day after. Then we'll go after him. Want to come with me?'

Huw continued with his ape-chat.

'Huw!'

But he took no notice. He was living in his own little world now, she'd have to leave him at Dolfrwynog… but what if he dug into the graves? Dear God, what should she do?

They went into the cave and Mari allowed the bones to slide

slowly from the bag, onto the ground, which was covered in dry sheep droppings. There were also ancient tools, rusty spades and pickaxes. Within seconds Huw had reconstructed an entire skeleton, as if he'd been doing it professionally for years. Mari was astounded.

'Well, Huw lad, you've got a real talent there, haven't you?'

And it was true, he had just demonstrated an exceptional ability; in no time at all he'd recreated four skeletons, all asleep on the floor of the cave.

He could have obtained a first class degree in anatomy. But of course, there were no medical schools in existence now, nor universities. Perhaps Huw might have been a top class surgeon in different circumstances, thought Mari. If the world had carried on in the way it had.

They stood in the gloom of the cave, surveying their handiwork.

'Not bad at all,' said Mari. 'All I need now is a story to go with them.'

The residue of a story in her subconscious had taken her in the direction of a king and his soldiers asleep in a cave like this one. The king had woken… but she'd forgotten the rest. It had been an important story in Welsh mythology. Perhaps Uncle Wil could be the king who'd been asleep in the cave with the skeletons, but he'd risen; Mari was aware that she'd have to come up with something better if she was going to convince the pilgrims, once they'd had their fill of her grave stories.

They returned home slowly, with Huw dancing around her like a young chimp. Then he stopped suddenly and looked towards the mountain with a long hard stare. Mari followed his gaze, and her heart began to beat like a drum… had the boy seen someone? Nico? Another gang of ruffians? But then he reverted to the dance, and all the way home he aped around, circling her and making *whoo-whoo-whoo* noises.

214

Time passed terribly slowly over the next couple of days. Mari slept by the well every afternoon; Huw had realised somehow that she was famished and started bringing her little titbits of food: a scorched strip of rabbit meat, or some hazel nuts, or berries.

By the next day they'd completed all their preparations and Mari moved to live in Wil's old home above the stable. It felt totally different, because there was no immediate link with Nico there; that was better in some ways but worse in others, because the pain of living without him brought a heavy curtain of despair over her eyes at times. She decided that if he didn't come on the following day she'd go after him, no matter what that entailed. At least it would create a bit of hope. Hope: without it there could be no future. Staying at Dolfrwynog would be a living death. Her stomach was expanding, but she feared that something was wrong; surely there should be more movement in there. Had lack of food affected the baby's growth?

For hour after hour in the heavy heat, Mari waited for Nico, or for a shift of weight inside her womb; she kept an eye on the hill above, on the mountain road; she listened avidly for a neigh or a bark, any sign of him. She longed to hear the sound of his voice again. To see his dead body would be better than this torture, she thought, but then she changed her mind rapidly. She started to prepare her backpack, ready to go. She searched for hours for an old plastic bottle to hold water, in vain. She found a hot water bottle and filled it hopefully, but it dribbled water all over the floor.

'I'm off tomorrow,' she said to Huw, who was sitting on the upper step of the stable loft as he used to do when he lived there with Uncle Wil. He was playing with one of the pups. 'Do you understand me?'

He said nothing, as usual.

'I'm going to look for Nico tomorrow. Over the mountain. You can come with me if you like, but I won't be coming back.'

The little pup followed her into the stable loft and licked her hand when she stooped to tickle it; then it let her play with its belly fur, and took hold of her finger with its sharp little teeth.

A gun… she'd have to take Uncle Wil's shotgun. She'd have to walk as far as she could at night and sleep by day. Nico had given her some idea regarding the location of the shanty town – it was about five days to the North, over the mountain, and then two days to the West. She'd take more time than him, so she tried to work out the differential.

An enormous moon sailed over the farm that night, and Mari could hear a fox barking at the far end of the cwm – or was it the sound of a war band approaching? She heard an owl flying over the paddock, hooting; it was the first she'd heard in ages, and she took it as a sign. Was it Nico's soul, begging her not to leave the following day? It was very hot in the stable loft and she slept most of the night naked on her woolsack, which was coarse and smelly; she was covered in fine sweat whenever she woke. Lying there in the silvery light of the moon, she heard mice running around in the walls, then the owl hooted again just above the roof, loudly. The fox continued with its lonely cry. All in all she had a bad night of it, tossing and turning, worrying and sweating. The last thing she heard before going to sleep was Huw whispering, *The water… the water,* over and over again in his sleep. So he could talk then, thought Mari. That was how the night drew to a close, with Huw whispering, *The water… the water,* and Mari, half-asleep, feeling surprised that her crazy little brother could still talk.

36

THE WATER... THE WATER...

Huw was at it again. Mari could hear his voice coming from somewhere far away. Then she woke suddenly: he was by her side, shaking her and shouting, *The water, the water...*

It was morning, and Mari had overslept. Then she realised she was naked so she grabbed her T-shirt to cover her swelling body. Huw was pointing through the door and hissing, *The water, the water...*

He looked wild, as if he'd seen a ghost.

'Go away,' said Mari, 'and shut the door after you.'

As she dressed hurriedly a train of thoughts and fears swept into the station of her mind. Had the lake risen again? Had a whale arrived in the cwm? Had another gang come to kill them all? She rushed down the steps from the loft and ran past the muck-heap. When she reached the gate to the lower fields she felt an electric current shoot through her – a charge which was half-fear, half-hope. At first she could hardly believe her eyes. Because down by the water's edge she could see a sailing ship, totally white from stem to stern, glittering in the early sun. Two men were moving around quickly, furling the sails, and there was a line of people standing along the rail, looking up at the farm. Huw had already reached the shore; Mari could see him running along the water's edge in his little red football shorts... he reminded her of a dog chasing passing cars.

Then one of the sailors who'd been busy with the sails jumped down from the ship and stooped to Huw's level, probably talking to him. Mari recognised the slant of his body, she'd have recognised it anywhere. That body belonged to Nico. She was certain of it, and a wave of warm relief suffused her being. He'd returned, as he'd promised he would. But she stayed completely still, unsure what to do next. She noticed that Huw was racing up the field towards her like a greyhound, and when he arrived he said two words over and over again: *Flowers, graves, flowers, graves...* he sounded like a parrot.

In a daze, she watched him run away from her again, towards the slopes above the paddock, where he started to pick wild flowers manically. Mari understood now what was going on, so she joined him, picking any flower she could find. They moved down to the hedgerow and managed to collect enough to make a show, and since there wasn't enough time to fetch water from the well they scattered their pickings on the graves like confetti. This created a nice effect, and Mari compared the site to an Indian temple strewn with holy garlands. By the time they'd finished and returned to the farmyard, six people were walking towards them in a line up the field. She could see Nico on the right, holding hands with a girl... *holding hands with a girl?* She almost passed out. Mari felt nauseous and weak. There had to be a reason. It was some sort of hoax or chicanery. Why would he come back to Dolfrwynog with another woman? She concentrated hard on controlling herself. She'd have to act as if nothing was wrong; she'd have to behave as if Nico meant nothing to her. *Have faith...* she whispered a mantra to herself. *Have faith...* she'd have to keep alive the flames of faith and hope.

They were nearing, and she could scrutinise their bodies and their clothes now. But they were nothing like she'd expected – they were far removed from the muscled, tattooed, gun-wielding banditos of her imagination. Indeed, they looked more like cartoon characters, a bunch of urban misfits on the prowl, or a party of men dressed up as women for a stag night. They were the rats of the dump, and presumably she was looking at the king rats. So this was how civilisation ended. Not with dignity and grandeur, but in knockabout farce. Surreal comedy. Twenty thousand years of human science and culture were coming to an end – in a comical line of Disney characters, straight from a video game. It was laughable.

The main man, as far as she could see, was a small, barrel-chested geezer who looked like a wrestler forced into retirement by age and injuries. His big dome-like head was shaved to the skin, he had a nose like a road crash, and he had a beer gut. His clothes were even more comical: he wore a pair of candy-striped pantaloons and blue flip-flops, with a loose robe which rippled around his corpulent body like a too-big dressing gown. It was bright red, with a golden dragon clambering all over it. Stubbled and ugly, his face was slashed across by a cruel little mouth which displayed a dazzling double row of gold teeth whenever he opened it. He looked more like an extra in *The Thief of Baghdad* than a gang leader, and Mari could hardly believe her eyes. Was this really happening, or was she watching an old movie, riddled with clichés and caricatures?

Next to him was a dark young woman in tight-fitting Lycra sports gear which hugged her body like a second skin; her black hair was cut very short and she wore no make-up or jewellery. In her white trainers – where on earth had she got hold of trainers? – she looked fit and athletic and boyish; she was a good six inches taller than the fat wrestler by her side, ridiculous in his red robe.

Next in line was a ferret of a man who had a pointy bald crown fringed with long, dirty grey hair which hung around his face like a decaying net curtain in an abandoned house. This hair wafted around like a wave of dirty water whenever he took a step, though the rest of him seemed to move very little because there was very little of him: he was a blade of a man, wholly unexceptional except for his footwear, a pair of enormous cowboy boots with spurs which jangled whenever he strode forwards. Finally, he wore a heavy black leather belt into which he'd stuffed a huge bowie knife. Close to him walked a large, dumpy woman with a froth of dyed blond hair, dressed in a ridiculously out-of-place pink tulle dress which spread out from her like an explosion in a chiffon factory. Even her nails and her lips and her high heels were pink; but because she was having to walk through a field she'd been forced to carry her shoes in her right hand, and she made no attempt to hide her disgust at having to pick her way through sheepshit and molehills, as if she were negotiating a minefield.

It didn't take a genius to surmise that she was a city girl with no experience of farm life; with her rings and her bangles and her heavy necklace, she complained every step of the way. Slightly detached from this group, Nico walked hand-in-hand with a girl who looked remarkably like Mari herself. She was almost her double in fact, with light brown hair and a pert little freckly nose. Slim and light, she was Mari without a baby sleeping inside her.

Huw and Mari stood waiting, but neither said anything until the visitors formed a ring around them in the farmyard. Mari suddenly felt like an animal at the zoo. They stared at her for ages, which made her feel even worse, a freak.

'Hiya, Mari,' said Nico, uncoupling his hand from the girl's. 'Glad to see me?'

Mari glared at him and tried to say something, but failed. She found herself staring at his hand, the one which had held the girl's. She could feel herself blushing, and worse still, she felt tears forcing their way to her eyes.

'I bring you some friends to see the saints,' he said quietly.

Saints? What the hell was he on about now? Was he the Devil incarnate, come to torment her? Had she woken up in Hell?

'Here, I have present for you,' he said, thrusting something into her hand.

She looked down at the gift without comprehending what it was. Then she forced herself to concentrate on the furry little lump in her hand. It was a little brown monkey, with a silvery chain ending in a snap-on device. She knew it well, this toy monkey, because she'd written *Mari* on its bald plastic bum with a biro one afternoon while travelling home on the school bus, and it was still there.

'Where did you find this?' she asked him.

He pointed in the direction of the water.

'In the sea, we pick it up on the shore. You like it? Present for baby.'

And he chuckled quietly. Then the whole group laughed, copying him. A family of apes had brought her a little monkey gift.

'Babymonkey,' she whispered, and she ran it along her cheek so that she could feel its furry little body, as she'd done a thousand times in her childhood.

'Babymonkey,' she said again. Because Nico had found the toy monkey which had fallen off her school bag one day, a long time ago, when she'd rolled down the hillock behind the bus stop and slapped Paul Symonds for trying to put his hand up her jumper, a week after he'd moved to the village.

But that was during another life.

37

THEY ALL WENT into the house, and an awkward silence
fell over the place while everyone tried to find somewhere
to sit. Most of them ended up at the long white table, but the
pink woman threw herself into Uncle Wil's big armchair by the
fireplace and immediately lit up a long black cigarette. Mari
hadn't seen a cigarette for years, and a sneaky memory returned
to her of sitting with Paul Symonds under a bridge and puffing
at a stolen ciggie. A rich aromatic smell spread over the room
– the tobacco had to be Turkish or Russian, if such places still
existed. Her name was Wilma, and when she asked, *Anyone
want a cigarette?* it became clear that she was neither Welsh
nor English, but possibly North American or South African
or from somewhere else. Mari wasn't very good at telling the
difference, and the woman's speech was rather loose. She had a
husky actress's voice, a voice from an old film. But despite the
bling and the girlie clothes she had clear grey eyes, intelligent
and inquisitive – she was certainly no fool, and she wouldn't be
easily cheated, thought Mari.

'Where's Mr B?' asked the woman in pink.

'He's still on the boat,' answered the wrestler in the red robe.
Mari wondered who Mr B was. The wrestler's nickname was
Jawsey, on account of his metal teeth. He was full of small talk
and dirty jokes, but under the surface one could sense a sleeping
psychopath. Mari watched him, transfixed with fear. He had a
Manchester accent and eyes like steel traps.

'Are we going to party or what?' asked Jawsey. He was

addressing the group, arms extended, jiggling his upper body and pretending to be in a party mood; his mockery brought a burst of laughter.

'Aye, why not,' said the blade with the monk's hair. He was a Scouser, with bad teeth and wolfish eyes. Indeed, every one of them fitted a cartoonish stereotype of some sort, as if they were in a casting queue. The Scouser was called Weasel and he was a credit to his name.

The tall athletic girl said very little, and that was because she had very little English and even less Welsh. Mari learnt later that she was Lithuanian, and she was Weasel's girlfriend; just like Nico she'd been trapped in Britain at the start of the troubles and had been unable to go home. She was called something like Drooba, and now she sat on the windowsill, swinging her legs to and fro. She was full of nervous energy and looked very short on patience.

'How about showing us the saints then, Nico,' said Weasel in his thin little voice. His sly half-smile seemed to indicate that he was incapable of taking anything seriously, and was here for the entertainment alone. It was just another day at the circus for him.

Mari felt her heart sinking. Dolfrwynog had turned into a freak show with her as the main exhibit. And who was this other girl, snuggling up to her Nico? His new girlfriend? Was he making fun of his little Welsh lover? Had she become a joke now, had Nico been laughing and joking about her throughout their journey here? Had he mocked her, his *little bit of fluff up the duff*?

Mari turned towards the door, intending to escape to her nest by the well.

'Where you going then, Mari?' asked Nico in a steely voice which she hadn't heard before.

She turned and looked at him helplessly, but said nothing in reply. She tried to look accusingly into his eyes.

'Are you going to be nice polite little girl and show our guests where the saints live?'

Her blood had reached boiling point by now.

'Yes, Nico.'

A wave of mirth swept through the room. The bastards were making fun of her. The hairy bloody baboons, they were enjoying the spectacle of seeing an innocent girl being insulted and demeaned, as if they'd replaced a bull with a gangly calf in the matador's ring. Had Nico brought them here for a bit of sport, was that the sort of man he really was?

Mari gestured towards the door and the rabble followed her, across the threshold, across the yard and through the paddock gate. She led them down to the shade of the plum trees, and everyone stood around the four graves. Silence fell over them as they took in the scene, and Mari began to hope she could convince them there really were saints underneath the soil.

'Who is who here?' asked Wilma. Her pink high heels were sinking slowly into Dylan's grave.

Mari named the dead one by one.

'This is Sara who saw the Virgin Mary by the well. This is…'

And so on.

'You start with Sara tomorrow perhaps?' said Nico.

Mari looked at him with as much ill-will as she could muster.

'If you say so, *master*.'

'Yes, I say so.'

Mari turned on her heel and started to walk away, but Nico called her back.

'Our company not good enough for you?'

Tears started to tumble down her cheeks.

'You not coming to our party, Mari?'

She stood before them, head down, with her heart in a thousand little pieces. And when they all moved off towards the farmyard again she trudged after them like a servant. Down they went, through the gate to the lower meadows, towards the ship on the water. Standing there waiting for them, like a basilisk on the deck of the ship, stood the biggest man Mari had ever seen. He was a giant, with a massive, muscular body and the head of a buffalo, black-skinned with tight curly orange hair. She couldn't see his eyes because he wore an outsize pair of shades. The man bowed to them clownishly when they reached the water's edge.

'Welcome aboard,' he said in a supercilious voice.

The gathering all laughed, everyone except for Mari. They were ready to party.

38

THE PARTY ON board the boat had reached fever pitch. The visitors had brought a large supply of alcohol with them for the journey: lager and wine and champagne; there were dozens of crates in the hold and the huge black man, Mr B, whose nickname among the rats was The Beast, went down below for more whenever Jawsey or Weasel issued a command – they were the only ones allowed to order more booze. The bottles they emptied came from the four corners of the old world: there were labels from France and Spain and Russia, plus several other countries. They'd all been pillaged – something which became clear to Mari as the night wore on. At some stage she noticed that the pirates' trademark flag, the skull and crossbones, hung from the mast. So that's what they were. Jawsey and Weasel and Mr B were joke pirates on a bit of a jaunt with their women. It was unlikely that they'd believe her saintly stories. But she'd have to go ahead with the farce and try her best to entertain them, otherwise they'd make her suffer in one way or another. If she couldn't convince them that the graves really did belong to the people in her stories – and that was highly unlikely – then it was important for her to tell the stories as convincingly as she could. But there was a difference this time; she'd told the original stories to keep Nico at Dolfrwynog, to waste enough time for him to stay with her and fall for her, maybe. But this time she had to tell the stories in such a way as to send this mob away satisfied, without prompting them to harm her and her baby, or anyone else who was still alive on the old farmstead.

Mr B had brought an old wind-up gramophone on deck, and now it was broadcasting old-fashioned music across the lower meadows. Uncle Wil could hear it from his deathbed, and he started to hum some of the tunes, though he didn't recognise any of them. It was music from the beginning of the twentieth century, long-forgotten melodies, but they were all the pirate-pilgrims had on board; they'd been found on a ship which had been boarded in the North Sea a month previously. The captain had asked for one last favour: to sit on the deck of his ship, sipping champagne and listening to his old vinyl records. Afterwards, Weasel had sent him to his death in the traditional manner, by making him walk the plank, glass in hand, while the gramophone blasted out an operatic aria. When the final scratchy note arrived he was pushed into the water.

Tonight, Weasel and Wilma were dancing close together on deck, while Jawsey had gone to sleep in a canvas chair. Mari couldn't take her eyes off the glass in his right hand; it had tipped over gradually and it was leaking red wine onto his silk robe. There would be all hell to pay when he woke; he was notorious for that sort of behaviour. Nico, plus his new girl, Drooba, and Mr B had gone below deck; she could hear their drunken voices rise and fall through the hatch. No-one had offered her a drink or a seat, and her legs were beginning to hurt.

This went on for an hour, until it grew dark. Eventually, Mari was able to sidle away when no-one was looking. She escaped homewards but when she arrived at the gate to the farmyard she was met by a terrible sight: Jess was licking the body of one of her pups, lying on its side in the dust. The other pup lay close at hand, in the same mangled condition. Mari leant against the stable wall and vomited. It was a revolting sight, but what had made her ill was the possibility that the double murder had been committed by one of the pilgrims. Who else could be responsible? Huw?

After she'd recovered a little she went to the well with the jug, to wash and to fetch some fresh water. She stayed there for a while, looking at the rising moon and listening to the night animals as they scurried in the undergrowth. When she returned to the yard she decided to leave the pups where they were, as a reproach to whoever had killed them.

She took the water upstairs, for her mum and Wil. Her uncle was asleep, but Elin was sitting by the open window, watching the pirates' ship on the water.

They could see lights appear on deck, and the music continued to seep up the fields towards them. The visitors could be seen dancing drunkenly, and they'd hear someone cursing occasionally when a foot was trodden on, or when an elbow hit the woodwork.

Elin had put some slap on her face and she had a bottle of nail varnish open.

'Mari love, will you paint my nails?'

It was difficult to believe that the skeleton sitting there, her own mother, wanted her nails painted. Why?

'I'm going down there,' said Elin, who couldn't help but notice the disbelief on her daughter's face.

'Well, why not? One last party. I might as well go out with a bang, Mari love.'

She smiled her crooked little smile and handed the bottle to Mari.

'Come on, I want to look my best.'

'But they're animals, Mum, they'll only make fun of you.'

'I don't care, Mari. A glass of champagne and one last dance sounds a whole lot better than dying in that bed.'

Mari lit a candle, and although she was having serious hunger pangs, she went about painting her mother's nails carefully.

'There you are,' said Mari eventually.

'Lovely job, thanks a lot, love,' said Elin. For the first time in ages the two of them felt close. Mari sat and chatted with her mother for quite some time, touching her sleeve, discussing this and that in the flickering candlelight. Then she helped her mother choose some clothes to go with the one remaining pair of shoes hidden at the bottom of the wardrobe. Elin wanted to look as nice as possible when she went down there, though her face was ghoulishly white and her eyes as black as a panda's.

'Will I do?'

'You look lovely, Mum.'

She looked like a dog's dinner, but so what. Then Mari noticed that the pink on her mother's nails was the same colour exactly as the pink in Wilma's frock. There would be a right to-do about that, probably. But Mari said nothing, it was too late now. As her mother said: *The show must go on.*

39

T HE PARTY WENT on all night. Mari stayed in her uncle's bedroom, consoling him or urging him to drink some water now and then. She'd taken the chamber pot from her mother's room weeks ago and given it to him; at some point in the night she emptied it in the garden. The music was still playing on the water. Afterwards she cat-napped in her uncle's corner chair, or talked to him in whispers – by now he either slept fitfully or reminisced about the past, his mind choosing to wander through his childhood rather than face the present.

Once upon a time, in the history of Uncle Wil and his home in Wales, there had been a North and a South and an East and a West. There had been hope. There had been somewhere to go to, either in the physical world or in the imagination. But like a sheepdog witnessing his kennel door being banged shut behind him after a hard day's work rounding up sheep, Wil's consciousness had been shut away in a dark little hut for some time. His world had shrunk, little by little, until there was nothing left but a bed, a pisspot, and a few woodwormed bits of furniture in a hot, smelly little room somewhere deep within nowhere. A little Hell on Earth. He could see now that man's only real requirements were food and drink and freedom and hope. Together with good health, of course. Simple things, but mankind had made the simple act of existence into something very complex. Wil could see it all clearly, but it was too late now. The human race couldn't deal sensibly with luxury or riches. They were greedy animals, but that was natural of course, since the urge to survive and succeed was so very strong. Like a squirrel, man had tried to find and hide as many nuts as possible to ensure survival. But with so many squirrels around, the nuts had become harder and harder to find. A few clever and greedy squirrels had stashed most of them away.

Sometime during the middle of the twenty-first century, scientists had published findings which claimed that the human race had divided into two main types, both going in different directions, as if evolution were conducting a grand experiment; half of humanity were becoming more and more greedy, unsympathetic and immoral, like the pilgrims on the boat, while the other half were going in the opposite direction. Humanity's future now depended on the outcome of the race between the two types. So far, the greedy ones were winning but no-one could predict the outcome. Whatever the result, it entailed the end of the old world. These considerations filtered slowly through Wil's simple consciousness as the music drifted up to him on the night breezes, as he listened to the manic laughter of drunken people and their hoarse chatter. He longed to take the boat from them and sail it away across the sea; he wanted to be Popeye again, before he went to the grave. He'd be able to re-live that afternoon at the youth camp when he'd tasted the fruits of paradise: when he'd realised he should have been a sailor. For one whole day he'd seen what it was like to be excellent at something, when he'd realised that he was a better sailor than anyone else around him. For one whole wonderful day he'd been the very best.

'Why the hell did I stay here on the farm?' he said to Mari in a semi-coma. He was mumbling in his sleep, on the edge of coherence. 'I should have gone to sea, that was what I really wanted.'

That's the way it was all night, with Wil talking in his sleep and Mari trying to catch some rest in the chair, or looking at the party through the bedroom window. Occasionally she could hear her mother's over-excited laugh; then, when the dawn came, they all fell silent and the valley reverted to its customary silence. Sometime in the early morning Mari was woken by a fox barking again at the far end of the cwm; then she lapsed into sleep again, though hunger pangs constantly gnawed at her.

She was woken by the sound of the front door scraping open, then someone climbing the stairs. She didn't recognise the footsteps and a sudden surge of fear went through her; the visitor certainly wasn't Nico. A shadow fell across the doorway, then Mr B entered. His enormous body filled the room like a stormcloud filling a winter sky. Mari stared at his perfect white teeth as he spoke.

'The master wants you to tell your story this morning.'

'Who's the master?'

'The master is Jawsey.'

'What if I say no?'

'Jawsey's in a very bad mood today. Party, you see. Too much champagne. Not a good idea for you to say no. And maybe you'd like to eat?'

She caught the flash of a smile from the giant, though she couldn't see his eyes.

'The master has an idea… he wants you to sing for your supper. Something like that?'

Mr B offered her a deep, rolling laugh as if he were a baddie acting in a James Bond movie. Yes, he was a film character, thought Mari. He was acting the part of a gangster in a Hollywood gangsta movie. That's what had happened gradually during the last century; people had stopped being themselves and had copied screen types to such an extent that they'd turned into cartoon characters, like their heroes on the screen, or in magazines. That's how it looked to her.

Every social interaction had become a standard scene in a movie. People had stopped being people, they'd all become actors. Every room, every space had been covered with a camera, either real or imaginary. Mari looked at the huge man standing in front of her: he could have been one of the minders seen in thousands of second-rate films.

The lives of the ordinary people had turned into a vast running soap or the plot of a pulp novel. Differences between living people had been rubbed out, traditions had melted like plastic in the furnaces of capitalism and globalisation.

'So *Jawsey* wants a story, does he?'

'Yes, he wants you to sing for your supper.'

'Doesn't look like I've got much choice,' said Mari.

'No, not much choice,' echoed Mr B. 'We start at twelve.'

'There's no clock working in the house,' said Mari, while struggling to her feet. 'What time is it?'

'It's ten now,' said Mr B as he turned and descended the stairs. Mari hurried after him so that she could wind up the clock downstairs and move the fingers to ten o'clock. How strange it was that time had returned to Dolfrwynog, after so many years' absence, and yet no-one had missed it much. She enjoyed the *tic-toc* of the clock again, it sounded sweet in the big room. Immediately, she was reminded of her grandparents in front of the fire in winter, many years ago in happier times, knitting or reading or just sitting there, while the only sounds came from the big clock in the corner and an occasional *phut* from the fire.

Mari returned upstairs and started searching through her mother's things. Somewhere at the back of her mind was a recollection of a long white dress which her mother had worn at a charity fashion show; after a while she found it hidden away in the wardrobe. It was wrinkled and smelled none too good, but it would have to do. Mari put it on and went to look at herself in the big corner mirror; she decided that the dress would be more suitable for the task in hand than her falling-apart jeans, which were too tight in any case. She'd have to look shy and virginal for Sara's story: it might be easier to tell a convincing tale if she wore the right clothing. She'd even look like the Virgin Mary herself, hopefully.

By mid-day the valley was baking once again and all the animals had gone to shade below the trees and the hedges; the heatwave had browned the whole landscape and the smaller streams had already dried to a trickle. As a heat haze clouded the atmosphere she observed a dishevelled group labouring up the fields towards the farmhouse, with Jawsey's sharp, whiny voice leading the way. Again, a nervous current started to run through her body; she began to feel dry-mouthed and faint, as if she were a first-time actress about to step on stage.

They arrived on the yard and formed a tight circle around her. She noticed that Jawsey's face was blotched and puffy.

'Well, Mari or whatever your name is, let's get on with it. If you want some food wench, you better come up with the goods.' He spat into the dust and looked at her challengingly.

Mari searched for Nico and found him; he was holding hands with that girl again, and looking at her very seriously... but did she catch a little wink from him? Surely he'd managed to tip her a half-wink, she was sure of it. What was going on? Was he on their side – or hers?

Nico's subtle gesture gave her enough courage to lead the group up through the trees above the house, towards the well. She took a stance by the cistern, with her arms held down by her side, palms outwards, as if she were an angel herself. She looked around her, at the blue sky above her, framed by the treetops, and noticed a squirrel on a branch above; she also noticed Huw, high in the branches of an ash tree, looking down on them in his little red shorts.

They all fell silent, and Mari started her story.

'Once, I had a sister called Sara. She was beautiful, with long black hair and dark brown eyes. Everyone looked at her, wherever she went, and one day an agent from a modelling agency stopped her in the street and offered her a contract there and then...'

At first her voice was tremulous and weak, but it strengthened as she warmed to her theme. She found herself adapting the tale as she went on; it was a total fiction by now, Sara's world had been completely different in real life.

But Mari knew that if she told her story convincingly she'd get some food, and so would everyone else at Dolfrwynog, hopefully. More important, she might make herself appealing to Nico again, and rekindle his love for her.

40

STANDING BY THE well in wilting heat, Mari was shaking uncontrollably – because of fear, or hunger, or maybe a combination of both. And towards the end, as she formulated a neat finish to her story, the baby sprang to life, burning her insides with pain. Fortunately her shakiness was interpreted as pure emotion, as was the *Oh!* which escaped her lips. Mari had woven an exceptionally good story, she had a talent for it. And the hoodlums around her had been fooled into thinking that grief and tenderness had brought on her emotional behaviour.

'And she was buried on her birthday, as the snow fell all around; a little robin redbreast landed on her folded hands in the grave, as we said our prayers for her, and it wouldn't fly away – not even when we began to put earth on her,' said Mari as she searched her brain for a suitable climax.

'Then a hawk fell from the sky and killed the poor little robin in a shower of feathers,' she added. She was being absurd now, ridiculously sentimental. But Wilma looked sad – at least one of them had swallowed the fiction.

'We screamed at the hawk and it flew away, but the poor little robin was dead; it lay on her hand, and a trickle of blood from its broken body ran slowly along her finger, onto to her snow white dress…'

The baby was playing a football game inside her, she could hardly breathe. 'We buried them both together and that night a great storm descended on the valley; there were massive peals of thunder and huge flashes of lightning; the wind howled and whistled through the trees, as if God above was raising His voice in anger at the death of poor Sara, as if the Virgin Mary herself was weeping tears for the lovely little robin redbreast which died that day in the snow.'

Jawsey and Weasel clapped sardonically in unison, but Wilma and the other girls were clearly moved, so the two men stopped being disrespectful and Jawsey said in a sober voice:

'Well done, Mari lass, you've done us proud.'

He was trying to sound sincere, to play along with the women, but nothing could hide the sarcastic edge to his voice.

'Where's my mother, anyway?' asked Mari suddenly. They weren't expecting the question, but Jawsey answered:

'Sleeping it off, duckie. Quite a party girl, isn't she?'

He smiled crookedly at her, then clapped his hands in front of his face, as if he were a sultan lording it over a troupe of servants, and said:

'For this, my friends, our good friend Mari deserves our thanks and our generosity. Mari, we humbly beseech you to be our guest at the dinner table tonight. Drooba – go and command Mr B to prepare the feast!'

Everyone except for Mari applauded, and then they returned to the farmyard.

'Mari, you shall be our guest at seven this evening,' said Jawsey in a patronising manner. Mari noticed that his temper had improved during the afternoon, but that could be due to the bottle bulging in the pocket of his pantaloons.

Nico led the men up the hill, to show them the upper meadows, while Mari took Wilma and Nico's new 'girlfriend' along the lower meadows, to view the pigs and the horses. Mari noticed that the pigs had left their lair below the great oak tree and had broken into the cornfield, partly destroying it. The pilgrims' food would be more important than ever now. But she hadn't anticipated having to plead for it, like a beggar on the streets of Delhi. She found the process demeaning, having to depend on the grace of others for a few scraps of food. And what about the baby? Mari feared increasingly that the constant hunger which was putting her own life in jeopardy was also threatening the life of her unborn child. She was convinced now that something was amiss.

At seven that evening everyone sat down in the cabin of the *Beagle 2,* with Mr B waiting on them in a red uniform with gold epaulettes. For this occasion he'd removed his dark glasses, and Mari was surprised to discover that he had nice eyes. In fact she rather stared at him because his eyes looked so out of place on him, as if he'd stolen them from someone else. They appeared to be kind and compassionate, full of humour. God, there was no understanding the world, thought Mari, it was absolutely bonkers. The end of the world was actually proving to be rather silly. It was supposed to be biblical and serious. The heavens were supposed to open and a very serious voice was supposed to speak to them from on high. But no, it was all madly childish. Here they were, coming to the end of summer, and they might as well be in Cairo; she was aboard a make-believe pirate ship in the company of a bunch of characters straight out of Disneyworld; and they were about to tuck into a feast while almost everyone else in the world was starving. It was all surreal; and adding to the sense of unreality was the fact that this boat was floating in a place where fields showed their greenery to the sun not so long ago. No wonder Elin and Uncle Wil had given up on life.

Caviar on toast, that was the first course they tasted – Mari had never had it and she decided it wasn't all that special, she couldn't see what all the fuss was about. But she ate it slowly, in case her empty belly reacted badly. Mr B wound up the gramophone periodically and they all munched away without saying much until the champagne took hold of Jawsey's tongue and he launched into a loud monologue, talking rubbish mainly and telling filthy jokes, while his teeth gleamed in the candlelight.

Next came lobster bisque. Mari didn't like it much and she sipped it very slowly indeed. Presumably lobsters had made a return to the seas after being fished close to extinction. A big shell holding a few mouthfuls of meat; it seemed hardly worth the effort. The taste lingered in her mouth for ages and burned her tongue. Yuch! Wasn't it strange, thought Mari, how distasteful she found posh, expensive food. What could be better than fresh bread and butter, with a simple wedge of cheese? She had no appetite for this sort of stuff. A huge piece of chocolate, that's what she really wanted. Mmmm, that would be lovely.

'You all right, Mari?' asked Weasel.

'Fine thank you, lovely food,' said Mari, who was close to bringing up her lobster bisque all over the white tablecloth. Her stomach had started to hurt again, but for a different reason – she wasn't used to so much food all at once. Steak and chips came next, and the pilgrims attacked this course like a pack of ravenous wolves. She managed about half her portion before she gave up.

'What's up, luv?' asked Jawsey in a pseudo-caring voice.

'The baby,' said Mari, touching her belly. 'It's had enough for now.'

Jawsey tut-tutted but let her be.

Mari looked towards Nico, but he avoided her eyes immediately. The little sod looked as guilty as hell. Damn him and all his fine words, thought Mari. Men! They were all bastards, really. They were off as soon as they'd got what they wanted. Only one thing on their minds, and he was just the same as the rest of them.

'Lovely,' said Mari when she saw the chocolate pudding. She wanted to swipe the bowl from Mr B's hands and plunge her face straight into it. For a moment she felt an urge to take her clothes off and smear the chocolate all over her. She'd look like Mr B then. Mmmm, lovely. She wolfed the pudding and burped loudly.

'Whoopsy daisy,' she blurted, and then sank another glass of champagne. What the hell, she might as well behave like a pig herself. She thought of herself and Nico lying naked under the oak tree by the river, happy and white with a pattern of blues and yellows on their skins, and her throat tightened into a knot. It had been the happiest time of her life. Nature's brilliant colours a kaleidoscope on her young hips. His lean body, his curly hair soft in her hands. Lying there with their eyes shut, drinking in the heat of the sun. Insects humming around them. A warm breeze caressing their bodies. Happiness was such a simple thing, really, wasn't it?

'Cheese and biscuits?' asked Mr B's big bass voice in her left ear.

'No thank you very much,' she answered politely, as if she were at a garden party at Buckingham Palace. She sank another glass of bubbly. Hey ho, life wasn't as awful as all that, was it? Then Jawsey rapped the table with his spoon and they all fell quiet. He cleared his throat.

'Ladies and gentlemen, it gives me great pleasure to thank our guest Mari for being here with us tonight.' They clapped politely. He continued:

'As a special honour tonight Mari, you may have three wishes.'

Three wishes. Good grief! What an honour. She shut her eyes as her mind raced through all the possibilities…

'Not those sort of wishes you daft bint,' said Weasel. 'Real wishes, things we can give you tonight.' And under his breath he said, 'Silly bitch…'

Mari opened her eyes. Her first wish was quite obvious.

'Plenty of food for the people in the house,' she said. 'Lots of it, to be taken up for Wil and Huw…'

'OK, OK,' said Jawsey. 'You can have some food. What else?'

'Have you got any medicine?' asked Mari.

Jawsey looked towards Mr B. 'Well?'

'Yes, we have some medicine, master.'

'Morphine?' asked Mari.

'Yes, we have some morphine, not much though,' said Mr B.

'Go on then, you can have some of that too,' said Jawsey. He was in a bad mood by now, he'd expected Mari to be more entertaining.

'And the third wish? Make it snappy.'

Mari closed her eyes again for a few seconds, then opened them again. She was feeling a bit drunk and stared straight at Nico, who stared straight back at her, looking alarmed.

'I would like,' she said slowly, 'I would like…'

But Jawsey cut across her.

'No, that's your lot girl. Now bugger off home.'

41

MARI GROANED AND held her stomach. Had it been the food, or the baby? The champagne, perhaps? One way or another, she was suffering today. She was by the riverbed, close to the well, under the hazel trees, a place which had been her toilet area ever since they stopped using the loo in the house because the septic tank was full. Normally she wiped her bum with grass or ferns or bracken and then covered the mess with a stone. Gradually she'd worked her way down the ravine, and she'd have to start on the other side of the river soon. She knew that Huw was watching her now, as he did on a regular basis; she had seen a glimpse of his red shorts in the tall ash trees above her. She also noticed that some of the trees appeared to be dying; the heatwave, which had lasted for weeks now, had seared the foliage and killed off trees such as the alders, which liked wet ground. Mari completed her toilet, without much success, and went down to the stream to wash her hands. The pain inside her was moving from one side to the other; what if her appendix was playing up? What would she do in an emergency like that? She had no idea, maybe she'd die. What had happened to the early Welsh people, living in their caves or mud huts, if their appendixes flared up? Or if they caught an infection? They had probably died in droves.

She didn't want to die. She was going to be a mother. She wanted to look after the little man growing inside her tummy. That's if he was growing. She hadn't been able to eat properly during the last few months, and perhaps the baby would be small like Dylan. Almost a midget. Perhaps Mari would start a line of Welsh pygmies living unobtrusive and shy lives in the river valleys, dark little things sleeping in vine hammocks slung between the trees around Dolfrwynog.

She made her way back to the farmyard, so that she could get ready for the visitors. First she'd have to empty Uncle Wil's chamber pot and encourage him to drink some water; he hadn't eaten for a while – he seemed to be living on fresh air. How could his body go on like that, day after day, with nothing to sustain it? The human body was truly amazing.

Wil had learnt the pirates' tunes and could sing them word for word; it was his second great talent, by the look of things. He joked to Mari that he could have been a famous operatic singer.

He smiled at her when she entered his room, he loved the girl. She fussed around him for a while, tidying his bed, and then she gave him a spoonful of morphine to assuage the pain inside him. She left the bottle by his bedside.

'Hey little Mari, listen to me singing their songs. I can remember them all!' And he started to warble in a faint tenor voice:

I think that I shall never see
A poem lovely as a tree...

'Hey Mari,' he continued, 'these visitors have brought a bit of life back to Dolfrwynog. Elin's a party girl again and I've shown a new talent. Can't all be bad. Don't knock it till you've tried it! You know what? Maybe I was a pirate like that lot in a previous life. Captain Morgan or Black Bart. I was always handy with billhooks and that sort of thing.'

'Billhooks, Uncle Wil?'

'Yes, a billhook is a bit like a sword, isn't it? And I was always a snazzy dresser, like Captain Morgan, when I used to go to the young farmers' discos.'

He started to sing again, barely audible this time:

A tree that looks at God all day,
And lifts her leafy arms to pray;
A tree that may in Summer wear
A nest of robins in her hair...

By the gods, he was good at this sort of thing. But Mari cut across him:

'Uncle Wil, we've got some food in the house at last. Would you like something to eat?'

He was astonished by the question.

'Food? What sort of food?'

'You won't believe this, Uncle Wil, but we have some caviar and champagne if you'd like some.'

He stared at her, open-mouthed. Caviar? He'd never tasted caviar, he didn't even know what it looked like. Was it some sort of meat? A cake, perhaps? No, surely it had something to do with fish...

'Go on then, I'll have a mouthful of the stuff and a glass of champagne to see what they both taste like,' he said. He'd drunk champagne at his sister's weddings many moons ago, when he'd compared it loudly to donkey piss. Not that he'd ever tasted donkey piss, of course.

And here he was in his bed at Dolfrwynog, about to drink the best Russian champagne – the drink of nobility. Popeye, drinking champagne. Ha! He started to laugh, then he started to weep silently. How sad it was, to be a little Welsh Popeye about to drink champagne on his deathbed.

Mari turned away and left the room, to spare his feelings. Like most of his countrymen he was a proud man, and he'd been able to be brave so far. But once she was on the other side of the door she too dissolved into tears. There was something quite striking about a rough and ready farmer drinking champagne while singing a long-forgotten song in a small room in the wild hills of Wales.

Mari had agreed to make an appearance in the paddock during the afternoon, to tell the second tale, which was the history of her father and the school incident which led to his hospitalisation; she'd have to describe how street gangs attacked the hospital and how they'd escaped to the farm with Jack at the wheel. But when she was actually reciting the story by the graveside there was consternation when she mentioned Jack's name.

'Who was he?' asked Jawsey.

Mari tried to explain.

Where was he now?

She didn't know.

Jawsey and Weasel looked around them in all directions, as if they feared he was hiding somewhere near.

No, said Mari, he'd been gone for months.

But Jawsey and Weasel weren't comfortable with this development. And soon it became obvious why.

'Were you there at the hospital, Weasel?' asked Jawsey.

'Yes, where do you think I got the morphine?' he answered.

'Which hospital was that?'

'Don't know – the big one in town.'

Mari interrupted them.

'This was a hospital miles away, in the South.'

But the story had unsettled them, because they'd attacked hospitals to steal drugs in the early days of the meltdown, and they both had unpleasant memories. It was the closest they got to feeling guilty.

'Don't think much of your story today, Mari,' said Weasel tartly, and away he went towards the boat, with the women following him. Wilma made a pathetic sight, rolling over the old tractor ruts like a sow who'd run higgledy-piggledy into a clothes line and emerged on the other side with garments draped all over her body.

Shortly after they reached the boat a family of dolphins appeared close by, playing and disporting themselves as they normally did, especially when Huw was around. Soon he was playing among them, riding on their backs and leaping from one to another acrobatically. All the pilgrims appeared to be laughing and encouraging Huw. Then, suddenly, a shot rang out, followed almost immediately by another. A double-barrelled shotgun had been fired into the water, and everyone went quiet. When they turned to see who had fired the gun, they saw Weasel on deck, reloading. A terrible scream came from the water: the scream of a child. And a dark red cloud could be seen spreading through the water around the boy. Mari ran down the field, thinking he'd been hit, shouting, *Huw... Huw...*

But by the time she arrived her brother had reached the shore and was running towards her up the field. Hit by a bad mood, Weasel had fired on the dolphins – leaving two of them dead, floating on the surface in a widening band of blood. The rest had escaped towards the sea.

They all stared dumbstruck at the bodies in the water, their glittering undersides already dulling in the heat. They stared too at Weasel, chilled by his act and the smell of cordite wafting around them.

'That'll teach you,' said Weasel through his clenched teeth. 'Nobody makes a fool out of me. Let that be a lesson to the lot of you.'

He turned on his heel and went down below deck, where he drank himself into a stupor during the rest of the afternoon. By dusk he was standing on deck again, swaying slightly and firing his gun indiscriminately into the darkening water.

246

42

W HEN DAWN CAME the following morning they saw their first cloud for months. A long grey straggle in the West was followed by a train of darker puffs, as if a hidden band of Sioux were sending increasingly frantic smoke signals.

'What an awful thing to do,' said Uncle Wil to Mari during their morning chat. He'd heard the shots and wanted to hear the full story.

Mari heard her own voice beginning to embroider the tale, as she was so used to doing by now, so she reined herself in and presented a reasonably truthful account. She described how Weasel had stood shouting on the deck of the *Beagle 2* with his smoking gun pointing towards the water. Then they'd seen the two dolphins floating on their sides in the red-dyed water. Cordite in the air. A blood-curdling scream.

Yes indeed, Wil had heard that scream, though he hadn't recognised Huw's voice: he thought one of the women had fallen overboard. He felt sad about the dolphins; they were so friendly and inquisitive – closer to man than any other animal except the apes, apparently. People who had swum with them reported a special rapport. Wasn't there a theory that dolphins had lived on land for a while, like man, but had returned to the water for some reason? But why would they do that, wondered Wil. Was it because of desire or necessity? Perhaps they'd been disappointed by the other animals on dry land; perhaps the earth-crawlers had oppressed them.

All sorts of outlandish ideas poured through Wil's inflamed

imagination that morning; perhaps it was the morphine, perhaps it was the change in the weather. He was feeling a bit better thanks to pirate medicine; he'd had a good night's sleep once that madman Weasel had calmed down and put his gun away. Silly bugger. Considering how cunning they claimed to be, the visitors could be very stupid at times.

On and on went Wil's ramblings and musings, so that by the time he'd finished the sky was beginning to darken.

'Change in the weather,' he observed needlessly.

'Looks like it, Uncle Wil, but we need rain badly,' answered Mari.

Both of them laughed. 'Here we are talking about the weather again,' said Wil. 'Some things never change.'

And in a nice family way they spent a pleasant half-hour together.

'I think I'll try getting up today,' said Wil. He had it in mind to walk to the centre of the farmyard again. To the centre of the universe. For the final time? There weren't any hens left, unfortunately. A pity. He missed the sound of Cluck crowing proudly in the morning, when the dawn arrived. One of the old sounds of Wales. And what had happened to his map on the wall? Mouldering away, probably, like the chart in Scott's hut, far away in Antarctica.

While Mari was drying her face after a wash, he asked:

'Do you know where Elin is?'

'She's still on the boat,' replied Mari.

'They must be having a hell of a party.'

'She's more likely sleeping it off – there are plenty of beds on board,' said Mari, who immediately thought about Nico and his new girl. She wondered if they…

Then her mind leapt in another direction, since it was best not to think about Nico right now. She went through today's tale: the story of Rhiannon. She'd have to change and adapt the story to suit Wilma and Drooba. She'd have to be extra careful, otherwise Weasel would shoot something or someone.

She'd decided not to mention Alun, the cruel husband from Pant yr Haul across the valley. Then she remembered that there had never been such a place or person. They had existed only in her imagination. That was the result of her weird double life – she no longer lived in full-on reality; hers was a jittery existence with an echo of mental illness, reinforced by the surreal, cartoonish nature of the pilgrims.

She'd start afresh with Rhiannon's story by the graveside, below the plum trees, with the crew of the *Beagle 2* standing around her again.

When they met in the paddock later on Mr B was absent; he'd stayed behind to look after Elin. Mari started to extemporise on the embryonic story in her head. The men were very quiet, Weasel especially so. Mari surmised that he was feeling guilty.

As she started, a big spot of rain splashed on her nose. Thank God for that, she thought, perhaps the rain would save her. As the water cooled her face she conjured up an image of Rhiannon in her mind's eye: tall, milky-skinned, beautiful, with bright red lips and dark hair cascading to her hips. She knew that she'd have to create quite an impression today.

'But Rhiannon was as cruel as she was beautiful,' Mari told them. She looked up at Nico and saw his eyes registering the shift in her story. It was a test of his feelings towards her, too. If he betrayed her and exposed her fiction she would know that he'd gone over to the other side. But if he stood there mutely she could take some hope from that. Mari felt like a spy leaving a coded message on a park bench; was Nico a double agent, or was he still faithful to her cause? He stayed as he was, head down, silent. He had taken her message without selling her down the river, and her heart leapt. Perhaps he was with her after all. She stopped speaking for a while since her mouth wouldn't obey her. Once again this was interpreted as pure emotion, and Wilma moved closer to her and put a big pink arm around her.

Mari continued with the story. Rhiannon had been cold and cruel since the day she was born. If unwanted newborn pups needed drowning it was she who did it. If there wasn't enough food for little kittens it was she who got rid of them. If the grown-ups found a spider without legs, or a butterfly without wings, they knew who was responsible. Then, one day, when she'd grown up, she met a man who was just as good-looking and cruel as she was. They were a perfect match, and they were married within the month.

They went to live in a grandiose house on a mountain, far away from anywhere else; their home was cold and perfect and white. Within a year Rhiannon had given birth to a perfect boy, white and quiet and beautiful. Rhiannon rejoiced in him; as he grew into a tall, brilliant, handsome man she became prouder and prouder. Of all the mothers in the world she was the quickest to extol her child and loudest in praising his many talents.

Mari looked around the group and saw that she was holding their interest. Wilma, the most openly emotional, was close to tears again and even Drooba was listening avidly; she was the first to switch off usually.

Then, one day, said Mari, the son went away from them without saying a word beforehand. They heard nothing for a whole year, and then a letter arrived all the way from India. Their son had opened a home for little orphans in the slums of Delhi, and he was happy, for the first time in his life, as he succoured them and improved their lives.

This sent his parents mad with rage. They flew immediately to India, begged him to stop his foolishness and return home with them.

But there was no point; he remained immune to their pleas. He was still there, as far as she knew. This time Mari was fairly sure that the pilgrims were enjoying her story.

One day, said Mari, Rhiannon went to the edge of the lake; as she stood there, despairing, Rhiannon decided she couldn't come to terms with her son's purity and generosity. How had such a thing happened, when she and her husband had been as cruel as possible towards their son and every living creature around them? For some incomprehensible reason their son was a failure. He was a good man. So Rhiannon walked into the water and her body was discovered the following morning. They buried her here with her family; that was Rhiannon's story. The End.

Mari looked from face to face, hoping that no-one would notice that Rhiannon was the complete opposite of a saint. The story had run away from her.

'Lovely story, Mari,' said Wilma. Mari noticed that one of her shoe straps had snapped, and there was a rip in her nice pink frock – the same frock she'd arrived in days ago. She was smelly. Yes, she stank. Mari realised that this woman by her side was suffering too; she had dark rings underneath her eyes, her skin was blotchy and spotty. Her hair was a mess. *Poor thing*, thought Mari, the new world order had driven her downwards too.

Next she looked at Drooba; as usual she appeared sly and moody, though it was almost impossible to guess what was going on inside her head. Drooba rarely said anything, but she continued to look at Rhiannon's grave while picking her teeth with a grass stem. The rest of them had started to walk away in a zigzag line through the paddock, led by Weasel, who was in a hurry to get back to the boat; last night's fun and games had left him with a headache and a parched throat. Mari could hear him talking to Nico's new lovebird; he was saying that they'd have to return soon or some other rats would take their place. Nico had held back, as if he was trying to get close to her… at one stage she felt his hand brush against her hip.

Mari was far away in her own world when the whole group jarred to a halt; she almost walked into Drooba. At first she was unable to see what was happening, but she could hear Weasel saying: 'Now don't be a silly boy, put it down. Go on, put it down.'

Mari stepped sideways so that she could see the whole group. Weasel had reached the gateway to the lower meadows and had opened it – but before he could walk through it, Huw had leapt out in front of him. The boy had been hiding behind a rusty old farm implement on the other side. Now he was standing a few feet away from Weasel in his dirty red football shorts, pointing Uncle Wil's shotgun straight at Weasel's chest.

Weasel made another attempt to calm the boy.

'There there, give it to me. I won't hurt you. Just a bit of a joke, I know.'

Huw was shaking violently, and there was a terrible look in his eyes. The bastard in front of him had murdered two dolphins, his friends, members of his new family. He waved the gun and squared up to Weasel, though that took a mammoth effort because the gun was too heavy for him.

Weasel took a step forwards, but that was a mistake. His last mistake. After the blast and the echo came a heavy silence, and the cordite aroma of death. He slumped slowly to his knees, then toppled onto his front with his hands still clutching his chest. Nobody moved for a while as all of them, including Huw, looked at his prone figure on the ground. Then the boy ran like a greyhound along the lower meadows, away from them, still holding the gun. In no time at all he'd disappeared completely.

Nico and Jawsey turned him over but Weasel was clearly dead. The strangest thing of all, thought Mari, was the fact that nobody screamed or tried to run from the boy. They'd all behaved like zombies, or as if Huw had merely tackled Weasel in a village football game. Perhaps they were all in shock. Afterwards they stood around, talking quietly. Next, they saw Nico's new love racing up the field towards them – she'd been helping Mr B to look after Elin all afternoon. When she saw Weasel on the ground she screamed and threw herself across his body. Mari thought she was over-acting until someone told her that Weasel was her father. Mari was shocked, she hadn't guessed that the two were related. The girl had wept with awful tearing sobs, and they gave her time to show her grief; then the body of her father was taken to an outhouse attached to the side of the farmhouse and laid out on one of the slate slabs used formerly to keep milk cool, with a blanket over him. They shut the door and then divided into two groups, some going into the house and the others walking down to the boat.

A deep silence spread over Dolfrwynog that night, until after midnight, when the wind rose and much-needed rain arrived to cool and refresh the old farmhouse. That night, as stealthy as a fox, Huw crept up to the stable loft and marked a big red cross on Uncle Wil's Anaglypta map. Where previously the activities of hens were recorded, a cold dead human was now remembered on the decaying paper. A civil war was about to erupt at Dolfrwynog, and by the end of the month there would be other crosses on the chart.

Mari was the only one to notice the new cross, when she went up to fetch some of Uncle Wil's belongings; she hoped to give him some consolation during his final days on Earth.

43

THERE WAS NO understanding people, thought Mari. She had watched the girl express deep and sincere grief; but how had her father, Weasel, deserved such love? How on earth could someone as unfeeling, vindictive, ugly and cunning as Weasel deserve such a sweet and sensitive daughter? The girl had shown dignity and true feeling as she walked to and fro between the outhouse and the boat. It was clear that she still found it impossible to believe that her father was dead. She'd sit by him, look at his face, and cover his hands with her own. His body was so very cold by then – it was unbelievable that flesh could be so cold. She'd cry quietly, sitting there alone, though the only obvious signs of distress were her red-rimmed eyes and her drooping shoulders. Mari didn't even know her name at that stage, but she took a jug of fresh water and a little white cup to her in the outhouse, and was thanked warmly. The girl revealed in a subdued voice that her name was Amber. Mari had many questions she wanted to ask her regarding her relationship with Nico, but realised that this was neither the time nor the place. The girl was heart-broken. It was strange that they should look so alike, thought Mari. They were almost carbon copies of each other; they were the same height, the same shape, and had the same mousey brown hair and bright blue eyes. Even their freckles were grouped in roughly the same places.

The father had been a complete bastard, but the daughter was an angel, and Mari soon forgave her for stealing her lover. How could she be to blame? That bloody Nico had a lot to answer for. Men, the usual story.

By the following day the civil war at Dolfrwynog had intensified. A meeting was held in the kitchen – without the talking stick – to discuss what should be done with Weasel's body. They should take him out to sea, said Jawsey, because that's what they did in the shanty town. There wasn't time to bury the dead, so they were rowed away in a boat and tossed in the water with stones to weigh them down. No, said Amber, she didn't want him to go that way. The notion of fishes and crabs eating her father was repulsive, and her eyes misted over; they became big and shiny in the light of the candle.

Perhaps they should take him to the Cave of the Braves, said Mari. She'd kept that card up her sleeve from the start, just in case; nobody knew about it as yet, except for Huw of course, because he'd helped her to assemble the skeletons. She had to explain where the cave was, though she didn't tell the full story. But Amber was dead against that too; wild dogs or foxes would be able to gnaw at the remains.

'So what can we do?' asked Jawsey. 'We've got to put the sod somewhere or he'll stink like a skunk by…'

Amber put her head in her hands, so Jawsey shut up.

Everyone agreed that Weasel should be buried. But where?

In the paddock with the others, said Wilma, who smelt almost as bad as the corpse by now.

No, said Mari. That was impossible. The graves in the paddock were family graves. Then she went to the foot of the stairs and shouted up to Wil:

'They want to bury that man in the paddock with our family, Uncle Wil, what do you think?'

'Not bloody likely,' he answered crossly. 'That place is for the Dolfrwynog family and no-one else, or I'll…'

He wasn't quite sure what he'd do. It was then that he noticed something was missing from his room; his eyes had made a quick search for the gun when he heard Weasel being mentioned. But then he remembered that the firearm had been given to Huw. So the die was cast. Silently, Wil nodded his approval.

Mari was upset by the plan. She didn't want a bad bugger like Weasel polluting the family plot.

In the end they accepted Amber's wish for her father be buried in the paddock, but in the upper corner, beneath the hawthorn bushes. With that agreed, Amber and Drooba went up to the corner the following morning to open a grave, while Jawsey kept watch with a shotgun. They feared another visit from Huw. Jawsey had been busy making plans of his own for Huw's future, and they didn't include birthday cards.

Jawsey had started his shanty town career as the chief fixer for the king rats; he'd killed men with debts, or anyone else who posed a threat. Then he'd killed the king rats and taken the top spot himself. The town was a warren of huts and narrow passageways, similar to the *favelas* of Brazil, only covered in serious rust and mud. The township was a brutal place, where no-one cared a button for anyone else and it was each man for himself; the more ruthless you were the richer you got. So Jawsey had become numero uno, and right now he was worried in case someone else had taken his place already, despite the fact that he'd left his henchmen there to look after the show. He was beginning to think he'd made a mistake by coming here – it had been a snap decision, made when he was drunk. Yes, the 'holiday' had done them all good, except for Weasel of course, but what sort of welcome would they get when they returned? Would his henchmen still be in power, and would they willingly hand back the reins?

On the other hand, Jawsey was looking forwards to the hunt; he would really enjoy tracking down Huw and exacting revenge for Weasel's death. One thing he had to be careful about: he wasn't used to hunting in open country, which gave Huw a slight advantage – the boy knew the terrain intimately and he'd be able to hide like a fox.

'Come on, hurry up,' he said unpleasantly to the girls. Although Drooba was fit and strong, the earth was hard and stony, which meant they were going too slowly for Jawsey's liking. It took them a couple of hours to dig deep enough, and then Jawsey and Drooba went to fetch the corpse. They took him there on the hurdle which Wil's hens had used as a perch in the hen house, and it was covered with hen shit; between that and the smell coming from Weasel's body the air was pretty rank.

They placed him in the hole, but before Amber could say anything, Jawsey shouted:

'Come on Drooba, let's go and find that little shit before it gets dark,' and off they went without a word of sympathy. So it was Amber and Mari who completed the ceremony. Between them they managed to piece together a simple service of remembrance.

'I know he was a sod to other people, but he was really lovely to me, and I loved him,' said Amber. 'It's hard to believe, but he was a brilliant father. Best in all the world.' By now her tears were falling faster than the rain, which was coming on with renewed intensity; the clouds had thickened during the day and now they were ready to disgorge their cargo over the valley.

As the two of them stood for a while by the grave, with flowers in their hands and rain running down their spines, they saw Nico walking away from them along the lower meadows, evidently following Jawsey and Drooba. He was wearing an old yellow sou'wester which made him look silly, and he had a gun slung over his shoulder.

'There goes lover boy,' said Mari. 'You two getting married?'

Amber looked askance. 'What, me and Nico? You've got to be joking. Whatever gave you that idea?'

'Well, you were holding hands, and that sort of thing…'

'No, he never wanted me like that. I think he was using me, to be honest with you. Trying to get into the gang. And I was flattered, he's so nice looking.'

'You mean there's nothing going on between you two?'

'No, Mari, nothing like that. He was just kidding me along. Haven't you seen the way he looks at you? He's only interested in one woman around here, Mari.' She looked down at Mari's belly. 'Or maybe that could be two… is that baby his?'

'Yes, of course it is.'

'You love him?'

'Yes, I love him… too much for my own good.'

In the distance, they heard shots. Then the echoes reverberated along the valley.

'I hope no-one else has copped it,' said Amber.

She noticed that Mari's face had tightened.

'Your brother… is he your brother?'

'Yes.'

'Don't worry, I've got a feeling it's not him. I saw his eyes when he was standing in the gateway yesterday. Very angry, and a bit crazy. Like a wild animal.'

They left the paddock together after scattering wild flowers on Weasel's grave. The rain had become intense by the time they arrived at the house. For some reason Mari decided to hide whatever food was left, and then she lit a fire because it was cooling quickly and she'd have to keep the place warm for Uncle Wil.

44

THOUGH WEASEL HAD been buried for less than a day, and though Drooba's body lay stiff and cold amid the bracken on the slopes above the lower meadows, there was worse to come. Another day dawned at Dolfrwynog, but there were no blue skies to buoy their spirits; after the heatwave a monsoon had poured a deluge of warm rain onto the land and covered it in jungle mists. Mari rose slowly – her swelling stomach was slowing her down now – but saw almost nothing from the landing window except a swirling milky soup, seeping through the fields. The outside scene could be somewhere from the jungles of Malaysia in the rainy season, with rain cascading in waterfalls and fog rolling over the house like cannon smoke.

Down on the water, appearing though the greyness occasionally, Mari could see a dark new shape – and her heart fell even further, right down into her boots. Because there was another boat out there this morning – no, this was a ship, much bigger that the *Beagle 2* and she was black, or grey, it was hard to tell in the conditions. As she loomed in and out of the fog, Mari counted three masts – two more than the *Beagle 2*; she squatted on the water like a big fat slug, waiting to crawl up the field towards them…

Mari upped the tempo and moved around the house as swiftly and carefully as she could, because she'd already seen the need for action. Realising that speed was of the essence, before the new visitors invaded, she woke Uncle Wil and told him the news. Then she packed all the essentials into two battered cases.

Fortunately she'd baked two loaves the previous evening using flour from the *Beagle 2*, and there were a few tins of food left over. When Wil had dressed they left the house, Mari leading the way. Wil paused shakily in the centre of the yard for one last time, and took a final look at his little kingdom while Mari lugged one of the cases towards the shade of the holly tree which marked the beginning of the hill towards the mountain. Then she went back for the other one.

'Come on, Uncle Wil, or they'll have arrived before we've started,' said Mari. She was breathless and hot, and she could feel the baby grumbling inside her.

'You go on ahead,' said Wil. 'I'm going to have a last look at this place, I'll be ready by the time you've finished with that second case.'

Then he realised he hadn't a clue what was happening, so he asked her where they were going.

Mari gestured behind her with her thumb and replied:

'The cave, Uncle Wil. That's the only safe place that's left.' She ascended the hill very slowly, moving the case yard by yard with plenty of rests in between. From the top of the hill she could see Uncle Wil still standing where she'd left him. Now he was looking towards the East, towards his old home in the stable loft. And he seemed to be talking to a ghost – yes, he was chatting to Cluck, because Wil could see his old friend walking around their domain and crowing proudly, leading his harem from one scratch-point to another. Once again he could see the dogs' keen, intelligent faces looking at him through the wire door of the dog house, keeping an eye on every little development and barking wildly if a stranger arrived on their manor.

Wil looked towards the South, towards the muck-heap and the gate to the lower meadows, which had been left open since the shooting. In the misty distance, on the simmering water, he could see the two ships appearing and disappearing in the fog. It was from the South that their troubles had arrived; first the land-gnawing sea, then the pirates, who'd wanted to steal their simple little lives from them. Turning to the West, he observed that the old farmhouse, weather-beaten and hunched, was rotting away; at one time its whitewashed walls and clean windows had told the world that its residents still had pride and a zest for life – but today it was sickening and dying. He could hear his mother's voice, calling him in to tea; he could hear his father's voice, calling on the dogs to follow him into fields which were full of healthy sheep and sleek cattle. And to the North he could see the hen house, doorless and empty. Inside it, silence, where once he had listened to the wit of his feathery friends. Farewell, said Wil. Farewell to old Wales, farewell to my home, farewell to my life.

By now, Mari had returned for the second case, and they went up the hill together like two centenarians creeping up to their rooms in an old people's home. When they eventually got to the top they had to take a long rest; Wil was completely exhausted and he had to lie down for a long time; he reminded Mari of a sack of potatoes which had toppled onto its side.

'We'll have to hide these cases somewhere,' said Mari. 'I'll never be able to carry them all the way to the cave today.' So she went in search of a nook in the heather, but Uncle Wil warned her that a wild animal might be able to get at them if they were on the ground, so Mary lugged them to a tree in a hollow and perched them in the lower branches; at least they were shaded and hard to find there. After another rest the two of them started again in the direction of the cave, moving extremely slowly because Wil was as weak as a kitten, often leaning on Mari for support. It took them most of the morning to get to their destination – the Cave of the Braves as she'd described it to the pilgrims. Finally they were able to sit in the opening, and look down on the farmhouse below them. Their coats were sopping wet so Mari hung them to dry on spurs of rock inside the cave. The skeletons, which showed no sign of having been disturbed, still slept peacefully in the dust and the sheep dung.

Here, they were much higher up and could get a clearer picture of the ship which had come to join them; she was much bigger that the *Beagle 2*, and was painted or tarred a sinister browny-black throughout; she had blood red sails, and Mari could see men walking around on deck. A dog, a big dog by the sound of it, howled and barked from somewhere in its intestines. Another boat – a tender – was tethered to the big boat. It was small and blue, almost lost in the shadows of the mother ship.

After resting, Mari went back to the house to fetch some bedding. She felt terribly tired by now and the journey took ages.

While sitting there in the mouth of the cave, Wil noticed that Jawsey and his crew had been alerted to what was going on and were now up on deck; soon enough they were making their way up the field towards the house. Wil's eyesight was none too good but he could see that they were carrying bundles and bags, and were therefore moving quite slowly.

He closed his eyes and nodded off for a while; that's the way his afternoon went, alternatively snoozing, waking, then snoozing again, because the journey to the cave had done him in completely. He felt, now, that he had very little time left; indeed, he'd have waited for the newcomers in his bed except for one factor: he knew that he'd be able to see the whole farm, or most of it anyway, from this vantage point. He was shocked by the state of the land; the trees appeared to be dying all around him and the pasture was scorched and brown. He felt a wave of nostalgia for the fields of his youth, the old Dolfrwynog, so very green and lush. Where had all the animals gone, and the birds? The fields were lifeless and the skies were empty. In that way he mulled for a while, then cat-napped. Wil's life was drawing to a close, and the world as he knew it was also coming to an end. When his eyes shut for the final time, old Wales would fall asleep too. A chapter in the history of his beloved country was coming to an end.

A shadow fell over the mouth of the cave. It was Huw, in his filthy red shorts, smeared with dirt and moss stains. Huw looked at his sleeping uncle, then he entered the cave and sat among the braves, with his gun resting across his skinny legs. This cave had been his home for weeks, but maybe he'd have to shelter somewhere else now. He didn't want to harm his relatives, but maybe they'd tie him up or lock him in the pantry.

While Wil slept fitfully in the cave entrance, and while Mari packed blankets and old sleeping bags into bedrolls, ready to be transported to the cave, the heavy rattle of an anchor-chain being lifted came up to them from the bay; then came the sound of men barking orders, while crewmen milled around the masts. They were clearly making preparations for a landing.

45

MARI STOOD AT the top of the stairs at Dolfrwynog, perfectly still, though her mind was racing around the house. Had she forgotten anything essential? Right now she was asking herself: *Should I take candles?* Then she remembered the morphine in Uncle Wil's room and went to fetch it; she was beginning to feel like a sheepdog trying to pen half a dozen stubborn sheep in a thunderstorm. On her shoulder she'd slung one of Elin's old bags, a baggy green affair with *M&S* on it, and every now and then she'd throw something into it. While wandering through the house she heard voices out in the yard, so she crept into her old room to see who was there; if the new pirates had arrived already she was in a right old mess. Would they kill her there and then? With a baby in her belly? That's the sort of people they were, after all. She started to shake, and was forced to sit down on the bed for a while. It was the bed used by her and Nico; their love-bed. She imagined the two of them lying in it, holding each other tightly after sex. Her mind drifted back to the film of warm dampness on his skin; and the way she'd lie with her hand still in his springy curls, listening to his heart slowing down and his breathing returning to normal. But what had love brought her? A baby, heartbreak and fear. She put a hand on her lump to feel the little man. She still felt sure it was a boy. He probably had curls already, like Nico, and brown eyes flecked with green, just like his handsome father. But what about the face? Would he have a mass of freckles and a dinky little nose like his mother? A strong current passed through her body, and with it came the certainly that she'd do anything, even kill whoever was about to enter the house, to defend her little bulge. She got up and started to push the bed against the door. Then a voice came up to her from the stairwell, urgently. It was Nico.

'Mari, you there? Hey, is that you, Mari?'

She relaxed, and opened the door.

'Yes, it's me.'

Nico surged towards her, taking the stairs three at a time. He'd grabbed her before she could move; and although she made an effort to push him away, his arms clamped her like a vice.

'Let me go, Nico,' she said shakily. 'Let me go, will you?'

'Mari, what's wrong?'

'Don't give me that shit,' she replied angrily. 'After what you've done to me.'

He moved away and held her at arm's length.

'What do you mean, Mari?'

'You know what I mean. Bastard. Coming here with that girl. Holding her hand like that, and me having to look at you both every day. Both of you together like that. You bloody sod,' and Mari hit him as hard as she could with her fists. He put an arm up defensively, but made no attempt to restrain her.

'Mari, you got it wrong…'

'Don't give me any of that shit. What were you doing on the boat together, then? Playing hide and seek? Think I was born yesterday?'

Nico moved in and put his arms around her again.

'No, Mari, nothing like that. I promise you. Nothing happen.'

Mari stopped struggling and stayed still. She looked into his eyes, and he looked into hers.

'I have to play game.'

She remained silent, gazing at him intently, looking for giveaway clues.

'Only way to get Jawsey here and Weasel. Pretend I am boyfriend of Amber. I talk to her, chat her up in street. That is only way. I try to make her fall for me, yes? Then I get to know her father, tell him about this place. Tell him about you, about the saints in the field…'

Still she didn't move, searching him with her eyes.

'Listen Mari, I tell you truth. Only way to get food here was with these men, only way to save you and baby. But they clever bastards, they see what I do, so I have to play game, pretend I am boyfriend of Amber. Understand?'

'No.'

'Mari, I tell you truth. These clever men, they see what I'm doing. So I can't show them that I'm…'

'Go on, say it… admit that you're the father of this little bastard in here.'

'No, I mean that I can't show that I am your boyfriend. Understand? Ask Amber, she tell you. I am saying truth. Honest, Mari.'

She relaxed. Nico's version wasn't important any more. Why should she worry if he was telling the truth? She'd already been hurt as badly as anyone could be, she'd reached the extremity of pain. Love was unimportant now, she decided, when their very survival was at stake. To live or to die, that was the only choice facing them now, if they had a choice at all. Nico, Mari, the family at Dolfrwynog were all in the same boat. Ha! *The same boat…*

Mari smiled weakly.

'Why you smile, Mari?'

She raised her eyes again.

'Doesn't make much difference now, Nico. We're all in the same boat. I don't care if you love her.'

She gestured towards the new boat.

'What are you going to do about them?'

He shrugged his shoulders. Then she told him about Wil, and the cave. She thought they should all take shelter there until the new boat departed – did he agree?

Yes.

So they worked together, bagging everything they thought essential. Nico went to the front door and called Amber. When she appeared it became clear that she knew what had passed between them.

'You have to believe us, Mari, nothing went on. He was just playing a game, but my father was too clever for him and there was no way out of it. He's all yours now.'

'Don't know if I want him,' answered Mari. Then she asked: 'Where's my mother?'

Amber and Nico looked at each other, but stayed silent.

Mari became agitated and made for the door.

'Where's my mother?' she asked again, in a stronger voice this time.

But before she'd reached the door, Nico stepped in front of her.

Mari stood looking straight into his chest, an inch away from Che Guevara's worn face. She noticed a hole where his nose had been.

Nico put a hand gently on her left shoulder and said in a low voice:

'It's no use, Mari, she was too weak to come with us. She could not walk, so we had to leave her.'

Mari pushed against him.

'Out of my way, Nico. I have to go to her.'

Amber moved closer to them and joined in the conversation.

'There's another thing, Mari. She didn't want to come back up here.'

'How do you mean?'

'Mari, she says goodbye to you. We were going to tell you tonight. Here's a letter from her. You read it.'

'Later,' said Nico. 'We have to go now.'

Quickly, they all left the house, carrying all they'd collected, and it was lucky that they'd moved when they did because the new pirates had boarded the *Beagle 2* and were ready to move onto land. There, standing on the yard, were Jawsey and Mr B. They both looked pretty down in the mouth, as if they'd been caught stealing sweets. They'd fled the *Beagle 2* without a shred of resistance, because they knew it was useless. The new boys were bigger and badder. Mari smirked as she passed them.

'So the rats have left the sinking ship,' she said sarcastically.

'Come on, quick,' said Nico, leading the way up the mountain road. The four of them laboured up the hill, then they turned to see what was going on behind them. The new pirates seemed to be having some sort of celebration. Up here they could hear whoops and guns being fired into the air. By the time the light was fading they'd reached Wil, who was still looking down on the farm. They were all wet and miserable, because the rain hadn't ceased all day. They couldn't light a fire either, in case they attracted the attention of the pirates. Everyone ended up with a bed of sorts in the cave, and as the light finally waned they shared a primitive picnic. As she ate a little, before darkness finally came, Mari took the opportunity to read her mother's letter.

Mari love,

The party's over. It was the best way to go – you know me! I've had a great time down here on the boat but it's all over now baby blue. Time to say goodbye. I can't come up to the farm, it's too much for me. Whatever happens, you know how much I love you. Get on with your life now, tell Huw how much I love him too, and the baby when it comes. If it's a girl can you call her Elin?! You can trust Nico, he's a good man. He loves you, stick with him. Say tata to Wil for me. Lots of love and kisses. Mam XXX

By the time she came to the kisses Mari was almost blind, but it wasn't because of the coming darkness.

46

Something from the past returned to her, a memory from her childhood, when everyone had sat around the television, some of them sitting on the floor, watching a major event. Nothing like that had happened for a long time. Mari thought of her family gathered all together, absorbed, conjoined, watching a Christmas film like *The Wizard of Oz*, or Wales playing rugby against the old enemy, with a parental arm around her; she recalled the texture of her father's pullover, the smell of sweets on her little hands. It had been a happy time, warm and affectionate. But the BBC had gone quiet ages ago, the army bulletins too, following years of social disorder. The emergency transmissions had lasted for a few months, then stopped suddenly. The silence which ensued on the airwaves had been more meaningful than the trillions of words uttered during decades of normality.

Watching TV together... yes, the memory came back fresh as yesterday as Mari and the rest of them sat in the mouth of the cave the following morning, watching the newcomers going about their business. They teemed like ants along the lower meadows, then they disappeared into the farmhouse and its outbuildings: they invaded the byre and the stable and the loft above it, before returning to their ship, still bobbing on the water, red sails furled. It cast a dark shadow over the white hull of the *Beagle 2* as the pirates pillaged and looted everything they desired; they even took furniture from the house, including the old grandfather clock and the long white table. They were at it for hours, then they rounded up the sheep and took as many as they could on board their vessel. Then a party of four, keeping close together, walked up to the upper meadows, passing underneath the cave. They went as far as the mountain gate and made a half-hearted attempt to round up a few sheep, but gave up and returned to the farmhouse; fortunately, they didn't spot the cave nor its human cargo. Another gang went along the lower meadows to round up the pigs, and they managed to catch some of the piglets; their squeals could be heard from the cave, but eventually the men gave up. They didn't try to catch any of the horses.

Late in the afternoon a hooter sounded and all the men on land returned to the mother ship, leaving Dolfrwynog in silence again. Mari saw one of the red sails being hauled up and then, after the anchor had been weighed, the ship moved very slowly across the water, to the far end of the valley. The small blue boat had been left behind, and now it was the *Beagle 2* which followed, in tow. Elin was still inside her presumably, either alive or dead.

'They'll probably strip the farmhouse over at the far end of the cwm,' said Mari to the gathering, though that was pretty obvious to all of them anyway. And since it was already late in the day, they prepared for another night in the cave. Wil had weakened even further, and his mind seemed to drift between dreams and reality throughout the night. He'd mumble a few words to Mari, then he'd seem to drift back to the past, and he could be heard talking to Cluck, and Megan, the dogs, and his sister Elin too, when they were children.

Watching the pirates from the cave had reminded Mari of viewing TV with her family when she was small. Mankind had lived in a virtual world for most of her childhood. Everyone around her had disappeared into their screens, as Alice had vanished into an alternative world within the rabbit hole. People had lived increasingly in a screen-world, either televised or computerised, and eventually that other world had become the real world; Mari and her friends no longer lived in reality, they lived in reality's secret compartments. She realised that now, as she thought about her life. One of the consequences was that a growing number of people were unable to cope with real life, either because they'd been absent from it for too long, or because it was so unforgiving. And when the screens went dead, millions were unable to live normally. They went mad, because the world around them was too blunt and cruel for them.

Mari slept near the entrance to the cave, close to Uncle Wil, with Nico alongside her, though she didn't let him cosy up to her. She wasn't ready to forgive him yet. Wil's breathing was irregular, he'd stopped mumbling but now and then he'd let off a hideous fart and then groan softly. The end was close at hand. During the last hour of the night, when a glimmer of light appeared through the gorse, he asked for a sip of water and Mari managed to pour some into his mouth. His voice was hoarse and feeble when they talked together for the last time:

'Mari, my little love, I'm going. Look after yourself, Mari, and the baby. Leave me here, where I am, will you? I want to see the farm for ever. I don't want to be under the soil, I'll never be able to see anything going on. Will you let me watch?'

She held him in her arms.

'Yes, of course, Uncle Wil, if that's what you want. You can look at the farmyard and the fields for ever and ever.'

She continued to comfort him through the coming of the dawn, then she felt the final shudder going through his body. She remained where she was, holding him, until the light was strong enough to illuminate the cave, then she woke Nico and whispered to him:

'Come and help me, Nico. He's gone. Uncle Wil is dead.'

Nico was exhausted, but after a slow start he helped to disengage the old man from Mari's arms, and he propped him up against a spur in the side-wall, so that Wil could look out over his former kingdom, as he'd requested. He was one of the old people, Wil, who had believed in the kingdom of heaven. Mari hoped that he was up there already, having a grand reunion with Cluck and Megan and his mates from the young farmers, and possibly Elin by now, too.

By the time they'd all stirred and woken, Mari and Nico had discussed the best way forwards. They'd have to return to the farm to catch the horses and to prepare; they'd have to leave Dolfrwynog because there wasn't enough food for the winter, and there was the baby to think of too.

'Hey,' said Nico to Mr B. 'Want to do this old man a favour?' He gestured towards Wil.

'That old man's dead,' answered Mr B.

'Listen, if we leave him like this the crows will get his eyes,' said Nico.

'You aint going to bury him?' asked Mr B.

'No,' said Mari, 'he wanted us to leave him like that, so that he can see the farm for ever.'

'Hey, aint that sweet,' said Mr B. 'So what's this favour you're asking?'

Nico looked at him with a smile. 'Let the old man have your shades. That way the crows won't get his eyes and he can see for ever. What do you think?'

Mr B didn't hesitate.

'Sure,' he replied, as he removed his glasses and popped them onto Uncle Wil's inanimate face.

'He looks kinda cool now,' said Mr B, and Mari was once again struck by his eyes: they were kind, and warm and intelligent. He was probably a nice guy, caught in a nasty world.

Mr B smiled back at her.

'I know what you're thinking,' he said. 'I'm not like the rest of them. This was the only way I could survive in that town, being the gorilla in the shades. That's the only way I could stay alive – by being a slave again. Back home I was a high school coach, but nobody ever asked me about that. All they wanted was a big black bum with a gun, so I played along...'

He looked forlorn for a moment, and his head dropped.

'But the real me passed away a few years ago in that shitty little shanty town, and I won't be that person ever again in this life, I don't think...'

Recovering slightly, he tried to cheer up by adding: I'll sure miss those shades though!'

They rolled up their bedding and collected the bits and bobs they'd taken with them. Then they stood around Uncle Wil for one last time, to say goodbye.

'You're the King of the Braves now, Uncle Wil,' said Mari, and she moved the shades on his nose to make sure they'd stay there.

Then they walked down to the farm, to see what was left. The old farmhouse was in a terrible mess, with clothes and possessions strewn all over the place, and breakables such as dishes and glasses smashed to smithereens. One of the pirates had lit a fire in the corner of the parlour by the piano but fortunately it had gone out, though there was a big smoky fan of burnt wallpaper around it. Some of the pillagers had written graffiti on the walls: *Oz woz ere,* in the kitchen and, *Black Bess Rulz the Wavz,* in the stairwell. That was the name of the ship, presumably. The place was a shambles and a big black cloud settled over poor Mari, who took it very badly; Dolfrwynog had been her home for many years, it had also been the ancestral home, and to see it like this was enough to break her heart.

'I'm going to sleep in the stable loft,' she said to Nico. 'Can't stay here, it's too depressing.'

On the way out she spotted a familiar item among the spillage on the floor: Babymonkey. Her furry little friend had waited for her all along.

'Get that for me will you, Nico,' she said. 'I can't bend down.'

He stooped and lifted the toy from the dirty floor.

'What you call him?'

'Babymonkey – he used to be on my school bag. You found him in the water when you came back on the boat, don't you remember?'

He shook his head. He didn't remember Babymonkey, but he would from now on.

'Come on, this place is getting on my nerves,' said Mari. 'Hopefully they haven't messed up the stable loft.'

Fortunately, the stable loft was in much the same shape as it had been when Mari had slept there in the summer heat, on that night when the original pirates had arrived. She lay down on one of the stuffed sacks because she had to rest for a while. Nico sat down near her and brushed her hair from her eyes with his fingers.

'Leave it, Nico,' said Mari. 'I just want to rest.'

Nico retreated from the loft looking cowed. When he returned, later, Mari was sleeping like a baby, so he gently draped one of Uncle Wil's old black coats over her and padded out again.

4 7

Mari slept quietly through the night. Pregnancy was really taking its toll on her body, and there had been so many knocks and shocks in the last few weeks, draining her slight physique. Nico slept close to her, but he had a bad night, tossing and turning, dreaming...

He woke before dawn and began to fret about their plans. They'd have to travel over the mountain, to the shanty town. That was their only option, surely. He would have to catch the horses, and that would be difficult because they'd become quite wild again. He'd have to fool them somehow. But what about Mari? Would the journey be too much for her? The birth of the child was getting closer and closer. And what would they do when they got there? Surely Jawsey and his henchmen would want revenge for the deaths of Weasel and Drooba. Nico stayed like that for hours, worrying, until Mari woke and opened her eyes. The first thing she registered was Nico's drawn face, staring back at her. The autumnal rain had given way to a cold snap and their breathing emerged in twin white balloons which met and fused in the air between then. The light coming through the dirty window was also whiter and sharper.

'Hiya.'

Mari looked into his face. Who was he, this man saying *Hiya* to her? Her lover, father of her unborn child, or a mean two-timer prepared to step on anyone who got in his way, including her, Mari?

'Hiya,' she replied.

Nico knew, now, that the little Mari he'd first met on the purple moors had gone for ever. Her face was so thin, it had set like cement into a cold white mask. This was another Mari; an older Mari, watchful and fearful.

'I want this baby, Mari. I want you to be safe. I want you to trust me again. Please, Mari.'

She looked at him for a long time, unflinchingly. What difference did it make if he was being sincere and truthful? They both faced the same future, whatever his motives. She adjusted her inner thoughts to take in the fact that there were three of them now. Nico wasn't going to leave her in the lurch, that was clear. He'd have gone by now if that was what he wanted. That, at least, was a positive.

'What are we going to do, Nico? This baby's had a bad time so far and I don't know if it's going to be OK.'

'How do you mean?'

'Nico, I've not had enough to eat these last few months, and stress isn't good for babies… it could be deformed, or too small to live, I don't know.'

'Is it still alive, can you feel it in there?'

'Yes, of course it's still alive, I can feel it moving now.'

'Can I touch it?'

Mari fell silent, then rose and went to sit on Uncle Wil's chair by the table.

'Not now, Nico, there's too much to do.'

She lifted a finger towards the two new crosses on Uncle Wil's Anaglypta chart – two big red marks denoting the deaths of Weasel and Drooba.

'We'll be lucky if Huw leaves it at two – he's on a mission. We've got to be careful. He's only killed strangers so far, but he could kill you too.'

'Don't worry, I can look after myself.'

'Yes, I can see that,' she said in a tired voice. He got up and went to her, then gripped her bony shoulders.

'Mari, I could have gone to the town and never come back. I could have left you here. But I came back for you, don't you see that? It wasn't my fault they were too clever for me. But I will take you out of here, we'll be OK. You understand? Mari, I love you. Understand?'

She remained rigid for a while, then she relaxed and folded in on herself:

'Yes, I know you came back for me. I understand that. But this has been a really bad time for me and I can't... I can't be normal about it now. I just need to have my baby, to see it alive... to see if it's OK, to be safe again. I want to feel safe again. That's all I can think of now. I don't care about love any more Nico, not right now. Do you understand me?'

He didn't, but he replied: 'Yes, I understand you, Mari. I do.'

They sat there in the chairs used by Huw and Uncle Wil when they lived here in their own little eastern kingdom; it seemed so long ago. And it had been such a crazy idea; had Uncle Wil started to lose his marbles at that point? Or had he been trying to redefine his world, as the real world disappeared?

'Nico, I have to tell the story of Dylan today. I have to finish. Do you understand?'

He looked at her full of wonder.

'Finish? How you mean?'

She took her time replying, because she herself wasn't completely sure why she wanted to end the story of the graves.

'I don't really know, Nico. I started the stories to keep you here, and then I had to tell them again to keep the others here... but I haven't finished. I need to tell Dylan's story again, because they haven't heard it.'

'You will have to tell the story then. Today?'

'Yes, today. Then we'll go soon. OK?'

Nico rose. 'You want me to get the others ready?'

'Not yet. I have to be ready myself first. Can you do me a favour?'

'Yes, of course, Mari.'

'Go to the house, see if you can find my white dress and the ring. You know, the story ring. Just in case those men missed them. I hid them under my bed... our bed. Can you see if they're still there? The ring's behind a bit of loose wallpaper.'

Mystified, Nico went to look for them immediately. And although a sleeping Jawsey was draped across the bed, he found Mari's things. He took them back to her, though the dress was creased and covered in dusty cobwebs.

'Now help me to get ready,' said Mari. 'Go to the well, get me some fresh water. Then I want you to brush my hair and tie it up. I want to look my best, OK?'

'Yes, Mari, I understand,' he said, and for once he did.

In an hour Mari was washed and dressed; the frock had been too tight around the middle so Nico had opened a couple of side vents with his knife; besides, it was only needed for a day. Nico brushed her hair and tied it up with a rubber band, because it was getting long; he'd failed to find her red bandana. Then he went back to the house and arranged for them all to return to the graves at noon; Jawsey hadn't been too keen at first, but then Nico had warned him gruffly: 'Listen Jawsey, I'm the boss around here now. You haven't got a chance of getting back to your town if you don't do what I tell you. Understand?'

Jawsey had no reply, because Nico was right. He'd be stuck there for ever, in a hellhole, unless Nico led them back to the shanty town.

'OK, OK,' said Jawsey. He'd had enough of the place.

'When are we going?' he asked Nico. 'Can we leave soon?'

'Don't worry, Jawsey, I'll get you out if you listen to me. But I'm in charge now, get it?'

Jawsey mumbled a response, with his eyes on his feet.

That afternoon they all met in the paddock, under the plum trees, with small white clouds bubbling from all their mouths. Everyone except for Huw, who was still missing. There was a fair amount of complaining at first because it was cold; Mr B was especially affected. He stomped his feet and clapped his hands together in an attempt to warm them up. Mari noticed that he looked comical because he'd found an old coat which was too small for him and his arms stuck out from the sleeves as if he were a badly-made scarecrow.

Mari stood by Dylan's grave, dignified and patient, until everyone fell silent. Then she went on with the story.

She began with a description of her younger brother. He was quite different to the rest of the family, with blond hair and bright blue eyes. He was small for his age, though perfectly proportioned. Yes, Dylan was a very special child. Mari described every aspect of his unusual nature: how he'd blow the hair from his face while making an appealing *brrrrrr* sound with his lips; how he'd dance along the lower meadows while turning and turning like a merry-go-round, with his hands floating around him like birds; and the way he'd make beautiful little dolls' houses for his sister.

Mari stood there, wondering why she'd created such a fiction. Was she trying to dramatise the truth, to make her dismal life sound more interesting than it actually was? Or was she trying to make the grim reality of her existence more palatable? She continued…

Dylan had been special to everyone, but there had been one person who was special to him – his great-grandfather. Dylan did everything for the old man; he'd take him his food, dress him, and take him for a walk around the farmyard.

Mari described how the old man had refused to eat any more food when he reached his hundredth birthday, because it was scarce. But Dylan had also refused to eat, because he was just as stubborn as the old man.

After two whole weeks of this, his great-grandfather had relented. Dylan and the old man had sat by the fireside that night, laughing and crying every other moment as they ate together.

Mari recited the fiction of the little boy and the old man, with Dylan leading his half-blind ancestor around the yard. Then he'd put him to bed, wind up a musical box and they'd both listen to the tune tinkling away until the old man was asleep.

That's how Mari started the story of her special brother Dylan, the way she'd told it first to her lover Nico. She was reiterating the story. She was reiterating her love for him.

48

MARI STOOD BY Dylan's grave, looking past the plum trees towards the water. It seemed to be rising again; the birch grove had almost disappeared, leaving just a few withered branches above the waves. In the silence which fell on them her mind wandered back to the past; she remembered a story heard by every schoolkid in Wales – the story of Cantre'r Gwaelod, a rich and powerful kingdom off the West Wales coast which was drowned and lost for ever one stormy night. And at high school they'd been told that their homeland, surrounded by water on three sides, had been wedded to the sea since pre-history. The epic *Mabinogion* myth described how the giant Bendigeidfran hauled an entire fleet of warriors across the sea to Ireland. The water off Wales had been busy with boats; saints had sailed hither and yon to sanctify the scarce people of the western world, then Viking pirates had ransacked the land for spoils. Once, a very long time ago, the Preseli hills had been higher than the Alps, only to sink below the waves, where they were rubbed out by the ocean's great eraser, before re-emerging once again as a set of worn-down teeth.

Then came Tryweryn, a tinnitus in the ear of Welsh history. A valley had been drowned to supply water for an English city, and the soul of the nation had been troubled ever since. *Remember Tryweryn*, said the slogans. And the Welsh had indeed remembered only too well, as if they were afraid the whole nation might be drowned one day.

Mari thought of the early Welsh seafarers in their little

wooden boats; they'd been famous for their bravery – only a few could swim. And that had been the nature of Wales's relationship with the sea: a mixture of fear and love, a bit like her own relationship with Nico. She loved him, and at the same time she feared him. It was like her relationship with water; she had to drink it to live, yet it could so easily kill her.

Mari returned to the present, to Dolfrwynog. She didn't know it, but Wales was an island now. The last little finger of land linking the country to England had sunk below the rising water. The scientific predictions had all been correct – and with a vengeance. Mankind's greed had destroyed the world, as the climatologists had foreseen a century previously.

Humanity had been born in Paradise and had turned it into Hell. And just as the mythical heroine Heledd had mourned the cooling of the hearth at Pengwern sometime in the first millennium, Mari now mourned the cooling of the hearth at Dolfrwynog.

She turned to face the present; she spoke again to the gathering by the graveside, and she finished the fable she'd built around her brother Dylan. Her fiction had grown stronger than reality. Was that because reality had been so painful and destitute?

She described how Dylan escaped from Dolfrwynog and followed his great-grandfather through the soggy fields. His wellingtons had become stuck in the mud and they'd stayed there for months because no-one could bear to touch them. Dylan had seen his ancestor on the roof ridge, shouting into the tempest. Dylan had joined him, he'd pleaded with him. But both had drowned in the storm.

She told the story almost exactly the way she'd told it to Nico that first time, in their bedroom. It was her way of writing *The End* on the last page of her life at Dolfrwynog. Without this coda the story of her family would have been incomplete; she had fulfilled her part of the bargain, she had kept the pilgrims at Dolfrwynog, and it wasn't her fault that the plan had failed.

When Mari finished the story, everyone stayed very still, looking at Dylan's grave. And then the silence was shattered by a tremendous blast close to them. As they reacted physically to the explosion they were deafened by another blast. With their hands over their ears, or with their arms wrapped around their heads, those who were unhurt tried to protect themselves instinctively while a double echo receded along the valley heights. Only Jawsey fell to the ground, and he fell across Dylan's grave. He didn't make a sound; he didn't say a word. He was the only one who didn't see a small red blur vanishing along the tractor ruts on the other side of the plum trees – a young boy holding a gun, running as fast as he could away from them, along the lower meadows. Huw, the filthy little wild boy, who lived nowadays with the pigs below the great oak tree. He was another Mowgli now, he looked like one of the Amazonian tribesmen in the *National Geographic* magazines on the windowsill at Dolfrwynog. Huw ran for his life, but everyone else was too shocked to move. Where had he come from? Where had he been while Mari recited her story? They surmised that Huw had crept towards them like a stalking hunter while his sister was absorbed in her story. But had she, Mari, actually seen him? Was it possible that she'd seen a small patch of moving red while she described Dylan's disappearance into the water? Was that a possibility, really?

Who knows… it's not important now. Like Jawsey's life, it was of no consequence. In the new world, nobody's life was of any importance.

They all left the scene in silence. A wave of shock had swept over them and numbed their emotions. But Nico and Mr B went with guns to the bracken slopes, to retrieve Drooba's body; they carried her back to the paddock, on the old hen roost, wrapped in an ancient woolsack. That evening they buried the bodies at the top of the paddock, with Weasel, under the hawthorn trees.

4 9

THEY ALL SLEPT in the stable loft that night, with someone on watch throughout, in case Huw decided to kill someone else. By now there were only four of them left: Mari and Nico, Amber and Mr B. Wilma had stayed aboard the *Beagle 2*, perhaps sensing that the new pirates were a better option.

Nico took the longest watch, mainly because he couldn't sleep. He had so much on his mind, starting with – how would they catch the horses?

They'd have to herd them into the paddock, either by trickery or fear, and then they'd have to be very cunning. They'd also have to prepare for the journey: was there enough food left, and what would they do for water?

Nico's mind ground away like a mortar in a pestle, all through the night.

He'd finally dropped off to sleep when the dawn came, sitting near the doorway, and they were all asleep when the sun sailed into view. This was a different sun in a different sky; it had gone cold suddenly and the high meadows were coated in a crisp white coating of hoar frost. Unbeknown to the others, Huw had moved back to the cave, to live with the four skeletons and Uncle Wil's body. Huw had taken the shades for his own use, and he'd gathered some clothes from the house, so that he was dressed properly for the first time in ages, though he still had nothing on his feet. Mari had left one of the sleeping bags in the cave – just in case, she said – and Huw slept in it every night. When he woke the sun was high in the sky; he still had a child's sleep patterns. After waking he sat opposite Uncle

Wil in the mouth of the cave, watching the grown-ups coming and going; he laughed at Nico and the big black man as they ran after the horses, whistling and shouting and waving their arms around like madmen. Finally, they corralled the horses in the paddock, and then cheated them into entering one of the sheds. He continued to watch as Nico leant against a wall with his head down, obviously recovering from all his exertions; the black man sat on his heels nearby, also recovering.

Hidden behind his new shades, Huw's cunning little eyes followed Nico and the black man as they walked along the lower meadows shouting *Huw!* as loudly as they could. Occasionally Nico shouted: 'Huw, we won't hurt you. We're leaving… we're going away Huw. You want to come with us?'

But Huw couldn't hear him, he was too far away.

Then Mr B shouted:

'Huwie, come on little fellah. Come on, man!'

But again, Huw couldn't hear a word. He was surrounded by silence in the mouth of the cave, except for the occasional mew of a buzzard.

The two men went up to the mountain gate, through the upper meadows, and this time Huw could hear what they were saying, their voices faint on the wintry breeze. They kept their guns at the ready always, and stayed as far as they could from the bracken and hedges, any place which could hide a crazy little gunman. Then they descended again, still calling out to him. They entered the cave for a last time and noticed that the shades had disappeared. So Mr B took off the balaclava he'd found by Dylan's grave and pulled it over Wil's lifeless face, so that his dead eyes stared out through the slit. He hoped that the garment would frighten off the crows and magpies, while allowing Wil to stare at his beloved fields.

Then they returned to the farm and started their preparations.

First they gathered every scrap of food they had left, though there wasn't much.

In the afternoon, while Amber and Mr B stayed behind, Nico and Mari went for a walk along the lower meadows, so that they could wander through the fields one last time. Mari wanted to visit the bathing pool in the river; she wanted to sit beneath the old oak tree again, and to bid farewell to a very important place in her life. She wanted to fix in her mind the one place on Earth where she'd been really happy; the place where they'd swum together in clear water before making love and sleeping naked together in the warm green grass. It was where Nico's skin had mirrored the many small flowers of the riverbank, casting blue and yellow and crimson shadows onto the white of his young body. They meandered slowly along, and she allowed him to take her hand – a small Welsh girl, heavily pregnant, traumatised by death all around her, and her Polish lover, still with her but living in a different world now. A different sort of reality; hard and cold and final. It would be the last time they would walk through Dolfrwynog's fields like two young lovers, looking for fish in the river, listening to the murmur of the water, glimpsing a sparrowhawk skimming the trees on the riverbank, or admiring a hare racing away from them along a field.

When they arrived at the pool they found two piglets in the shade of the big oak; they ran off to join the rest of their family when Nico and Mari sat down and rested against the huge, wrinkled trunk of the tree. It was much too cold to swim or to lie around in the grass, as they'd done in the past, and anyway the pigs had dug up the pasture. Neither of them would ever again lie in this secluded spot, under a hot summer sun, pretending to sleep while glancing covertly at each other's bodies. And that feeling of a bubbling, champagne-froth love foaming all over their unblemished skins – they would never feel that again either. Mari thought of their entwined love during that period, their agile innocence. Here, under the tree by the river at Dolfrwynog, in the lower meadows, they'd tasted paradise for a few short hours. And then, after only a few days' sunshine, that paradise had been seared before their very eyes. Neither said a word during their last visit to the oak tree. Then they rose and returned to the farmstead, hand in hand, knowing that their youthful love was already a thing of the past. By the time they reached the house, fine snowflakes were beginning to swirl in the air around them. Christmas was fast approaching, and the land would be white as they fled from the farm. Up on the side of the hill they noticed the mouth of the cave gaping black in a white mask of snow. The farmyard lost its shape; the buildings began to disappear in a white wonderland, the whole place began to be a non-place, erased from sight, as if a magician had said *Abracadabra*…

By the light of a single candle, the four of them shared the remains of a mouldy loaf in the stable loft, then they lay on the woolsacks like soldiers waiting for dawn, waiting for the big push in the morning, with a low wind moaning in the eaves.

'Christmas is coming,' said Mari to Nico, hidden under Uncle Wil's greatcoats.

'Yes, I know.'

'Can we go tomorrow?'

'Yes, let's go as soon as it's light.'

Nico moved close to her, and took her in his arms.

'Have we got any bread left?' asked Nico.

'Two small loaves, and a few tins. Not much. Just enough to get us to the town I think. What about Huw?'

'Mari, we have to leave him here. No chance of catching him, too much danger.'

'But he'll starve to death.'

'Maybe he live wild, who knows. If we try to get him maybe he shoot us.'

'Poor Huw. I don't think we did enough to help him, somehow…'

'Mari, we have been trying to stay alive, all of us. That's all there is now. Trying to stay alive, you and me and baby.'

They fell silent again, and Nico thought she'd gone to sleep when she mumbled in a sleepy voice:

'Do you love me, Nico?'

He squeezed her tight.

'I love you, Mari, always. You and baby, I love you both.'

Again, silence. But soon, Mari's breathing had slowed and her body had relaxed. She'd managed to catch some precious sleep.

50

WHEN THE FOUR of them woke the world outside was almost totally white, with a few outlines showing, and a few gnarled tree trunks black against the white-out. After searching the house they put on as many garments as possible, and Mari showed them how to make leggings from old sacking; Mr B found a set which seemed to curl naturally like corkscrews around his shins. They also made ponchos out of old sacks. Mari took just one luxury; when she put a hand into an inside pocket she could feel Babymonkey, warm and comforting, touching her fingers. He was rather dirty and bedraggled, but since he'd turned up in the most unexpected places, and since he'd been with her longer than any of the people around her, she'd decided to take him with her as a talisman.

The horses, kept in the byre overnight, were eventually caught after half an hour of patient cajoling by Mr B, who seemed to have a talent for dealing with them. Saddlepacks were made from sacking to hold the bedclothes, the remaining food, and the guns.

Then, as they prepared to leave Dolfrwynog for the final time, it started to snow heavily. Seated in the best saddle, with Nico leading her horse, Mari was full of trepidation. At the top of the hill they turned to look at the farm. The yard had disappeared, though the muck-heap still showed its Everest-shape under a cone of snow. There were no animals left: no dogs to bark, no hens to leave zigzag tracks in the white powder.

'Bye-bye, Dolfrwynog,' said Mari from her perch, and she waved a schoolgirl's goodbye wave.

They turned, and went onwards up the hill. They went through the mountain gate in Indian file. Nobody looked back.

In the cave, little Huw stood in front of Uncle Wil, still wearing the shades, saying *Dammit!* over and over again in a small childish whisper.

Hope. That was the only thing that drove them on. Hope was the only thing remaining. And they had youth on their side, of course. But the snow intensified by the time they reached the higher reaches of the mountain. Nico had been through this heathery wasteland previously, to get the horses and the pigs, so he knew where to find them shelter – in an old shepherd's hut. He also knew there was a farm which could be reached in three days; a farm once famous for its pigs. The bodies would still be there on the yard where he left them, probably. Or maybe just some bones; the crows and birds of prey would have stripped away the flesh. He remembered their faces: a middle-aged man and a girl of Mari's age. He remembered the way their faces had swivelled towards him as he walked towards them across the farmyard, with his gun raised in front of him. That was when his heart had hardened and turned to stone. That was what he'd had inside his body ever since, a heart of stone. From that day on there hadn't been much point in staying alive; only his survival instincts had kept him going. His life had been pared down to the basic acts: breathing, eating, drinking, pissing, shitting, and sleeping when he could. He had felt something towards Mari once upon a time, but what use was love in a loveless world? Something had left him, passed through the top of his skull like an invisible bird, when he killed those two innocents. Two warm bodies had lain in the cold mud, on a remote farm on the fringe of an obscure mountain range. Blood oozing from the girl's mouth had formed a dark question mark on the ground. So what was left after that, after the spirit-bird's departure through his skull? Nothing, except a cold wind blowing through his hair, passing through him on its journey to the far ends of a pitiless universe.

That night, as the snow piled up in drifts around them, Mari suffered racking pain. She hadn't ridden a horse for a long time, and since she was heavily pregnant she'd felt uncomfortable from the start. Nico had made a bed for her on the hut's earthen floor, using his own bedding too so that she could get warm, but she failed to settle and ended up weeping silently beneath her bedclothes; the pain in her belly was almost unbearable. The horses stamped and neighed in the night, as if some danger was approaching them in the darkness; and Mr B shouted Huw's name repeatedly in his sleep...

By morning she knew that she had to turn back. It was all too much for her, she couldn't possibly survive a long trek through the snow. Even if they made it to the shanty town there would be insurmountable problems. They'd been crazy to consider the plan.

Her vivid imagination presented her with a preview of life in the shanty town. There would be pigsties instead of houses, a mudbath instead of streets. Vile misshapen huts made of rusty old corrugated iron sheets and beachcombings, anything that came to hand. Black smoke rising into the air, packs of dogs baying like Arctic wolves. Mari saw a vision of Hell, not a town. She trembled at the thought of giving birth there, because she'd felt the baby move into position during the night.

As dawn came she called Nico to her side and told him. They'd have to turn back. Her body couldn't take any more. The dream of escaping from Dolfrwynog was over. Nico nodded slowly but said nothing.

When they were all awake Nico broke the news that he and

Mari were returning to the farm. Her body couldn't take any more. The others would have to choose what to do next. They could go on, or return. If Amber and Mr B decided to go on, the food could be divided between them. Nico urged them to decide quickly, so that Mari could be taken back to safety.

It didn't take long. After a brief conflab Amber and Mr B decided to continue onwards to the shanty town and to take their chances among the pirates. It was, after all, their home town. It was the place they knew best.

Fortunately, it had stopped snowing. Within half an hour they'd disappeared into the white wilderness. Nico had given them some rough directions, and a bag of rations. He stood by the door as they vanished into the drifts. He never saw them again.

51

THE JOURNEY BACK to Dolfrwynog was slow and difficult, but they made it before nightfall. Back at the farm, Nico lit a fire and made a bed for Mari in front of it. She was in great pain now, almost delirious. At some point in the night a son was born to them. Mari lost quite a lot of blood, and the baby was very small. He was also jaundiced, but he was alive. Nico washed him in cold water and dressed him in clothes which Mari had prepared for him. They named him William, after his grandfather, who was still sitting in the cave presumably. But their options were running out fast. There was very little food left. By now, Nico and Mari and little William had only one choice left in the whole wide world. They'd have to flee again. This time they'd have to escape another way, and there was only one way open to them. They'd have to take to the sea.

Nico knew that the big pirate ship had offloaded a small blue boat so that the *Beagle 2* could be towed away. He remembered it as a two-berth sailing dinghy in reasonable condition, and the sails had been left on it. There was no other option: they would have to collect what little food they had left, plus some water, and put out to sea. They would have to find other people. It was a slim hope, but that's all they had now. A little hope. They needed a sanctuary where Mari could recover.

That night, Nico and Mari prepared themselves for one last desperate bid for freedom. Nico stalked through the farmhouse, collecting anything which might be useful. Then he loaded his pockets with cartridges and settled down to wait for the dawn.

When the first rays of light came he would take all their supplies to the boat. They would finally leave Dolfrwynog, never to return. Both of them knew that this was their only chance of staying alive; they would sail along the coastline, looking for another refuge – a more civilised place, where they could settle and bring up William in decent surroundings. If there was such a place left on Earth.

Mari managed a little sleep, but Nico sat planning and preparing himself throughout the night. When a dim light began to appear in the windows he took all their supplies to the boat. Then he roused her and they went, stumbling between the molehills, down to the water's edge.

Nico half-carried her towards the little boat, with William on his other arm. Mari could hardly walk, she was too weak – she loped along like an injured animal. The pain of childbirth had never left her and she knew that something was wrong with her. A grey mist fell over her eyes as she took in the liquid shape of the boat in the distance. Nico reached the water, then vanished. She panicked – where was he? It felt like years before she too reached the boat. Nico had put the baby on deck and he was already untying the ropes which held the boat to the shore. Mari crept up the swaying gangway, winded and almost doubled up, then lay down by her baby on the planking. Staying very still, she waited for her breathing to ease, though she felt sick and her heart was beating hard against her chest. The baby started to cry, but she was unable to move; the most she could do was to stretch out an arm to touch the little bundle close to her. She prayed for some strength, just enough to allow her to take him in her arms and to say a few words of motherly comfort. Then she detected movement; the boat beneath her began to rock and sway. It started to move through the water, she could hear the hull hissing through the waves. Nico seemed to be running around the deck insanely, pulling ropes and engaging levers; she watched the sails dropping down in canvas gloops, then rattling in the breeze. Eventually, Nico moved the baby close to her side and went to stand by the rudder, so that he could steer them towards open water. Mari went in and out of a thick sea mist, a mist in her mind. The pain inside her was unbearable one second, then it vanished for a while, then it came back again with renewed force. She probably slept for a while, she couldn't be sure, or perhaps she'd descended into a coma. She was aware of the baby crying or whimpering occasionally, and she made a superhuman effort to move, but failed; her whole body seemed to be held down by a powerful magnet. Now and then Nico's voice drifted towards her, reassuring her softly.

At some stage, it could have been hours later, the fog lifted from her brain, and she saw Nico clearly for the first time that day. He was holding the baby against her exposed left breast, and William was suckling her.

They'd have to find a sanctuary soon, thought Mari. She had only so much to give, and she wasn't producing much milk.

She started to whisper. She said, *Dolfrwynog*, and again, *Dolfrwynog*… could he hear her? She lifted her right arm and dragged his attention towards her. He stooped and put his head as close as he could to her mouth. *Dolfrwynog*, she repeated.

'What you saying Mari?'

'Dolfrwynog… the farm… milk…'

He lifted her left arm and draped it around William, pinning him in place, then returned to the rudder.

Had he heard her? Mari continued to whisper the name of the farm.

Nico steered the boat away from the shore, but what

now? He had little experience of sailing, other than the few manoeuvres he'd picked up on his original journey from the township to Dolfrwynog. He'd watched Mr B move their boat around effortlessly, but Mr B wasn't with them now. Perhaps he should have brought him too. Nico cursed himself. What should he do next? Perhaps Mari was right. He'd heard her whisper *Dolfrwynog*, and maybe that was the answer; what other option was there, really?

Perhaps he should follow the coastline, in search of another shanty town. But that would be dangerous, and they didn't have much time, since they had only a negligible amount of food and water. He was almost demented with worry by now. And because he'd spent the last couple of hours in a state of confusion and indecision, he'd steered the boat well away from the land, so that Dolfrwynog had become a tiny dot.

The breeze slackened and the sails lost their shape, becoming limp and crinkled. They were becalmed, and for the rest of the morning the ship swayed gently on the water, going nowhere particularly, though they were drifting further and further away from the land because at some point it disappeared altogether. From one horizon to another, Nico could see nothing but water now.

He left the rudder and went to lie by Mari on the deck, after wrapping the sleeping baby in a blanket and putting him between the two of them. He fell asleep for a while, then he lifted himself on his elbow so that he could look into her face. She was very pale, and her breathing was shallow.

'Mari.'

No reply.

'Mari,' he said again, a little louder this time.

She turned towards him and tried to focus on him, but her eyes seemed far away. Could she hear him?

'Mari, I want to tell you…'

He hesitated, then realised how stupid it was to feel constrained, so he said to her:

'Mari, I love you.'

Again, there was no answer. Perhaps… had he seen a flicker of recognition in her eyes, just for a second?

He waited for a few minutes, then he said:

'Mari, I love you. I always love you, Mari. Sorry it end this way. I want to say sorry to you… for the way things happen and we have no way to stop them. But Mari, I love you…'

He continued to stare at her unmoving face, then her eyes flickered open again. This time she recognised him, and made a desperate attempt to say something, he could see her lips move.

'What you say, Mari?'

Her lips rippled again. But nothing came out.

He lay on his back again, and continued his inner search for an answer to their predicament. What on earth should he do? He closed his eyes, and took refuge in his imagination; as the boat drifted towards the edge of the world he drew a mental picture of himself and Mari standing outside a beautiful cottage, with William as a young boy between them, holding hands with them. They all looked happy, well-fed, there were roses round the door. They lived in a land of peace and plenty…

Nico heard a sound, and sat up quickly. What had he heard?

Gripping his shotgun, he swung onto his knees and looked out over the side of the boat. Out on the glassy sea he saw another vessel coming towards them in the distance, a ship ten times the size of *Beagle 2*. Its deck, alive with activity, reminded him of a leaf floating in a stream, covered in black ants. Still kneeling, Nico took in the red flag above the new ship, rippling as she moved towards them. They were better seamen than he was, they'd managed to find a breeze to stir their sails.

The ship was closing in on them now, he could hear voices and occasional laughter.

Nico relaxed. He felt a wonderful calmness flowing through his body. His movements by now were almost leisurely, fussless and precise. After taking a last look at her sleeping face he dipped down to kiss her on the cheek; he did the same to William, with his left hand knotted in Mari's light brown hair. He looked at her little nose, her freckles.

There was just enough time for him to rise to his feet, for him to greet the oncoming ship with a wave of his gun, before the first bullet zipped into his body.

52

在西欧海域进行船只巡逻的"荷花3号"，其《航海日志（或报告）》 1/1/11 写道：我们在韦尔士古国--现为逃犯（人数不详）之家的1个岛屿--海面的 1 条小船上发现3名西欧人。我们假定原居民已遭灭绝或根除。船上 2 具尸体，是1名纹身男子和 1 名妙龄少女的。还有 1 名男婴，仍然活着，被带到了"荷花 3 号"上，并（照他胳膊上玩具的名称）取名为猴子。他的大脚趾上一直戴着 1 枚戒指。这孩子被送往上海孤儿院 6B（科），以评定可否作为司空见惯的灭门案或军事间谍职业生涯方面的案例。2 具尸体则留在水中。

[Entry from the log of the patrol boat Lotus Blossom III somewhere off Western Europe on 1/1/11: 'We came across three westerners in a boat off the coast of the old country known as Wales (?) – an island today harbouring refugees (numbers unknown). We assume that the original inhabitants are all dead. Two bodies in the boat, a white man with a tattoo and a young woman. Male baby alive, taken aboard Lotus Blossom III and named Monkey (because of a small toy tied to his wrist). A ring on one of his toes. We have been ordered to take this child to Orphange 6B at Shanghai for the usual assessment regarding extermination/military training. The bodies were left in the water.']

Also available from Y Lolfa:

"Richard Gwyn's memoir – his down-and-out vagabondage around the Mediterranean – takes us on a terrifying, funny and erudite journey through alcoholism, insomnia and liver disease to a redemptive and self-accepting wisdom. One hell of a good read."
Desmond Barry

The Vagabond's Breakfast
Richard Gwyn

£9.99

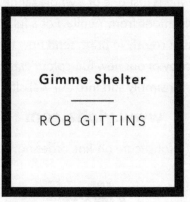

Gimme Shelter

———

ROB GITTINS

£8.95
£17.95 (hardback)

Water is just one of a whole range of
publications from Y Lolfa. For a full list of
books currently in print, send now for your
free copy of our new full-colour catalogue.
Or simply surf into our website

www.ylolfa.com

for secure on-line ordering.

TALYBONT CEREDIGION CYMRU SY24 5HE
e-mail ylolfaylolfa.com
website www.ylolfa.com
phone (01970) 832 304
fax 832 782